Praise for Books by L.V. Ditchkus

The Sasquatch Series—Science Fiction 1ˢᵗ Prize Winner, Colorado Authors League Book Awards 2021

"I thought this was a well-crafted and enjoyable tale and imagine that the sequel will be just as entertaining."

—Judge's feedback for *Crimes of the Sasquatch,* Writer's Digest Book Awards

"Her character development is excellent, with the reader quickly feeling he/she *knows* these people."

—Arlene Shovald, Book Review for *The Sasquatch Series* in *The Mountain Mail*

"The author's ability to put readers in astonishingly creative settings is nothing short of delightful."

—Laurel McHargue, Award-Winning Author

"I was immediately hooked."

—David Kramer, Author of *Entering the Real World: Timeless Ideas Not Learned in School*

BY L.V. DITCHKUS

Crimes of the Sasquatch: Book I of The Sasquatch Series

Mission of the Sasquatch: Book II of The Sasquatch Series

Legacy of the Sasquatch: Book III of The Sasquatch Series

SOON TO COME:

The Chrom Y Chronicles

Passage
of the
Sasquatch

Book IV of The Sasquatch Series

Passage of the Sasquatch

Book IV of The Sasquatch Series

L.V. Ditchkus

Pinon Press

Colorado

Passage of the Sasquatch: Book IV of The Sasquatch Series
Copyright © 2021 by L.V. Ditchkus
All rights reserved

Published by Pinon Press
Colorado

Library of Congress Control Number: 2021918280
ISBN: 978-1-7342125-3-2
Subjects: 1. Sasquatch—novel 2. Bigfoot—novel 3. Science Fiction
4. Paranormal
Cover design by Tina Pickell and executed by Rafido.

To Ms. Whited, a fourth-grade teacher who nudged a timid
writer

Chapter 1

I stood erect and braced against the storm. Sideways sleet and snow whipped my fur and obscured my view. But I sensed what lay beyond. Last season's downed needles confirmed towering pines existed—their unmistakable scent aroused by moisture.

My gut clenched. I was *not* supposed to make this trip. Only Dylan should have traveled back to Porgu—his dimension. Halveks did not know how to transfer between our worlds. So a Sasquatch needed to help him, and I attracted the requisite lightning bolt.

When Sasquatches journeyed between Reval, our dimension, and Porgu, we focused on the destination. I had instructed Dylan to visualize a spot in Porgu where he would be welcomed and safe.

Conditions in Reval had been perfect, with the moon at its fullest. When I raised my arms to capture the energy from a bolt, I imagined my world with blue nutrient pools, bushes filled with flowers as big as my head, and my soft sleep site. Logically, I should have stayed behind.

But no one had ever tried to send someone forward and remain behind. Most of us went alone. Or Sasquatches might travel in pairs if they were bringing a deformed newborn to Porgu. I considered all possible scenarios of what had happened before and what might have occurred. Then my situation became clear. When a close pair attracted a bolt, they both transferred—irrespective of their intended destinations.

I must return to Reval immediately.

Months ago, when I took the lives of two halveks, I knew the act was horrific. But their violations against defenseless children were worse. Severe charges waited for me back home for intruding on Porgu's citizens, and I felt obliged to accept the penalty.

In our society, my actions were inexcusable. Without explaining the circumstances, I had requested the High Council euthanize me.

Despite my pledge, I would not be there to accept my sentence. Representatives of the Council were probably already looking for me. They might assume I transferred to avoid them.

Despite my thick fur, I shivered when a gust nearly blew me over. The wind storms of Reval might be more intense but lacked precipitation and never came with plummeting temperatures. My world remained constant—never too hot or cold. Porgu's weather was as insufferable as the halveks who lived here.

If *I* considered the conditions distressing, how did Dylan feel? I cursed myself for thinking of only my predicament. Had he lived through the transfer? Was his virtually hairless body capable of surviving in these conditions?

"Dylan?" I called in my hoarse whisper of a voice.

No response.

Telepathy, the Sasquatch way to communicate, might work better. Dylan spent a month in Reval and learned how to send, receive, and block messages. Despite my higher intellect, his progress to communicate in our way far exceeded my meager attempts to speak out loud in his language.

I sent a broadcast mixture of images and words, including Dylan as he looked when he arrived in Reval, with little body fur and his head hair cut short. I followed with visions of how he looked before we left, with hair down to his shoulders and a shadow of fine fur sprouting across his chest and arms. While he remained short by our standards, his doughy skin had tightened over chiseled muscle. His transformation, accelerated by our nutrient pools, masked the deformities typical in halveks. I sighed, recalling the hours we spent in intimacy and sharing details of our very different lives.

With a forceful crack, a branch not far away broke under the strain of newly fallen snow and snapped me back to reality. There was no time for reminiscing. I focused on my transmission. Our way of talking was remarkably faster and rarely gave a false message. Halveks needed words to describe emotions, places, and beings. With a few rapid-fire visions, a Sasquatch could convey an idea in an instant.

I knelt and hoped to gain a better vantage of what lay nearby. Nothing moved except the boughs and desiccated autumn grasses bowing against wind and snow. If we transferred together, Dylan must be close. I crawled on all fours in a circle but could not make out a prone body.

I stopped my search to sit cross-legged, my back propped against a rough tree. Where could Dylan be? Suddenly, I jolted upright and leaped to my feet.

What if I transferred, and he did not?

If Dylan had remained in Reval, he was in grave danger. Until I had convinced Dylan that Kalev planned to use him as collateral to gain influence with our High Council and curry favor with his brother's wife, the naive halvek believed Kalev to be a friend and mentor.

Our hasty effort to transfer Dylan back to Reval was meant to get him out of Kalev's clutches. My attempt to save Dylan from Kalev may have put us both in the wrong place.

I looked up into the boiling storm. If the moon remained near its fullest point, I might transfer back to Reval.

My flawless memory held specifics from all previous Sasquatch transfers. I rifled through the recollections and could not think of a single attempt to return immediately. Others had waited until the next full moon or, more commonly, a year or two later. Sasquatches had come to Porgu for thousands of years to silently observe the flawed halvek race and track their decisions and development. I could recall them all.

Without the luxury of time, I needed to face my sentence in Reval and confirm whether Dylan had successfully left there. If he had not, I might delay my execution and help him find a safe hiding place, away from Kalev and those who would search for him. With another month of practice, Dylan could try the transfer on his own at the next lunar cycle— twenty-nine days in Dylan's terms.

I stood to raise my arms toward the moon I could not see. Despite the unrelenting gale, I envisioned Reval. Mild temperatures and the faint fragrances of home enveloped my body. I could almost feel Porgu's atrocious storm dissipating. An electric pulse tingled my fingertips and tracked down my torso. My hair stood on end. I willed myself to leave Porgu behind.

Time slowed. A serrated lightning bolt spiked from the sky to detonate a massive tree near where I stood. My muscles collapsed as wood splinters shot in every direction.

The blast threw me to the ground. My head snapped against a boulder, and I heard the crunching collision of granite against my skull.

The world went black.

Chapter 2

NOVEMBER 20

Something licked my cheek. How long had I been unconscious—just the night, a day, two? Blurry thoughts crept through my mind. Pain. Throbbing agony pounded my temples.

I tried to open my eyes, but they were stuck. Or maybe they would never open again. I tried prying them with my fingers, and finally one eyelid popped free. Ice had sealed them. Brutal cold nearly froze my tears as I tried to focus. Heat and insects tormented me on my first trip to Porgu—now snow wanted to bury me. How could halveks live in such brutal conditions?

Another lick, this time along my temple. I rubbed my eyes to clear them. Something with a pointy nose and ears. A fox. I shooed her away, and the animal scampered to hide behind a nearby bush. Despite my roaring headache, I smiled when she peeked around the branches. Did the fox want to play, or was she confused about what she'd seen?

I sent her a message to leave. But she stood firm. She should have immediately responded to my command. I repeated my directive, and she dutifully obeyed. But her delay made me question—had she grown weary of observing me, or did she react to my order? Her fluffy tail was the last bit of fox I saw as she darted into the forest.

Ever so slowly, I propped on an elbow to survey my surroundings. My head lay next to a dark, blood-soaked rock. I touched my temple—fur crunched between my fingers. I pulled out a clump of something hard and saw crusty blood.

Would the pounding headache ever stop? Despite my muddled state, I tried to recall what prompted my fall. I wasn't clumsy by nature. I had strength and speed beyond many of my peers.

Aha. I attempted to do a second transfer on a full moon—back to Reval. *Lessons learned? Don't try that again.*

As I moved to sit, I brushed snow off my shoulders and thighs. The falling flakes had stopped, but several inches lay on the ground. Even if Dylan had traveled with me, finding him under a blanket of snow could be challenging. My throat constricted. Without a natural fur coat, he'd be long dead by now, and if he were not incapacitated, his tracks would be buried.

If Dylan were my Sasquatch friend and lover, I would mourn his passing. But I did not know the halvek customs or whether they honored their dead. Better to assume he was alive.

I leveraged a hand against the rock to rise and stand, staying careful to avoid the smear of blood and fur. Vertigo made me sway, and I braced my feet far apart to steady myself. If Dylan transferred nearby, I needed to contact him. I used all my might to concentrate, but my transmission failed to coalesce. Each time I tried to capture visions or words, they disintegrated like dust thrown to the wind.

One more try. I rubbed my temples. A brutal pain shot through my forehead before I could consolidate thoughts and images. An hour of soaking in one of Reval's pools would help me recover from the head blow, but that wasn't an option.

Surely my injury would heal on its own. Reval's natives looked unkindly on Sasquatches without telepathic communication. We were too social to accept anyone in our midst who could not engage. But in my case, what did it matter? Soon after I arrived home, the High Council would euthanize me, and my disability would be irrelevant.

I grabbed a tree to steady myself, realizing my injuries might preclude me from searching for Dylan. If I could not broadcast a message, I must find him. And what if he was still in Reval? Maybe a better idea was to stay hidden until the next full moon in twenty-eight days.

Struggling to gain strength, I collapsed. Wind whistled in the branches, and bundles of snow fell from the treetops to plop on the ground. From deep in the forest, I heard animal sounds. A hearty squirrel, likely still gathering winter food, reprimanded a deer as it passed. A truck's faint engine sounded from a roadway, and in the other direction, a domicile door slammed. If Dylan had transferred with me, would he have tried to find a road or a shelter? A vehicle could provide transportation to a town, but a halvek home might offer him immediate protection and clothing.

Again, I stood on shaky legs. If Dylan had gone to the road and hailed a driver, he would be far away by now. But if he'd walked to the domicile, he might still be close. I decided to try the house.

The bitter scent from incinerated pine logs mingled with a repugnant odor from rotting refuse established my route. After a few deep inhalations, I sensed the residence was close.

Once I managed several rickety steps, my balance improved, and I followed the horrific smells.

Ice caked my feet, and I left huge tracks in the snow. But anyone following me might believe my prints looked like a rambling bear, awoken from his winter nap to search for grubs. To promote my ruse, I rolled a few fallen trees along the way and scratched at the trunks' undersides.

When I reached the domicile, I noticed similarities to the one Dylan had shown me in his memories. He called his place Augie's cabin. Both structures were made from stacked logs with a center door and a chimney that belched smoke. While Dylan's opened to a wild exterior with naturally growing shrubs and grasses, this one had snow-covered furniture and planters with stems from last summer's flowers poking through the snow.

Careful to remain unseen, I skirted the trees at the clearing's edge until I found a path to the cabin with limited views from the windows. After listening for halveks opening doors, I crept to a side window and inched up from below until my eyes were level with the sill.

Horrors! Inside was a despicable display of animal heads and skins. Each wall had at least four mounted heads—decapitated deer, elk, moose, and one colossal bison stared into the middle of the room from their high perches. Some gaped with open mouths. All had shiny eyes. Skins in brown and blinding white lay across the backs of furniture. A massive bearskin rested on the floor with its teeth exposed as if the animal wanted to take an ankle bite from anyone who passed.

I stared, mesmerized.

It could have been my shock at the room or my recent head injury, but I'd lost my keen awareness. Before I sensed him, a bulky halvek came around from the back of the house with an armload of wood. His age and bald head reminded me of one of the men I had killed earlier in the year— during my disastrous first transfer to Porgu.

His eyes widened, and his jaw fell slack. "Wha-wha-what?" he stammered.

In a flash, I bolted toward the woods. I was not as fast as my usual pace, but I gave it all I had.

"Stop!" He called after me. I heard a muffled clatter as the logs fell from his arms onto the frozen ground.

After making the tree line, I zigzagged between bushes and trees, trying to find a previously trampled path. His footfalls faded as I outpaced the halvek's awkward stride. While scampering, I intently listened until I heard a stream gush not far away.

I bounded through two dry gullies and circumnavigated an open meadow before finding the creek and splashing into its center.

If he tracked me, the halvek would want to believe I traveled downstream—it would be easier for him. But I turned uphill to spring over rocks and felled logs, thrashing through the freezing water.

My thighs screamed under the strain. But I kept moving until dusk fell, leaving the halvek far behind.

Spent from my run and angry with myself for nearly being caught, I dropped to the ground and rested until night closed in. I stared at the sky, finally clear after the storms. First one and then another star glimmered.

Ever since we started to explore Porgu, Sasquatches had watched the stars. Our unfailing consolidated memories of terrain and celestial bodies helped us navigate in Porgu.

Dylan had shown me his memories of physical maps—both on paper and on a small handheld device. At the time, I marveled at halveks needing complex tools to find their way. A Sasquatch could navigate anywhere— as long as another individual had traveled there before.

Sadly, prior Sasquatch journeys had not come here. Yet the longer I stared at the night sky and faint distant hillsides, the more familiar it became. I was not far from a location previously traveled.

Good to know, but if I do not know where I intend to go, how is my current location valuable?

I sighed and dragged some branches over my body in hopes they would provide warmth. Dylan had talked about a place not far away—a town called Jamesville with a small domicile owned by a person named Destiny.

Dylan's memories included a house with colors I associated with the forest's leaves and bark. There was furniture on the porch and a swing that moved in the wind. Dylan sat on that swing after one of his jogs through the neighborhood. He shared that memory with me because he wanted to express his appreciation for fitness and his passion for running.

I recalled his route and the house's position within the town. At night there would be few halveks roaming around. I could go there to see if Dylan might have approached Destiny for help while he recovered from his month in Reval. While halveks were not as social as Sasquatches, he might have contacted her.

Dead tired from my nearly disastrous encounter with the halvek at the cabin, I allowed my leaden eyes to close. I desperately wanted to sleep. But the longer I considered my plans, the more I knew better. Traveling by day was fraught with detection risks. The darkness gave me cover and an advantage. Most halveks moved around exclusively in the daylight hours, and—according to Dylan—my night vision was far superior to any halvek.

Forcing myself to sit, I pushed away the branches and rubbed my eyes. Sleep could come later. I must travel to Jamesville.

With hesitancy, I strained to stand. My head still throbbed, and my stomach constricted. I had not eaten in nearly a day—since my transfer to Porgu. I'd need to keep up my strength for this journey.

The bushes were devoid of berries at this time of year. The last time I visited Porgu, I transferred into a hot, swampy terrain. That area was full of sweet grasses and flowers—not enough to satiate my hunger, but I could survive. What did these woods have to offer? I pulled off a bunch of pine needles and stuffed them into my mouth. They tasted bitter and stuck to my gums.

"Pthat." I spat them out and rubbed my tongue with the side of my hand. There had to be something more edible or better tasting than that. I recalled memories of other Sasquatches who had visited these environs.

Some had called on trash dumps to look for discarded vegetable matter. Others ate plump berries when they were in season. Still others chewed on nuts and seed cones. I dug in the snow under a tree to find a cone and took a bite.

Crunchy but better than the needles.

I grabbed a few more and tucked them under my arm before I set on my way to find Jamesville and, hopefully, Dylan.

Chapter 3

LUCAS EDWARDS

Lucas paced the cabin, too excited to sit or stand, his heavy lug boots scraping the polished hardwood floors. He had never before walked around his home without exchanging his outdoor shoes for slippers. Lucas kept the place clean, and some would say immaculate. But on that evening, he was too frustrated to care.

Stupid firewood—I couldn't even grab my phone to take a photo before I lost her!

Who would believe him without proof? He'd spent the early evening hours poring over websites about Bigfoot sightings. Oregon ranked fifth in the most Sasquatch reports. Articles talked about glimpses from cars or campsites—but this one was right outside his door. How many times had she come to his cabin without him realizing? She must be curious. He had caught her peeking in his window. In his book, that made her intelligent and inquisitive.

Few online reports mentioned the gender of a Sasquatch, but she was undeniably female and not at all gorilla-looking like the cartoons and supposed photos. She was close to seven feet tall and had a body like a top female basketball player with broad shoulders and a tiny waist. Her face had delicate features with caramel-colored eyes that went wide when he startled her. A photo would have been priceless.

Damn that firewood.

Hours ago, when he first spotted her at the window, Lucas ran as fast as possible, tripping on logs hidden under the snow and relying on his superior tracking skills. But before long, he shivered in the damp cold as never before. He'd left without his coat and needed to go back to the cabin. His hunt for her would not end in his hypothermic death.

Once geared up and armed with his rifle, Lucas followed disturbed needles and recently snapped low-lying branches to a creek. He looked both directions but could not decide whether she had taken the easy route downhill or a more thoughtful approach up the hillside. He considered her peering into his window and her shocked reaction when he caught her. Definitely, she went uphill.

Staying out of the creek as best he could, Lucas followed the water and struggled along the bank at a snail's pace. She'd covered her tracks well. He occasionally spotted a broken branch or snow sluffed off a fallen log where it should have been pristine. But otherwise, she'd made no mistakes.

Once the shadows grew long, Lucas's opportunity to find her was fading. Bathed in darkness, her minute mistakes would be impossible to spot—even with his headlamp.

"Son of a bitch!" He had called into the woods before turning to retrace his steps back to the cabin.

But that was hours ago, and after all that time, she was likely miles away.

Lucas planned to get an early start and climb back up the creek bed in the morning. In his heart, he knew his efforts would be for naught. Lucas had hunted animals on four continents and knew that the strategic advantage changed once a beast caught a whiff of pursuit. The prey gained an edge—especially if the game was highly intelligent like a big cat. A Sasquatch might even be more cunning, which would make his pursuit all the more rewarding when he took her down.

I have to regain the upper hand.

In Africa, he hired guides to help him track big game. Their knowledge of the terrain and his quarry's habits always facilitated success. Without their expertise, he would have come home empty-handed.

How would he find a serious hunting guide for a Sasquatch? Lucas had no confidence in the websites touting Bigfoot hunts for all comers. They catered to people chasing a fantasy who would be satisfied to hear whoops or thumping in the woods. Lucas needed to find a guide with experience tracking a Sasquatch. He was unimpressed with what he saw online and had no time to start an exhaustive interview process.

Lucas considered posting his sighting on one of the Bigfoot Internet sites to see if others might have seen her. But broadcasting his experience could attract a hoard of attention. If the woods around his cabin filled with believers, someone might find her before he did or obliterate all traces of her.

Better to keep his experience to himself and scout the area on his own. But the believer societies' postings could help him. If someone reported seeing her, Lucas could use *their* knowledge—sharing was another matter entirely.

Chapter 4

In the dank, dark alley, I fist-bumped the air when I reached Destiny's house. Dylan always made that motion when pleased with himself. Without another Sasquatch to share in my success, I co-opted his solitary celebration technique.

After circling the domicile, I could see the windows were all dark, and nothing moved along the street. Quiet for Porgu, but with different sounds than the forest with its unrelenting insect chirps, birdsongs, and animal rustling. I heard traffic from a nearby thoroughfare and sounds from houses with lights on.

Woodsmoke and auto exhaust saturated the air.

While not hesitating too long in front of the windows, curiosity ate at me as I desperately wanted to know what was inside. The contents in halvek homes were relatively foreign to all Sasquatches, as we generally stayed in wooded areas. The exposure to Dylan had fostered my longing to understand their creations. Sasquatches lived in absolute simplicity and halveks in abject complexity. Why did they need so many things?

Thinking back on the remote cabin scene brought a sour taste to my tongue, and a chill spread across the skin under my fur. What would possess a halvek to kill an animal and display its carcass? They should be embarrassed to kill another being—not proud. I had no doubt he wanted my head to join his collection.

As I stood alone in front of Destiny's home, I decided I would never understand them. While Dylan seemed passive and kind in Reval, would he want to display a conquest in his house? Unless I visited his home, I would never know.

Something clunked in an alley a block away and brought me into focus. Enough about the cabin. I needed to find out whether Dylan might be inside.

A directed transmission to Dylan might wake him if he was sleeping. Assuming my head had not fully recovered from my fall, I braced myself for the pain. As I strained to consolidate my thoughts, I imagined floating with Dylan in a cleansing pool and making love in the slick fluid. But the images I tried to formulate would not coalesce, and the transmission faded before it left my head. A throbbing ache pounded my temples.

The transmission would not work. What was another way to attract Dylan's attention? If I threw a rock into a window, it might wake him. As an overprotective halvek male, Dylan would come to find out who broke the window—not Destiny.

A fist-sized rock lay next to a walkway. Once I hefted it in my hand, I decided it had an appropriate weight. With a smooth arc, I hurled the rock into an upstairs window. Glass spilled from the frame, and I scurried behind a bush to watch what would happen.

Nothing. No lights came on. No heads peered out from the broken glass. I puzzled over the lack of response. Either the rock did not awaken anyone, or they did not care. Now what?

Maybe I should go inside. I'd only once entered a halvek structure. At that time, I burst into a barn armed with a halvek weapon and shot two men I caught abusing young girls. Those circumstances were dire, and I protected the youths from further harm.

In *this* case, I was only entering the dwelling on the slim chance Dylan was inside. The mentors in Sasquatch transfer training hammered us with a consistent message—*never* go inside a halvek building. They were dangerous, and the risk of detection was too great.

With a shrug, I stepped to the backdoor and climbed the porch to peer into the window. Glossy wood and metal boxes lined the walls. I had no idea how halveks would use them. But I noticed no clutter or apparent signs of halvek life like discarded clothes or shoes.

After weighing the risks against finding Dylan inside, my desire to reunite with him won out. I grabbed another rock and smashed the handle.

When I pushed against the door, it swung wide. After pausing to listen for sounds of movement, I entered the house.

Surprised at how warm it was inside, I kneeled to press a hand against a metal grate. Warm, dry wind rushed from somewhere deep inside the house. A low rumble and the floor's faint tremor led me to conclude the halveks had created a machine to provide indoor heat. I scoffed—another device to dull their natural resilience.

My heart pounded as I tiptoed through every room. The place smelled dusty, and the floors were devoid of furniture or adornments.

No dead animal heads on these walls.

Not only was Dylan not here, but his friend Destiny was not in the house either. Without furniture, like the pieces I'd seen at the cabin, I could not imagine any halveks were living here. Had I entered the wrong house? No. Based on Dylan's memories, this was the correct location. But Dylan and Destiny must have gone somewhere else.

I squatted on the floor in the front room. The light from outside lamps played against the walls, shining through leafless bushes and the bare windows. Maybe this was a sign. I had twice tried to find Dylan and failed. The first time was at the cabin where I was nearly caught and the second in this vacant house.

Where did he go?

I recalled Dylan talking about a place called Salida. Destiny lived in Salida for a time, and Dylan had met Kalev there at the structure called Augie's cabin.

I pieced together the terrain from Sasquatches, who had traveled in the area between Destiny's house and Augie's cabin, and from maps Dylan recalled for me. The distance between Jamesville and Salida was great. Dylan would have traveled by vehicle, but I would go on foot. I calculated the expanse and how much ground might be covered in a night. If I hurried, I could reach Salida before the next full moon.

As I picked at a bit of debris that clung to my fur, I wondered if it might be easier to stay nearby and hide until I could transfer back to Reval at the next full moon. I weighed my options. Confirming whether Dylan had safely transferred with me or had remained in Reval was essential. I would know whether I was returning to a disaster or merely fulfilling my promise to the High Council. Further, making the journey to Salida might teach me more about the brutal halveks—I'd already learned about their propensity to display death. I could share some of these details with the High Council, adding my knowledge to the collective.

I rose and slipped out the open back door. After rounding to the house's front and moving into the street, I decided to send one more broadcast message. Maybe this time, Dylan would hear me.

Staring hard at the front of Destiny's home, I braced my hands on my thighs.

Ignore the pain. I must make contact with him.

Despite a knife-stabbing agony at the back of my skull, I focused on the house and silently screamed my vision into the Oregon night air.

Chapter 5

RURAL OREGON
LUCAS EDWARDS

After another day of slogging through the woods, Lucas had nothing to show for his efforts except blisters and soggy clothes. Back in his cabin, he yanked the belt on his terrycloth robe tight around his middle. Lucas inspected a cut crystal glass for any remnant fingerprints or water spots and poured himself a generous portion of Scotch. The whiskey burned his throat as he swallowed, and he hoped it would dull his frustration over not finding the beast.

Lucas crossed the room to the computer sitting on the dining table. He had clients who needed his attention, and he had not responded to any emails for the entire day. *She* had hijacked his focus. While his customers represented healthy commissions, she embodied fame and a prize no one had ever achieved. Not just another sighting, but a highly-coveted treasure for his trophy wall.

He drummed his fingers on the glass. Lucas had seen her in a way not described on any website. Their reports were rote or suspiciously detailed about interactions between a mother Sasquatch and its child. His sighting was unique and genuine. Despite being skunked that day, Lucas knew he would find her. She would become his favorite trophy. Probably smaller than a male. But hunters everywhere would clamor to see her sandy-colored hair and delicate facial features.

A neat stack of hunting magazines sat next to his computer. As the whiskey took effect and diminished his frustration, Lucas mused—how would he decide which media outlets would receive his first interviews?

Maybe he'd hire an agent. Perhaps one of his clients could help him find a good one.

After another swallow, Lucas set his glass next to his computer. *Time to quit wallowing in future plans and get to work.*

He brought up a program designed to render a 3D representation of Earth based on satellite imagery to trace his route. Lucas quickly found his cabin and the stream where he first tracked her the previous day.

With the nail on his pinky finger, he traced the creek as it peeked between the trees. Early that morning, he followed the stream up several cascades to its source. For miles, Lucas clambered over fallen logs in and adjacent to the creek.

By midday, Lucas had spotted a matted bush where she might have rested. But after further inspection, he detected elk prints close by. The wapiti had likely made its bed there and not his Sasquatch.

Lucas zoomed in on a clearing where he recalled taking a break for coffee and a protein bar. Shortly after his stop, the creek withered into a trickle and finally disappeared altogether. He searched the surrounding topography on his computer screen, unable to find another stream uphill from the one he had followed.

Lucas slammed a fist on the table, nearly toppling his glass.

Where did she go?

She might have left the creek at any time, long before the stream's source. When he left the headwaters and retraced his steps back down the stream, Lucas inspected each side and found no evidence of her route. He checked bushes for broken limbs and piles of ungulate scat for unusual density or shape but found nothing.

Lucas tapped the screen to widen the view and evaluated the roads in the vicinity. A few dirt tracks and one highway crossed within a five-mile radius of the clearing where he'd given up his search. At ten miles as the crow flies, Jamesville was the closest town to the west. Another village sat twenty to the east. A Sasquatch would certainly avoid civilization. So she would, more likely, head north or south.

Tired of scrutinizing the aerial views, Lucas considered other clues about which direction she may have taken. If they weren't solitary animals, she might hook up with another—perhaps her mate. Two roaming Sasquatches could attract greater attention. Maybe someone had posted something new on one of the websites Lucas found.

The first one only included old reports from days or months earlier. The second had a new comic on the home page with a cartoon Bigfoot driving a sports car and one onlooker commenting, "Well, you don't see that every day." While another said, "Yeah, I've never seen that model in red."

Lucas smiled and tapped on a link for reported sightings. After the page switched, he straightened and leaned in to gain a closer look at the most recent post:

> 11/21: (Jamesville) Caught a glimpse of a BF on my way to work the midnight shift last night. I took a shortcut down an alley and saw a tall, skinny upright BF leap behind a dumpster. I stopped the car to take a picture, but it was long gone before I got there. I never thought I'd see one so close to town.

Responses accused the poster of seeing a dumpster diving vagrant in the middle of the night, but Lucas knew better. The Jamesville resident described the Sasquatch as tall and thin, while all the other postings had depicted hulky hominids.

This fellow might have seen my beast.

Lucas drew a breath and held it in before he clicked on the post to send a message asking the Jamesville spotter to contact him. His luck was changing. Lucas asked for more details about the animal's height and anything else the spotter had seen. He also wanted to know precisely in which alley in Jamesville the sighting occurred. Any details might be helpful.

His second message went to a friend at a nearby cabin. Lucas had hunted with the guy's dogs in the past, and his buddy would not ask questions if Lucas asked to borrow one or two again.

Chapter 6

The first rays of sunshine brightened the peaks when I decided to stop for the day. Exhausted and not thinking clearly, I'd suffered a few mishaps on my first full night's journey from Destiny's house to a sizeable lake where I planned to find a cave or some other place to hide for the day.

The first near calamity happened in the alley near Destiny's home. In my haste to be on my way, I ignored the sound of a car passing on the main road. Who knew it would come down my alley? The minute it turned, I jumped behind a metal container full of rancid waste. When the car stopped, I needed to run before the halvek could catch me. I squeezed between the box and a wall, jumped a wire fence, and escaped through a yard.

"Wait! I won't hurt you," the halvek had called after me. But I kept running until I no longer saw any illuminations from the town.

My superior eyesight did not need the halveks' artificial lights. I had made excellent time by leaping over rocks and creeks that would slow any pursuers. The event left me unharmed, except for a bit of fur I'd lost at the first wire fence. No matter. It would grow back.

My second setback came hours later. I realized I could make better time if I used the halveks' roads to travel and stayed on the paved, painted track unless I heard a vehicle approach. Then I would hide in the forest until it passed.

Without warning, deep into the night, my thighs turned to lead. No matter how much I pushed, they would not respond. Finally, I stopped in the gravel at the side of the road and collapsed. I recognized my calamity—my body needed food, or my journey would end abruptly on that roadside.

I crawled to the forest edge and scraped the dirt, looking for anything consumable. Under a drooping tree, I found seed cones and gorged on a dozen despite the way they scratched my lips and gums. My stomach cramped after I swallowed, and I knew my system would struggle to process the roughage. However, based on my last transfer, strength would return after a few days of absorbing Porgu's scant nutrients. My initial days in Porgu would vacillate between hunger pangs and digestive cramps. But the cones would lessen my need for nutrients.

The rest of the night had passed swiftly with minimal interruptions from halvek vehicles.

A bitter fragrance from submerged rotting leaves and the sound from rustling swamp grass told me a lake was nearby. I paused at the roadside in front of a sign with the symbols WELCOME TO DETROIT LAKE—whatever that meant.

I stared at the notice with its carved letters over a scene with mountains, flowers, and a sky-blue lake. The halveks were informing others about something important, and I wanted to send my own message as well. While my other attempts to send a transmission had failed miserably, maybe I could broadcast with a distinct image rather than multiple rapid-fire visions as was typical for a Sasquatch.

With my fists balled, I leaned toward the sign, taking in every color and detail. I closed my eyes, hoping to let the image fly to anyone who might pick up my transmission. It should have felt like the vision whisked from my thoughts. But instead, I dropped forward as if someone had struck the back of my skull.

My open palms took the brunt of my fall. Besides needing to pluck a few small stones out of my hands and fur, I suffered no injuries from my mishap.

Altogether spent from lack of sleep, I left the highway, crested a gentle slope, and spotted what might have been a lake at a different time of year. A water trickle snaked through a rocky ditch as if a giant had sat at the river's end and sucked the lake bed nearly dry. On the hillsides, cabins and docks sat far above the waterline.

Needing a resting site away from the halvek developments, I struck out to the north and skirted the dwellings.

Before the sun rose in earnest, I found a shallow cavern devoid of other inhabitants and crawled inside to collapse into a sound sleep.

Distant barking niggled and forced me out of much-needed slumber. When the sound came nearer, I tensed. There would be no more sleep until I could rid myself of the interruption.

I rose to sit cross-legged in my shelter. Dogs had chased after Sasquatches since the beginning of time. Fortunately, they were one of the easiest of Porgu's animals to control. With a few well-placed thoughts, I could send them in a new direction or encourage them to stop their pursuit and lay still—much to the chagrin of their halvek masters.

Their voices grew louder, and it was time to chase them off. I drew a deep breath and focused on their barks. Before my initial visit to Porgu, I'd practiced this technique for hours. Once in Porgu, I found directing lower animals a simple task.

While I expected the dogs to stop barking, they did not. I tried again with more force. Ouch! My concentration was met with a stab near the place I'd collided with the rock. Massaging the sore spot, I thought back to the previous day when I directed the fox to retreat. At the time, it seemed to ignore my command. When it left, I assumed the animal delayed her response. What if she had never received my directive, and she went away on her own accord? The fall compromised my ability to send transmissions. What if my other telepathic animal control skills were similarly damaged?

I scrambled into a crouch, ready to leave my cavern's safety. Listening intently, I noted the dogs' distance and strained to hear who or what accompanied them. I heard only footfalls and no sounds of an engine. They must all be on foot and not far from my hiding spot. Once they found me, I would be trapped.

Time to move.

After slipping from the cave, I headed northeast and farther from the lake. I needed distance between the dogs and me. Without my ability to redirect them, the dogs would continue an unrelenting pursuit.

I loped uphill to the top of a rise and expected to run down the other side. Much of the terrain I experienced the previous night was rolling, and the cliff at the top shocked me. My feet slid to the edge. Loose rocks skittered over the edge. They clacked on boulders jutting from the near-vertical wall until I heard them splash into a shallow stream far below.

With deft concentration and without looking back, I heard the dogs and their master as they grew closer. One glance over the edge told me down was not a good option. The scant stream at the bottom would not help break my fall if I jumped.

A frontal assault on my pursuers seemed ill-advised. The dogs' master might have a gun. I'd seen first-hand what a halvek weapon could do to flesh and bones. Since I'd used a gun to kill the pedophiles on my last transfer to Porgu, perhaps my destiny was to die by a hunter. I would be the first Sasquatch slain at the hands of a halvek. Future Sasquatch transfers to Porgu for observation and research might be forever compromised. This mistake would be a bigger disaster for the Sasquatches than my initial crimes.

"Come," the master encouraged the dogs.

His voice—I'd only heard a few words when I first saw him, but I knew in an instant this was the halvek I'd seen at the cabin with the dead animal display.

I straightened and gained courage through my rage. He would not add *my* head to his wall.

Gently, slowly, I lay on my stomach and dangled my feet over the edge of the cliff.

Chapter 7

SALIDA, COLORADO
DYLAN COX

Unwilling to abandon his dreams of days spent with Kati in Reval, Dylan kept his eyes shut and adjusted his head on the wadded-up fleece jacket propped against the car window.

"You can wake up now." Destiny gave Dylan's shoulder a soft shove. "We're finally back in Salida."

The Subaru no longer rocked from the highway's uneven surface. Dylan took a deep breath and stretched his arms above his head. Despite remnant light from the late afternoon sky, Augie's trailer was fully illuminated with two barn lights—one on a pole near the ramshackle garage and the other above the aluminum screen door.

"Thanks for coming to get me in Oregon," Dylan said.

"It was my pleasure. But I thought we'd have more time to talk along the way." Sarcasm laced her voice.

"Sorry I've been asleep most of the last two days. I don't feel tired, but my trip to Reval must have taken a lot out of me." He placed a hand on his chest. "It surprised me when you showed up instead of Tom."

"It was the right thing to do. Tom stayed here to keep working on Augie's cabin and watch Trip while I was away." She bit her lip. "Tom and Trip get along great—they probably both appreciated having a bachelor pad while I was gone."

Dylan looked out the side window at Augie's trailer. On his last visit, Dylan had lied to Augie and told him he was taking a short-term investigative job in Colorado Springs. At the time, Dylan expected to follow the Sasquatch Kalev into the woods and have a brief meeting with his pals. That encounter lasted over a month.

"I promised Augie that I'd take him to Chicago to see my home and meet Tom." A lump formed in Dylan's throat.

"Augie asked you to take him to Chicago?" Destiny reached across the seat to squeeze Dylan's arm.

"Yeah. The day before I left with Kalev, Augie said he'd like to see where I lived. I told him we'd go. Now I'm not sure he'd want to visit me there." Dylan smoothed his jeans over the tops of his thighs. "I'm not even sure *I* want to go back right away."

With Tom's promising romance with Destiny, Dylan figured Tom was in no hurry to leave. The restorations on Augie's cabin, formerly Jen's cabin before Kalev orchestrated her death by a mountain lion and bear, would take weeks or months. Kirk Steadman's fire had made the place uninhabitable but left it with the bones for a new life.

Dylan longed for time to reflect on his experience in Reval, and a quiet life in sleepy Salida might be the ticket. Rent from Dylan's turn-of-the-twentieth-century greystone home in Chicago would cover payments to Augie and their modest living expenses until Dylan felt like returning to his detective work. But all that depended on whether Augie could forgive Dylan.

After my lies and unexplained disappearance, does Augie still value our friendship?

"Augie suggested I stay with him?" Dylan turned to give Destiny a sideways glance.

"He did. If you'd rather, you're welcome to stay with Tom, Trip, and me—but we don't have an extra room. You'd be on the couch." She rubbed the top of the steering wheel with her palm. "When Augie found out you were coming back, he proposed you stay with him. Augie made the offer right away. You know he's got a spare bedroom in his trailer. He and his Aunt Peg lived there for years. There's plenty of space."

"He's always been upfront and honest with me. Even if he forgives me, I don't know if I can forgive myself." Dylan picked at the seam on his jeans, newly purchased at a resale shop in Oregon. "This year has been a string of failures. Jen and Nate died because Kalev eliminated them to get to me. Kati will face terrible consequences in Reval for helping me."

Destiny interrupted Dylan's self-deprecation. "Kati decided to take euthanasia as punishment for killing two men who were brutalizing children. I understand how you felt about her, but you can't take her decision on yourself. She made her choice before you met her."

"What if the High Council decides to refuse her petition and do something worse to her for helping me transfer back here?"

"What's worse than ritual suicide?"

Destiny had a point, but Dylan countered. "They could banish her. Sasquatches aren't hard-wired to live solitary lives. She'd rather die than humiliate her family and live alone on the frontier."

"You've got me there. I'm not an expert on Sasquatch customs and politics." She placed a hand on his shoulder. "Are you thinking of finding a way to go back to her?"

"It's crossed my mind." Dylan wanted to see her again more than anything. But he'd never transferred alone. Would that even be possible?

Destiny checked her watch. "You don't need to make any life decisions right now. Augie's waiting for you, and I'd like to get home before dinner. Tom and I didn't want you traveling alone after all you've been through. But four days is a long time to be away from both my boys."

"I appreciate your sacrifices for coming to get me." Dylan leaned in to hug her. "Tell Tom I'll see him tomorrow up at the cabin. I want to help him with the repairs. Being outside and physical should clear my head."

"I'll tell him. Please, give my best to Augie and apologize for not stopping inside."

"He'll understand," Dylan offered without knowing if Augie would understand or forgive anything.

Destiny waited in the car while Dylan crossed the sidewalk and stepped up the four wrought iron steps leading to the center entrance. He glanced over his shoulder. When Destiny made a knocking motion, he turned back to the door. Dylan barely had time to retrieve his fist before the door opened.

Augie stood in the opening, backlit from pole lamps that made his home operating room bright. Augie's unlined face held no trace of emotion—derisive or otherwise.

"Hi, Augie. Thanks for inviting me to stay," was the best Dylan had to offer. He waited for Augie to respond. But the slight, middle-aged man stood like a statue with thin arms dangling at his sides as he stared from behind thin-framed glasses.

"It's cold outside. You need to come in." Augie pushed open the screen, and Dylan walked through. Before Augie could close the door, Dylan turned and waved at Destiny, and she pulled away from the curb.

Augie took a long look at Dylan from his face to his shoes. "Whose clothes are those?"

"When they released me from the hospital, Destiny took me to a thrift shop. I bought this T-shirt, jeans, and a quilted down jacket. Don't you like my new style?"

"No." Augie smiled. "You look like Tom."

Augie left the room without another word and returned with the duffle and backpack Dylan had left behind when he traveled to Reval with Kalev. Augie dropped them on the floor at Dylan's feet. "These are your clothes. Do you need to change now?"

"I appreciate your suggestion. But I'm fine for now. Thanks for holding on to my things. It'll be nice to dress like myself tomorrow."

"You need a haircut."

"You should have seen me before I had it cut in Oregon."

"How could your hair grow so long in a month?" Augie cocked his head. "It's as long as Tom's hair."

"Tom has dreads. Mine's not as long as his."

"Sit down." Augie turned to claim his recliner and elevated his feet. "We should talk."

"You're right. I owe you an apology." Dylan crossed to sit on the plaid sofa after he moved a crocheted afghan to one side.

"Tell me why you're sorry."

"Fair enough. I'm sorry I lied to you about taking a job in Colorado Springs. I didn't go there. I went with Kalev to Reval and couldn't come back until a few nights ago."

"Reval is where the Sasquatches live. Tom told me." Augie tapped a thumb on the arm of his chair. His eyes never left Dylan. "Why didn't you tell me you were going to Reval?"

"I didn't know where Kalev was taking me. I assumed he'd take me into the woods to meet other Sasquatches. When we got to the top of Church Mountain, Kalev tricked me into transferring to Reval with him. I didn't have a choice and needed to wait until the next full moon to come back." Thankfully, Dylan and Kati had left Kalev behind in Reval.

"Can you take me to Reval?"

Dylan did a double take. "You want to go to Reval?"

"Can you take me there?"

"First off, I don't know how to go there without a Sasquatch to help me. But I'm surprised you'd like to see it."

"Why?" Augie cocked his head.

Great question. Dylan could not imagine taking Augie to a foreign country with strange food, undecipherable languages, and unfamiliar customs. Any oddities from a country in *this* dimension would pale in comparison to what Augie would see in Reval. "They eat different stuff, live outside all the time, and don't like humans."

"No burgers?"

"Nope." Dylan smiled. "No fries, no shakes, no bagels, and—worst of all—no pizza."

Augie's foot moved back and forth like a windshield wiper, a sure sign he was in a good mood. "Well then, I'm not interested."

"Not surprised. You told me you wanted to visit Chicago sometime. Maybe we can start with that when I move back there."

"Why don't you stay in Salida? Tom said he might move here to be with Destiny."

Dylan raised a brow. "He told you that?"

"Yes, but I thought he might stay here even before he told me." Augie had an uncanny ability to read people. "Tom and Destiny are in love."

"Have you drawn their pictures? I know you like to draw people's emotions. I'd like to see if you've captured how they feel about each other."

"I'll show you." Augie stood to leave the room. "Stay here."

Dylan heard Augie rifle through papers in the other room. He returned with a blue spiral notebook. Augie moistened a finger and flipped pages until he stopped to double them back. He held out the book.

As Dylan expected, Augie had captured an intimate moment between Destiny and Tom. Their heads tilted together, nearly touching as they huddled over Destiny's son Trip. The boy held an open book. Destiny's mouth captured a word from the story while Tom stole a glance at her, his eyes full of adoration.

"This is perfect." Dylan envied his roommate for finding love in an unexpected place. "Destiny told me you drew some Sasquatches. Can you show me those?"

Augie pulled away the sketchbook and flipped toward the front before handing it back. "Here," he said and returned to his recliner.

The likenesses were impeccable. Dylan followed Augie and pointed. "This is Kalev, and this is his brother Alevide." He looked up at Augie. "Alevide died while I was in Reval."

Augie's brow creased with concern. "How did he die? Did animals kill him like they did Jen?"

"No. A falling tree crushed Alevide. There are terrible wind storms in Reval, and sometimes trees fall without warning." Dylan saw no reason to tell Augie that Kalev likely had a role in causing his brother's death or that Alevide was Dylan's father. He pointed to a Sasquatch standing next to Alevide. "This is Tiina."

"Kalev is in love with her."

Stunned, Dylan asked, "How do you know that?"

"Sometimes I have the dreams. I see what Kalev sees." Augie looked into the kitchen as if his words had no consequence.

"But how do you know he loves Tiina?"

"I can feel how he feels."

"When was your first dream about Kalev?" Could Augie tap into Kalev's thoughts only when the Sasquatch was in Porgu?

"In May."

"When was the last?"

"Before you left."

Augie's leg started to wiggle. The conversation had lasted too long and breached territory that made Augie uncomfortable. But Dylan was determined to uncover more. "You haven't had any dreams like this since I left with Kalev?"

"I said I didn't have any more dreams about Kalev." Augie took back the book and turned to the final page. The whole chair trembled from Augie's movements by the time he handed the notebook to Dylan. "I had this dream last night."

Dylan's jaw dropped when he saw the photo-likeness of Destiny's rental house in Oregon. Augie had captured the image in darkness. Long shadows crossed the yard where trees blocked the light from street lamps. The sky was charcoal gray, and stars speckled the sky. Dylan ran his palm across the page before tapping a FOR SALE OR RENT sign drawn in the corner.

"Did Destiny tell you her old landlord was planning to sell the house in Oregon?" Dylan asked but guessed Augie's answer before he could respond.

"No. I saw the sign in my dream."

"Was this Kalev's dream?" Dylan held his breath, waiting for Augie to respond.

"No. She is someone else. I never had her dreams before."

"She?"

"Yes. Her dreams are different from Kalev's."

"Different how?" Dylan gripped the afghan, knotting his fingers into the loose yarn. There could be other female Sasquatches sending broadcast messages. But how many would send one of Destiny's Oregon home?

"She was sad nobody was home."

"Who was she looking for?"

"I don't know." Augie's leg wiggled harder. "I see the dream and know what she feels. But I don't understand why."

Dylan crossed the room to kneel next to Augie's chair. He placed the notebook on Augie's lap and patted his hand. Augie's leg slowed, but his creased forehead reflected his anxiety.

"Don't stress over my questions. I appreciate everything you've told me."

Dylan glanced at the notebook, still open to the page with Destiny's former home. The vision must have come from Kati. They did not intend for her to transfer with Dylan. But somehow she did, and they were separated when they entered Porgu. If she went to Destiny's house, she was trying to find him.

His mind raced, considering what to do—what he *must* do.

"Tomorrow, I'm helping Tom at your cabin, but after that, I'm going back to Oregon. Would you like to go with me?"

"Yes." Augie grinned, his legs still and relaxed. "Can I meet your girlfriend?"

Dylan rubbed his stubbly chin. "Girlfriend?"

"You look like Tom when he talks about Destiny."

Chapter 8

DETROIT LAKE, OREGON
KATI

Sharp rocks and brittle brush gave me purchase on my climb down the cliffside. I inched my way, finding a new toe or finger hold before moving.

Once, I dislodged a nest and nearly fell when a bird flew at my face. If I had my transmission skills, I would have calmed the stressed animal. But in my disabled state, that option was not available. No matter. It would find another place to rest.

Nearly halfway down with one foot securely planted on a protrusion, I dangled the other to search for a lower toe hold. Nothing. In a smooth motion, I swung my leg to the side, flexing my toes and expecting to feel a solid surface. Only air. After my third unsuccessful sweep, my shoulders began to shake. The secure foot trembled.

Keep it together—another expression from Dylan. I drew a long slow breath.

Leaning out, I could see I'd climbed to the top of an overhang. A glance to either side told me sideways was not an option. The slight crack I'd followed offered more protection than the smooth walls an arm's length away.

My heart thundered in my ears.

Ever so slowly, I transferred full weight to my arms and lowered my body below the jutting rock without knowing what lay underneath— besides the long drop to the creek below.

When most of me hung unsupported, I kicked a foot forward to sway my hips toward the wall. With a leap of faith that a nearby ledge might stop my freefall, I released my grip.

"Oof." I slammed into the wall and crumpled onto a tiny shelf. I smoothed the dirt under my hands and smiled at my good fortune.

Seconds later, pebbles cascaded from above. The stones, some the size of my fist and others as small as dust, skittered from above my overhang. They cascaded into the abyss like a sandy waterfall. A dog yelped, and my heart sank—the chasers must have reached the cliff-top.

"Hey!" the master yelled from above.

His voice echoed off the other side until the sound faded into the canyon. The dogs whined in frustration. My nose instinctively wrinkled in response to their fishy aroma—a sure sign of their excitement. More stones fell—the dogs might be running in circles, knowing their quarry was near but out of reach.

"Come!" The halvek yelled to the dogs. "We'll find another way down. We may even beat her to the bottom." His voice paused. "Maybe she'll fall, and we'll only need to recover her body."

His callousness about my death made me yank grass from my ledge and fling it over the edge. With a sneer, I resolved to outrun him or outsmart him. He would not beat me. Halveks are naturally slow and stupid.

The noisy hunting team was long gone before I felt secure enough to rise and sit on the ledge to inspect for injuries. Some scrapes and a missing fingernail, but the rest of me seemed in fine shape.

On the far canyon wall, water trickled down the sides. Pockets of snow and ice clung in crevices. In a few weeks, both sides might be covered with snow. I was fortunate to be sitting on the sunnier side.

Shadows filled the canyon. Despite the blue sky above the rim, only a few hours of light remained. As long as I reached the bottom soon, the darkness gave me a significant advantage over the halvek. For one thing, my night vision was far superior. Also, if he kept the dogs close, I could stay ahead of them. Eventually, the dogs would tire, and the halvek would require rest. By keeping up my strength with occasional seed cones, I would outdistance them.

I crept forward on the ledge to peer over the side. Maybe it was my optimism, but the remainder of my journey to the creek seemed more straightforward than what I'd seen so far. I took a huge breath and turned around to continue down the cliff.

Other than an unstable vegetable hold that came loose in my grip, forcing me to scramble and find another handhold, I made good progress. Soon I was within three Sasquatch lengths of the bottom.

Bits of debris, moss, and mud covered my fur. I glanced at the stream. How might it feel to lay in the icy water and bathe before continuing?

The rock under my right foot let go. I froze.

How could I be so careless? I should have known better than to daydream about cleanliness when I still had a ways to go. Until that point, I'd tested every foot and handhold on my way down. My lack of focus left me precariously perched on one foot.

I lifted the unsecured foot and slid it across the granite face to find a rock or bump to give me purchase. Nothing worked. Muscles spasmed around my knee, and I took a deep calming breath.

Subtly, I adjusted my secure foot to change the rock wall's pressure points. Whether from fear or fatigue, the shaking spread to my core and arms.

I struggled to gain composure. My hands trembled, and I fell backward—away from the wall.

Time seemed to slow.

As I dropped, I grabbed a sapling to help right my body. But the meager branches peeled off, leaving a shredded stick in my wake.

A foot smacked the ground, and I slid.

With each whack down the slope, I floundered to find anything secure to slow my fall. Loose rocks and plants joined my bounce to the bottom.

Immediately before my feet struck the creek bed, I pointed my toes to land on the balls of my feet. My bent knees absorbed the impact. Once stopped, I fell forward into the water onto my extended arms. When they collapsed, my face unceremoniously submerged.

After pushing my arms to raise my head and shoulders out of the water, I spat to clear out sand and mud. My faint reflection in the stream seemed grossly distorted by the water dripping from my fur. With a mighty shove, I heaved myself onto the shore to lay on my back and catch my breath.

Above, the canyon rim looked incredibly distant as I traced the cracks, sheer walls, and outcroppings of my path. How had I made it down without killing myself? I had no energy to replicate Dylan's celebratory fist pump. Breathing seemed enough of a reward.

One at a time, I wiggled my hands and arms with a good result. Afterward, I lifted each leg. My left felt strong—no remnant tremors. But the other, the one that gave me trouble in the first place on the insecure rock hold, was not quite right. The knee bent properly, but when I tried to rotate my ankle it tingled, then flared with pain.

I stared up at the top of the rim and saw no trace of my pursuers. They may have found a more accessible route to the river, but I felt confident my progress put me ahead.

Keep moving.

A stout tree offered leverage to help me rise. When I tested the weak ankle, stabbing pain shot up my leg. I balled my fists in frustration.

First my telepathy and now my body. Porgu is full of danger and frustration—no wonder halveks are brutally primitive. I want that gun from my first visit—I'd shoot the dog master and stop him in his tracks.

I needed to calm and focus. Strength and persistence would get me to Salida.

A gentle push from a tentative finger confirmed the joint had started to swell. I took a step to cross into the stream and winced each time I put pressure on my foot.

How would I keep ahead of my pursuers if I could not run?

Bracing for the cold, I stuck my foot in the icy water. The chill soothed the throbbing, but I could no longer depend on my speed. I glanced up at the canyon walls to estimate how long the dog and master's detour might take.

To compensate for my weaknesses, I chose a new route built on solid reasoning. Based on my recollection of the area, I figured Salida was to the southeast, and upstream in the canyon should be east. I pushed forward in the creek bed with a painful but manageable limp, heading against the current.

By the time the canyon sides sloped to nearly meet the creek bed, daylight had ended. My feet were almost completely numb, but the compromised ankle did not hurt as much. Fear of pursuit and inertia drove me onward.

As I left the stream and turned southeast, I heard an unfamiliar sound.

Other Sasquatches had brought back memories of halvek music, and while I'd never heard it outside of a vision, I recognized the rising and falling notes. These tones were intentional sounds from a halvek-made instrument. I searched memories about music that Dylan had shared—irritating noises with banging and blasting tones. Those tunes were very different from what I heard in the darkness.

I needed to put more distance between myself and the dogs, but the irresistible melody drew me nearer. The notes' pitch and duration formed complex patterns—some repeated and others innovatively fresh. When I tried to break away, I could not and limped ever closer to the sound. With each step, I longed to hear more.

When I saw a female halvek sitting in the clearing under the light of the waning moon, the numbing comfort I'd felt in the icy stream had completely worn off. My pain grew unbearable. I hobbled around the edge of her clearing and dropped next to a thick pine.

Seed cones littered the ground below the tree. I grabbed one and gnawed it to bits, hoping to regain strength but feeling I might not ever stand again.

Between the trees, I could see her sitting, straight-backed and cross-legged. She blew into the mouthpiece of a long wooden pipe. Her fingers flicked over holes as they created a melody that filled the night sky. From the way she shifted on the rock, I sensed she knew I was there.

Mesmerized by the sound, I nearly forgot about the dogs.

Chapter 9

LUCAS EDWARDS

The minute Lucas heard the music, he blew the ultrasonic whistle to call the dogs to him. No need to warn the musician about his arrival. Lucas had seen the posted signs and knew the land was private property. If he were hunting local game, he would have called the owner and asked permission to cross. But this was no ordinary hunting trip. He'd been on the run all day to catch up with the beast, and he would not stop to make a courtesy call.

Earlier in the day, his plans had clicked into place. His friend generously gave him two healthy hunting dogs and supplies to keep them fed and under control. Next, he rendezvoused with the guy who had posted the Sasquatch sighting in Jamesville.

The plaid-wearing fellow was an Oregonian to the core—beefy, honest, and chatty.

When the man pulled up behind Lucas in the alley with his white, extended cab dually, Lucas knew he could be trusted. They both had great taste in dual rear wheel vehicles. But Lucas's truck had the sheen of a daily washed model while the other would be due for a new paint job in a year or less.

"That you, Lucas?" the man asked as he muscled himself out of the truck.

Who else would meet you in an alley at six in the morning? But Lucas said, "It's me. Thanks for meeting me. I want to hear all about your sighting. Is it your first?"

The guy tipped up the brim of his cap with a thumb. "Yeah. I would never have believed it if one of my friends told me the story. But when it happens to you, it must be true."

"Tell me." Lucas braced himself for a longer-than-needed story.

"When I turned into this alley," he pointed to the entrance, "I could see the outline of something big over by this dumpster. At first, I thought it might be someone hauling out trash in the middle of the night. But then I caught a better view when I hit the brights."

"Show me where."

The man walked to the back of the dumpster and jabbed a finger toward the ground. "I only saw it for a few seconds, but it was right here." He sidled up next to the trash bin. "What do you think? This side is about five feet tall, right?" Lucas nodded, and the man continued. "I'd say Bigfoot was three feet taller than the top."

"Are you sure? That seems pretty tall."

"It was huge and skinny. But it didn't look like any drawings or photos I've seen before. All of them picture Bigfoot like a big hairy ape. This one was lean with a narrow face."

"Could it have been a tall homeless guy? I saw some response posts from people who were skeptical about your sighting."

"Yeah, I guess it's possible." He shrugged. "But it wasn't wearing clothes and had long hair all over its body. Except maybe on its face. Seems like its face had shorter hair and maybe lighter. I knew it was a Sasquatch right away—you can just tell." He cleared his throat with a deep cough. "Look, I only saw it for a few seconds. By the time I parked and jumped out of the truck with my phone, it was gone."

"Which way did it go?" Lucas gestured, urging him to show where the beast made her exit.

He pointed behind the dumpster. "It must have squeezed through here and jumped that fence. When I searched in the back, there was no sign of it." The man looked from the spot where the Sasquatch had disappeared back to Lucas. "Have you ever seen one? What's your interest?"

"Nope." Lucas shook his head. "I found your posting and was fascinated by your description. All the other postings mention a big bulky animal that walks with a clumsy gait. Your story sounded different, and I wanted to hear your account first-hand."

"Happy to help." With that, the man nodded toward his car. "I've got to get to work. Great to meet you."

Lucas waited until the guy's taillights disappeared before he clicked on a flashlight and maneuvered behind the dumpster. He squeezed to the fence, where he knelt and examined each twisted wire.

"Bingo," he called to no one. *She's left me a gift. The dogs are going to love this.* Lucas pulled strands of fine beige hair out of the crimped chain link and walked to the kennels in the back of his truck.

After about an hour of tracking the Sasquatch's trail through the back alleys of tiny Jamesville, the dogs led Lucas out of town and parallel to the highway headed southeast.

The farther they got from Lucas's truck, the more disheartened he grew. If he made a kill, Lucas needed the vehicle nearby to transport the carcass. With a less valuable trophy, he might hide the body until he retrieved his truck. But Lucas could not risk another hunter finding her while he was away.

Could the Sasquatch be smart enough to understand the convenience of staying near the roadways? Bridges would help avoid major water crossings, and the graded terrain would be faster than navigating through gullies or canyons.

Lucas returned to the truck and drove to where the dogs last had her scent. He spent a minute there to keep them interested before re-kenneling them. After a few miles farther down the road, he released the dogs again. When they picked up the trail right away, Lucas smiled. His Sasquatch was indeed following the road.

Lucas repeated the process every few miles, the dogs confirming her commitment to stay near the highway. She probably appreciated the cover of darkness. How far could she travel during the night if she left Jamesville near the time she was spotted? Lucas pulled out his hunting GPS and measured the distance. He would continue confirming her trail with the dogs, but Lucas figured she might stop to rest somewhere near Detroit Lake. The area had an abundance of water and hidden coves offering protection.

When he reached a point where the dogs no longer picked up her scent,

Lucas doubled back until they found her trail as it headed north and away from the lake. He locked the truck and confidently hefted his rifle, knowing she couldn't be far.

That was how his long day had progressed. By late afternoon, they'd only caught her scent and had a near-miss when the dogs chased her over a cliff. At nightfall, the dogs picked up her trail upstream from the precipice. Lucas did not know whether to be pleased or frustrated. While he preferred to catch her without a ripped hide or bruises from a fall, his taxidermist could work miracles. Better to trap her quickly—before she escaped forever.

Music floated from the meadow as he broke through the trees. A woman in a gauzy ankle-length dress and an oversized quilted hunting jacket sat on a low, flat rock in the center of the clearing. Her lips firmly gripped the mouthpiece of a foot-and-a-half-long recorder.

She seemed harmless—probably a peace-loving earth muffin with a thick braid draped over a shoulder.

Lucas knew he could talk her into permitting him to search her land.

Chapter 10

KATI

Low branches helped me hide as my pursuer stumbled into the clearing and called to his dogs. My superior night vision gave me an advantage over the halvek. He would not see me.

The dogs were another matter. Based on their galloping pursuit with tongues wagging and legs scrambling, they had picked up my scent. I pressed further against the pine's prickly trunk. Sticky sap glued me to the bark. Or maybe lethargy kept me from jumping up to flee.

In one swift motion, the female halvek laid aside the pipe and grabbed a firearm resting at her side. My jaw dropped when she leveled the gun and called to the dog master, "You're on private property. I'm asking you to leave right now! And take those beasts with you."

"Come!" the dog master called as he slid to a stop in the wet grass. The dogs passed the female and completely ignored her. My body tensed, anticipating their assault. If they attacked, I could toss them out of the meadow or crush their throats. But they did not deserve mistreatment—the dog master commanded them, and they were simply responding to him.

"Come!" he called again, louder. On his second attempt, they responded. The dogs tumbled forward with their front legs reacting before the rear—nearly plunging end over end before they stopped only a few feet from my side of the clearing.

I dared not breathe as the pair whimpered but obeyed his directive. They returned to sit next to him and squirmed, knowing their quarry was near. Their instinctive movements were subtle, and the halvek ignored them—likely unaware of their anxiety.

"I'm sorry to bother you." His condensed breath puffed in the chilled air. The halvek laid his gun on the ground near his feet and rose slowly with his hands open and wide apart.

"My name's Lucas, and I've been tracking an animal for days. I'm certain it's nearby. May I have permission to cross your land?"

The female threw back her head and laughed. Did she find *Lucas* or his request humorous? She waved the tip of her gun toward him. "Our property line started a mile back. You have the nerve to ask permission after you jumped a fence and ignored at least three no trespassing signs to get here?"

"You're right." His crooked smile seemed designed to deceive. "I should've tried to contact you before I came onto your property. Please, forgive me." He rubbed his hands together and blew on them, ostensibly to warm them. "This animal would be an amazing find. I can tell you're a hunter by the way you're holding that Browning. We could look for it together and share credit for the discovery."

"Discovery?" She cocked her head.

He paused as if considering options. "You might not believe me, but I've been tracking a Sasquatch."

She showed no sign of interest or surprise. He continued. "I saw her near my cabin a few days ago and found traces of her hair. These dogs are tracking her scent. She may have been injured in a fall over a cliff. If you help me, we can find her."

The female halvek shifted her weight on the rock. "Her?"

Without clearly seeing her face, I did not know whether she was intrigued or playing for time. I peeked through the branches at Lucas and twisted a fingernail between my teeth to extract a bit of cone.

Listening. Waiting.

"I caught a good look at her. She's definitely female."

Lucas stood for the longest time, waiting for her to respond. Finally, he asked, "Well, will you help me?"

Again, he waited. The tip of her gun never faltered and stayed centered on his chest. "No. I don't think so. Leave your rifle where it is and take your dogs."

"But…" he tried to interrupt.

"Go back the way you came in. Don't even think about circling the property. You're right. I'm a damn good hunter. If I hear you or your dogs, I'll come after you and won't warn you before I shoot. I have a right to protect my property."

My stomach fluttered—pleased her actions helped conceal me but unsure of her motives.

"I'm guessing you don't believe me." Lucas placed a hand against his breastbone. "I swear I'm no crackpot. Before I saw her, I didn't believe they existed." When she did not respond, he took a step forward. "You don't understand."

"I completely understand." She raised the gun butt to her shoulder and looked at him over the length of the weapon. "You take one more step, and I'll shoot you dead."

"Okay, okay. I'll leave." He raised both hands and took a step back. "There's no need for violence."

When he leaned down to retrieve his gun, she said, "Are you deaf? I told you to leave your rifle on the ground."

"But it's been in my family for years. I can't part with it." I detected a hint of deceit in his voice. Was he trying to influence her?

"I'll drop it at the county Sheriff's Office the next time I'm out that way."

"Tomorrow?"

"Not likely." She scoffed. "Salem's an hour from here. I might get there before the end of the year."

"Whatever you're comfortable with." Lucas balled his hands into fists, ostensibly struggling to bury his aggravation. He lifted his cap and swiped a hand across the top of his head. "Can I take out a flashlight? There's plenty of light in this clearing, but the woods are dark."

"Take it out slowly so I can see what you're doing."

Lucas held one side of his jacket open with two fingers while he slowly slipped the other inside and retrieved a metal cylinder. After he clicked a button on the top, a beam of light splayed on the ground.

"Now go," she commanded.

The man called the dogs and strode into the woods. She waited, and I listened to their fading footfalls.

After a few moments, she dropped the front of the gun and leaned forward as if to listen for their return. They had left, but her hearing was likely not as keen as mine.

"Hmph." The halvek returned her firearm to its resting place next to the rock. She continued to stare at where the dog master had stood as she smoothed the front of her skirt.

Moments passed before she picked up the instrument and ran her fingers over the holes without putting the mouthpiece to her lips. Was she still thinking about the interruption or something else? She glanced toward the tree where I hid.

I hunched my shoulders, trying to look smaller but knowing there was no use. Even though she had looked away, the halvek knew I was there.

"You can stay right where you are. I'm not going to hurt you," she called over her shoulder. "I'm guessing you were enjoying my recorder. It's Bach, and I'm not ready to go inside yet. Stay and listen if you'd like."

She started to play a melody with steady shifts in the tune that made the music animated yet hypnotic. I tried to keep my head firmly upright and propped against the tree, but it kept nodding forward with a jerk.

Focusing on her as best I could—eventually she faded into a mist.

My eyes shut as I gave in to fatigue.

Chapter 11

NOVEMBER 23

The sun's rays tried to pierce my eyelids, but I was loath to open them and face another disappointing day. I had dreamt of my sleep site in Reval with its forgiving ground and a soft blanket leaf for protection from the wind. But Porgu's unrelenting birdsongs and penetrating pine needle fragrance forced me into reality—I was far from home.

While my dream of Reval quickly faded, I still felt a leaf cover resting on my shoulder. I did not recall hauling tree boughs to build a nest. My memories from the previous night were exclusively of the female halvek chasing away Lucas the dog master and his beasts—and falling into a deep sleep while listening to her spellbinding music. I opened my eyes to discover a halvek blanket covering my body.

I snapped to attention and raised on an elbow—no halveks within sight. I heard no footfalls or clothing rustles, only chirps, clicks, and chatter from Porgu wildlife.

With a sigh of relief, I lay back to consider whether to find a hiding place until the next full moon or continue to Salida and reconnect with Dylan. That is if he *was* in Salida and not in Reval dealing with Kalev and other horrors.

I rolled onto my back. In the same motion I might make with a leaf cover, I pulled the hefty fabric up to my neck.

Wait. Where did it come from?

The blanket smelled like a mixture of Porgu's most fragrant flowers and looked like hundreds of fabric squares bound together into a vast flat covering.

But who put it here?

I would have noticed it if it was under the tree when I dove beneath the branches. I struggled to recall any details of the evening where a halvek might have delivered the covering. All I could remember was feeling saved when Lucas left the clearing.

Could the female have approached my hiding spot and covered me without waking me? If I were at full strength, a halvek could never surprise me. I would hear their approach either from their clumsy footsteps or ragged breathing.

My exhaustion and injury had left me vulnerable. Without rising, I could feel my swollen ankle and sense the pain that would come if I tried to stand. *I must find somewhere to hide and heal.* Away from the sly female but also far from the dogs.

After flipping the cover off my shoulder, I struggled to sit upright and banged my head against a low branch. The blow sent a tremor down my spine, reminding me of the injury that robbed me of my telecommunication and animal control skills.

I balled my hands into fists. These injuries would not defeat me. After a sweeping glance around the open meadow, I decided to send another broadcast message.

Through the faint morning fog, I could see trees, the clearing, and a faraway fence with a sign. Halvek symbols were grouped into the words YOU'RE STANDING ON PRIVATE PROPERTY—EXIT HERE. NOW! While Dylan gave me an extensive range of halvek verbal vocabulary, he never taught me how to translate their written language. The symbols and their meaning were lost on me. I closed my eyes to help focus on the vision. Images swirled in my mind instead of forming an articulate message.

Giving up, I dropped into a curled lump and pulled the blanket over me.

Maybe I would lie here until the female halvek changed her mind and joined forces with Lucas the dog master. They would find me and shoot me full of holes before carving up my best features for the wall. The two primitive halveks could share my corpse with my head mounted next to Lucas's moose and my skin on her floor.

When I heard bipedal footsteps swishing across the grass, I ignored them. Let her come and kill me. If I were still in Reval, I would already be dead. What did it matter?

"Hello? Don't be afraid. I'm not gonna hurt you." She spoke with the soothing voice from the night before—not harsh commands like she gave to the dog master but with the tone suggesting I listen to her music. I lay still under the blanket. Maybe she would assume I died in the night and go away.

"I don't know what you eat, but I brought you breakfast." She jiggled a pan, and the cover rattled. "It's scrambled eggs. But I put some sausage, fried mushrooms, and peppers on the side. I don't know if you eat meat— that's why I separated them. Joe made the sausage himself. He adds fennel seed to the ground meat, and that's the most predominant spice. If I were a meat-eater, I'd probably love it. But I turned vegetarian a few years back. I still enjoy cooking meat for Joe. The smells are to die for."

Despite her constant verbal assault, most of which I did not understand, the fragrance in the pan overwhelmed me, and my mouth filled with saliva—a sensation I had never experienced before. Sasquatches did not salivate before entering a nutrient pool in Reval.

With great difficulty, I sustained my simulated death. My stomach growled, begging me to accept what she'd brought.

I heard her kneel in front of the tree and shove away the branches between us. "Your cheeks are hollow, and your skin makes me think you're dehydrated. I brought a pitcher of water. Can't I convince you to take something? You'll need to get stronger if you want to keep ahead of that asshole hunter."

What could she mean? Was she aligned with Lucas the dog master? Her tone when she used the word *hunter* told me otherwise. I searched through Dylan's shared memories and pictured a sphincter. Surely, this image was not a positive reference.

The food's scent grew more potent, and my resolve weakened. The High Council prohibited engaging with halveks. Yet I'd already killed two, buried the bodies with another, and tangled with the dog master. How could one more interaction be worse than what I'd already done? I could either die in this spot from a lack of food and water or regain my strength and continue my journey to find Dylan. The second option seemed preferable.

When I rose to sit, she fell backward on her behind and nearly dropped the pan and pitcher. The female's laugh came out with the grace I would associate with a self-deprecating Sasquatch who found humor in a mishap. Not a response I would expect from the clumsy, short-tempered, and ill-mannered halveks.

"I'm Tansy," she said as she recovered her position. She opened the black pan on the ground in front of me and pulled a metal implement from her coat pocket. "I brought a fork but have no idea if you need it." Tansy inspected the fork from the front and back. "You know, forks are funny looking. Aren't they? I never considered what they look like to someone who might not use them regularly. If I didn't know how to use one, I sure wouldn't put it in my mouth. It looks dangerous with all those points on the end."

I looked from her to the food and back.

"Try some." She nudged the pan closer and sat back to wait—shockingly silent.

My stomach growled again, urging me as much as she had. I reached forward and grasped a piece of the yellow mass between my fingers. Most fell apart and landed back in the pan. But some remnants stayed, and I brought a finger to my lips.

"Do you like it?" Tansy moved slightly closer.

Before she could take it away, I grabbed the pan and devoured nearly everything—the yellow mush and the chunks of slippery brown, red and yellow. The gray bits she called sausage I left alone after one whiff. Its scent made my stomach lurch. There was something very wrong with that item. After I'd finished, I stuck out my tongue and licked the greasy coating from the dish, being careful to avoid the sausage pile.

My eyes closed in satiated delight. The flavors and textures were new and exciting. My body tingled as it had years ago with my first sexual encounter. That experience gave me a hint at what pleasures my body could feel. Halvek food came a close second.

"I guess you liked it?" Tansy asked as she handed me the water pitcher. "You must be dehydrated, and I'm not nervous about adding salt to my eggs. Please, drink this. I can bring you as much as you'd like. I suspect you've been drinking from the streams. Joe says you can get giardia from unpurified water. This is from our well. It's completely clean. I can't even remember the last time I drank city water. Joe says it's full of chlorine and other chemicals. They think it's okay to treat water with stuff to strengthen your teeth. But they don't know who might be allergic. Seems like they should leave it alone and allow folks to make their own decisions about what to put into their bodies."

I gulped several mouthfuls before I set the pitcher on the ground.

This halvek had many words that needed saying. It made me think of Sasquatch transmissions with rapid-fire still images and clips with moving pictures. She could talk nearly as fast as we could transmit.

I liked her.

"Kati," I said in my hoarse whisper of a voice. "My name is Kati."

Chapter 12

Sun poured through the cabin windows and reflected on bits of sanded drywall mud circulating in the air.

"You must be glad you put the new roof on before the cold weather hit," Dylan called over his shoulder as he dipped drywall tape in the compound and smoothed it on the wall with a putty knife.

"Wasn't an option." Tom worked on the other side of the room. "I wanted to keep snow out and run a heater while we did the indoor work. The place should be move-in ready before the new year."

"What's the hurry?" From Jen's description of winter in Salida, Dylan knew that most days were sunny, and many had temperatures into the sixties. While there would be some snow in the valley, most fell on the high peaks and spared the town.

"Augie agreed to let me live here rent-free for six months in exchange for doing the repairs. I have a personal deadline to move in full time after the holidays."

Dylan swiped a loose lock away with the back of his arm. A gob of mudding compound hung from the ends of his hair.

I'm making a mess of myself and the wall.

One glance at Tom reinforced which of them had done this before. Tom's jeans and zipped-up hoodie were as clean as when they started the project hours ago. Dylan looked like he'd lost a food fight with pancake batter.

"How does Destiny feel about you moving out?" As soon as Dylan asked, Augie peeked around an archway from the back hallway. He held a sanding block in his hand.

"My living with Destiny was always a temporary situation. I needed a place to stay while I waited for you to come back. Making our arrangement permanent shouldn't be a matter of convenience. A decision like that deserves a well-thought-out conversation."

"But you treat her nice," Augie piped in, "not like Nate."

"Don't forget, she only became a widow six weeks ago. Destiny needs time to find herself again, work out her future with Trip, and set up her business." Tom finished the drywall joint and turned to face Dylan. "We're not calling it quits. I'm giving her space to see if I fit in her plans." The corner of Tom's mouth ticced up. "That being said, you don't see me headed off to Chicago and letting some other guy muscle his way in."

Augie disappeared around the corner, apparently satisfied with Tom's answer.

A sharp knock on the front door caught their attention.

"Expecting someone?" Dylan asked as he picked at a blob of drywall compound on his sleeve.

"I could always use another pair of hands." Tom set down his joint knife and wiped his hands on a rag.

Tom opened the front door, and Cynthia Waters burst into the room—a bouncing mass of auburn curls and jiggling breasts. She crossed the room to envelop Dylan in a massive hug around his waist, ignoring the smears of drywall mud on the front of his sweatshirt.

"I'm so happy you made it home safely," she said into his chest. Cynthia eased back to raise on her toes and plant a lipstick-laden kiss on his jaw. "I was so worried about you."

Out of the corner of his eye, Dylan saw Augie reappear with his lips pulled into a tight line.

Cynthia continued her explosive monologue, oblivious to a lack of salutations from the men in the room. "Erle and I waited all night for you to come back to the top of Church Mountain. You can't believe the horrific snowstorm that night. By morning, the ground was covered with six inches of snow. I thought we were going to die up there. You've heard about people on Everest who were buried under snow and suffocated inside their tents, right?"

Without waiting for Dylan to respond, Cynthia wrenched something out of Dylan's hair and continued. "I made Erle go out every half hour and shake the accumulation off the tent. We wanted to be there when you returned. But what's the point in being there if we were dead when you got back?" She took a step back to stand with feet apart and hands on her curvy hips. "How could we help you if we were dead?"

"Did you want me to answer that question?" Dylan asked.

"Of course not." Cynthia flicked the wad of dried mud to the drop cloth. "You should know, Erle and I wanted to help you in any way we could. We would have taken you to the hospital, given you food, or anything. Who knew you'd show up in Oregon?"

Cynthia stopped her barrage and stared at Dylan, obviously waiting for him to divulge any tidbits she could use for an article or whatever she might be working on. Dylan was not playing her game. He had no intention of letting her know about his month in Reval or the relationships he'd formed with the Sasquatches.

Dylan swallowed hard. "Thank you."

"I'd love to hear about your adventure." She tipped her head. "Erle told me you left Salida in mid-October with a giant Sasquatch named Kalev. After a month, you showed up naked in rural Oregon. The world should know your story."

"How did you hear about my condition in Oregon?" Again, Cynthia proved herself to be a better detective than Dylan. He'd read the meager accounts in the news. They spoke of a disoriented man found walking along a deserted Oregon highway, but none mentioned his lack of clothes.

"I've done my homework."

"Who did you con into talking?"

Cynthia knew how to play the angles and get people to share details that eluded him. She stayed one step ahead of him last summer in his hunt for Trip's abductor.

"I don't divulge my sources." Cynthia flipped a handful of hair behind a shoulder and tipped her head toward him as if they were compatriots. "I promise not to release any part of your story to the public until you want me to."

"Okay." Dylan turned to his drywalling supplies but jerked back when he considered the full extent of her words. "I don't want you to release anything—ever."

"I understand why you'd be reluctant to work with some local hack or even a national reporter looking for fame and glory. That's why I want you to give me an exclusive. We can work together, side-by-side. I'll write it exactly the way you want. If you'd like a running story with installments every month for a year, I can do that. If you'd rather we create a full-length book, I'd be happy to write it." She laid a hand on Dylan's forearm. "This is *your* story, and I can help you inform the world."

Dylan batted her hand and picked up the end of a piece of drywall tape to watch it unspool. Did the public deserve to know about the roots of the human race? If so, would a book written by Cynthia Waters be the best way to unveil the truth?

Tom broke into Dylan's thoughts. "You don't need to make a decision today."

Wise words.

"Can you give me some time to think about it?" asked Dylan.

"Take as much time as you need." She hooked a curl behind her ear. "But consider writing down some notes about what you saw and did. Our memories fade faster than you can imagine." In a swift movement, Cynthia extricated a card from a pocket. "Here's my contact info. I'm staying at the Palace Hotel. You can reach me there anytime."

Dylan held the card between a thumb and finger, bending it into an arc. "I'll let you know when—or if—I'm ready to talk."

"Just assure me you won't give your story to anyone else, and I'll leave you to your work." She glanced around the room. "Hard to believe this place was a burned-out shell only a few weeks ago."

"Kirk Steadman's criminal handwork," Tom chimed in. "It'll never be the same as when Jen Rickard lived here. We had to scrape all the charcoal off the log walls, wash them down, and cover them with smoke sealing paint before we drywalled over what's left of the logs. I liked the natural look, but it wasn't possible to save them."

"I hear Steadman's in custody for arson." Cynthia shifted to a pained look, but was her empathy genuine or fabricated? "Maybe they'll put him away for a long time."

"Unless it's for life, it won't be long enough for me." Tom tipped his joint knife toward her. "He's a career criminal who tried to turn this place into a warehouse for stolen merchandise. When we upset his plans, he decided to destroy it.”

“Sounds like a cut and dried case to me,” offered Cynthia.

“I won’t be satisfied until I hear his sentencing. He’s a slippery bastard with a propensity to avoid prison.” Tom glanced down at his mud pan. “If you don’t mind, we want to finish our work before this stuff dries out.” He turned to the wall and started another piece of tape.

“Stay in touch.” Cynthia squeezed Dylan’s arm. “I’ll hold you to our agreement about exclusivity.”

Dylan nodded, not to agree with her verbal contract but to indicate he’d contact her if he *ever* decided to tell his story.

When the door closed, Dylan glanced at Augie, still standing in the back archway. “I guess Cynthia forgot to say goodbye to you. Or hello, for that matter.”

“That’s okay. Cynthia is not my friend.” Augie tapped the sanding block against the side of his hand and watched dust fall to the floor. “She’s not your friend, either.” He turned to walk down the hallway.

“As usual, you’re right.” Dylan crossed the room to his partially finished wall and nodded toward Tom. “Augie and I are headed to Oregon.”

“Leaving me alone to finish up the drywall?” Tom asked with a snicker.

“We’ll help today. But after we finish, we’ll clean up at Augie’s and take off. The drive will take about twenty hours. If Augie and I trade off sleeping, we can make it in one go without stopping overnight. If we get there early in the afternoon, I’d be okay with that.”

Augie appeared again. “I’m driving half the way? You drove before.”

“That was a rental car. This time, I’m hoping we can take yours.”

“Sure,” Augie agreed with a shrug and went back to sanding.

“May I ask why you’re hurrying back to Oregon?” Tom asked.

“Augie’s been intercepting transmissions.”

“From Kalev?”

“I don’t think so. They were from Destiny’s rental house in Oregon. Augie and I want to find out who’s sending them. Our best bet is to go to Jamesville.”

Dylan clamped his mouth shut when he heard a board creak on the porch outside. He ran to the window and spotted Cynthia hurrying to her car.

Had she lingered on the porch to gather her things? Or maybe she hovered next to the partially open window and listened to their conversation.

"That's unfortunate." Dylan shook his head before turning toward Tom. "I think Kati may have transferred from Reval with me. She wasn't next to me when I appeared, but she might have come with me by accident. If she's still in Oregon, I need to find her."

"Then that's where you should be." Tom nodded. "I'll hold down the fort here while you're away."

Dylan tipped a thumb toward the window. "Try to keep Cynthia off our tail if she comes back."

Chapter 13

DETROIT LAKE, OREGON
LUCAS EDWARDS

After an hour of scouring the property records in the Marion County Assessor's Office and more time talking to the locals in cafés and coffee shops in Mill City and Detroit, Lucas had found what he needed. People around there loved to talk, especially if they thought you had a similar mindset. At midday, Lucas sat in his truck at the crossroads between Detroit and the dirt road where he'd tracked the Sasquatch.

His Sasquatch had run onto an eighty-acre tract of land owned by Joseph Palmer, a sixty-three-year-old recluse. Rumors spoke of a bohemian woman named Tansy, who had lived with him for decades.

Twenty-seven years ago, it was quite the scandal in sleepy Detroit when she moved in at age seventeen. Joe was over twenty years her senior. But that was then. Recently, no one batted an eye at their relationship.

The first encounter with territorial Tansy had not gone well. While she might be a fine solo musician, she would be a tough nut to crack and had his favorite rifle. Not a family heirloom, but a beloved firearm nonetheless. Good thing he'd brought several from the cabin.

Lucas drummed a thumb against the steering wheel. He needed an excuse to enter their property.

Hmm. Joe might be easier to manipulate than his common-law wife. Lucas turned north toward the Palmer property. Somehow, he'd gain access.

For all he knew, the Sasquatch could be long gone by now. But something told him she might have sought refuge on the property.

Forty minutes later, Lucas pulled into the gravel drive, clearly marked PRIVATE PROPERTY, NO TRESPASSING, NO SOLICITATION, NO KIDDIN'. Compared to Lucas's remote retreat, Joe Palmer's residence was a compilation of discarded parts and pieces. The place looked like an abandoned junkyard.

As Lucas opened his truck door and stepped to the drive, he called, "Anybody home?"

A rusted single-wide trailer stood at one end of the yard and must have been the property's first structure. In every direction from the trailer Palmer connected something to increase the living space. One side had a screened-in porch, topped with a living roof of moss and small shrubs. Another connected to a railway container with holes punched for windows. The top of a geodesic dome peeked from behind the trailer, and a well-patched canvas yurt stood a few yards to the side.

Lucas waited for a response but heard nothing except the hum from a heater beside the yurt. A thin plume of gray smoke snaked out of the trailer's chimney. People were likely living in both places.

Stepping over dried weeds, Lucas approached the trailer's rickety porch. Consistent with the mishmash of structures, a veritable treasure trove of collectibles littered the yard. If hillbillies bragged about having an out-in-the-back for their junk, Joe Palmer could boast of having both an out-in-the-back and an out-in-the-front. Lucas counted sixteen cars and trucks in various stages of disassembly.

The most interesting were two dilapidated International Scouts, a vintage Willys Jeep, and a hippy van with a retro paint job circa 1960s. None bore a license plate, and most looked as if they did not work.

Disinclined to roam the property without permission for the second time in as many days, Lucas crossed onto the porch, carefully avoiding gaps and hoping the flimsy boards would support his weight.

He knocked.

No response. Lucas pushed the door with a closed fist. Much to his surprise, the door swung open.

Why would anyone predisposed to privacy and sensitive to invasions leave a door unlocked?

Lucas did not take the bait. He stepped back from the porch and yelled. "Sorry to open your door. It was unlocked and came open when I knocked.

I'm unarmed and only want to talk."

He listened for any sound—a watch dog's nails skittering on the floor, the pump of a shotgun slide, or running footsteps. Nothing. Off-the-grid people were unpredictable, and Lucas needed to exercise caution.

Before giving up and returning to his truck, Lucas considered one more approach to attract attention. Strolling around back to check out the dome seemed a hair's breadth from an intrusion, but the yurt stood next to the driveway and in plain view. Someone must be inside. Why else would they keep it heated?

"Joe, are you around?" Lucas approached the canvas structure. "I'd like to speak with you."

Two brilliant orange and blue painted doors were affixed to the front of the yurt. Lucas raised a clenched fist to knock when the door flew open and nearly hit him square in the face.

He stepped back as Tansy slipped through the opening. While Lucas strained to see behind her, she shut the doors before he could peek inside.

"Why are you here again?" She gave his shoulder a shove. The woman could not have weighed more than a hundred twenty pounds. But what she lacked in girth, she made up for in aggression. "I told you last night to go away and leave us alone."

"I was hoping Joe was around." Lucas raised his hands in surrender and backed up several paces. "As I told you before, my name is Lucas. I'd like to talk with him."

"How do you know Joe?" Tansy's eyes narrowed.

"I think my dad might have worked with him on the pipeline up in Alaska in the seventies." Lucas straightened, hoping Tansy did not see through the ruse he'd designed after talking to the locals.

"So you want me to believe you're here for a social call?" Tansy stood with feet wide apart, defending her territory. "After the shit you pulled last night with your dogs and crossing our property boundary without permission?"

"I understand why you're apprehensive." Lucas dredged out his most obliging smile. "The truth is, I'm visiting the area for a couple of days. One of my objectives was hunting and the other was to find Joe Palmer and see if he remembers my dad." Lucas looked down at his feet, attempting to appear contrite. "He died last year, and I've been tracking down his old friends to piece together more of his history."

"Why didn't you mention this before?"

"At that point, I wasn't sure this was Joe's property. My priority was hunting, and I believed I was on the trail of a Sasquatch. But it's probably long gone by now." He waved a dismissive hand to let her know he no longer cared about searching her land. "Now I want to continue my research about my dad."

Her puzzled expression led Lucas to believe she might be buying his story.

"Joe's not home right now, but he's on the property. Why don't you leave me your father's name and a way to contact you? If Joe wants to talk, he'll let you know."

Score. He'd hooked her. "Sure. Do you have something for me to write on? I didn't bring a card or a pen."

"Based on your haircut and clothes, you look like the type to always have a business card ready." She scowled at him and pointed to his truck. "Wait in there. I don't want you roaming around while I go into the house. I'll bring you some paper." Tansy stood in front of the yurt and waited until Lucas hauled himself into the driver's seat and shut the door.

He opened the window and waved. "I'll be right here until you come back."

Tansy drew her quilted jacket tighter around her middle and marched up the front steps to the house.

While tempted to jump from the truck and see what Tansy was hiding in the yurt, Lucas stayed put. Once he befriended Joe, they could look around together.

In less than a minute, she came out of the house and crossed to Lucas's truck. From under her arm, she extracted Lucas's rifle and handed it to him through the window. "I took out the bullets. But I'm sure you've got more. Do not bring a loaded firearm on our property again."

"Yes, ma'am." Lucas leaned the rifle on the passenger seat, suppressing the urge to wipe her greasy fingerprints from the barrel and stock.

Tansy handed him a pad of yellowed paper with a logo from a hotel in Pennsylvania and a half-chewed pencil with a rock-hard eraser. Lucas grimaced as he held the pencil, imagining what kind of person would put a filthy pencil in their mouth.

Lucas scribbled his cell number and a barely decipherable name that looked like Mike Johnson.

There had to be somebody by that name among the thousands who worked the pipeline in the '70s.

"When do you expect Joe home?" Lucas asked as he handed back the pencil and pad.

"That's none of your business."

"Any chance you can call him to let him know I stopped by?"

"We don't have cell phones. Joe's done the research—they cause brain cancer." Tansy bit her lip as if realizing she may have said too much. She cleared her throat. "I'll give him your note, and if he wants to talk, he'll call from our landline. If not, you won't hear from him." She looked at the truck from front to stern. "Do *not* enter our property again without an invitation from Joe."

Lucas gave her his most sincere smile and a two-finger salute. "I hope we can arrange to meet again soon. I'd like to see if Joe remembers anything about my dad. He talked about a few memorable guys, and Joe Palmer was the name he brought up most often."

Tansy mumbled something indecipherable as she turned. She threw a hasty glance at the yurt on her way to the house.

What was she hiding in there?

Chapter 14

KATI

The cast on my ankle was still wet when Tansy washed her hands in a bowl and left to deal with Lucas the dog-master. We had heard him pull into the driveway and call out. Tansy was confident he would leave if she did not respond. But when his footsteps crunched near the yurt, where I lay on a cot with my leg propped with pillows and foot draped in plaster and fabric, Tansy jumped into action to chase him away.

Trapped inside, I intently listened to their conversion and understood some of what Tansy and the hunter said, but the term *business card* was completely lost on me. When I found myself stuck in Porgu, I had been confidently armed with the vocabulary Dylan taught me. But halveks used expressions without context.

My kind's telepathy—a mixture of rapid-fire moving and still images—was always clear and complete. The halveks' verbal language was just one more disadvantage that kept them from fully developing their intellects.

The day before, when Tansy ushered me into the cloth-covered domicile, she called the place a *yurt*. At my blank expression, Tansy clarified. "A circular tent. Ours is made of canvas, but the originals were made of animal skins." She scrunched her brows. "Not sure, but I think nomads in Mongolia or some other Asian countries use them. Buying one was Joe's idea. There's plenty of room for us both in the main house. But Joe saw an ad in the paper and couldn't resist. Someone was practically giving the yurt away. I wanted to leave it folded up in the bag. But Joe said it might mold if we didn't set it up." Tansy looked around the room. "It's a good thing we did. You're probably more comfortable here than inside our trailer."

Tansy used more words in one conversation than Dylan did in a day. From other Sasquatches' memories, I understood these structures but had never associated a name. If a Sasquatch wanted to reference the structure to another Sasquatch, they would simply transmit the image. Mongolia must be very far away since Dylan had never seen such a building before. At least he had not shared a memory of one with me.

When the hunter's vehicle left the yard, I let out a huge breath.

"It's me," Tansy called before she came through the door and bolted it behind her. "Well, that was surreal."

Unsure of her meaning, I whispered, "What?"

"That asshole Lucas claims to know my husband Joe." She scratched her cheek. "Well, not directly. His father knew Joe when he worked up on the Alaska pipeline in the '70s."

I shrugged and shook my head.

"You probably have no idea what a pipeline is or where Alaska is. Right?"

A single nod served me better than trying to strain out a sentence she could hear.

"Alaska is a huge state north of here, and the pipeline transports oil across that state so they can haul it by ship to where they need it." She laughed at my blank stare. "Never mind. I can tell your knowledge of U.S. history is a bit weak."

Tansy came and sat on the cot. After checking where she'd washed the crusty blood from my head wound, Tansy gently poked at the plaster. "I haven't had to apply a plaster cast in a long time. Joe took a fall a few years back, and he taught me how to set his broken arm. We've got a good stash of cast kits in our bunker. Joe wore his for about five weeks. If I've done this right, yours may last that long. But I'm guessing you plan to walk with yours. I've added an extra plaster bandage to be sure it's thick enough. Of course, I have no idea how long it will take your bones to heal."

If I had access to the healing pools in Reval, my bones would mend in a day. In Porgu, the timing was likely the same as for the halvek. How did they endure the pain and inconvenience from prolonged injuries? No wonder they were prone to erratic behaviors.

Tansy's reference to weeks made me wonder how long I had until the next full moon. Twenty-nine halvek days expire between the full moons. I'd been in Porgu for four. That left twenty-five until I would transfer. Four weeks was twenty-eight days—three beyond my time in Porgu. Whether she wanted me to wear it for four or six weeks, it would not matter. The cast would help me continue my journey, and Dylan would help find a way to break it off my ankle before I transferred.

"I'm glad you decided to come inside and rest." Tansy patted my leg. "It would be best if you slept some more. I'll bring you scrambled eggs in a while. Joe probably won't be home tonight. He's camped out to hunt elk on the north end of our property." She paused. "At least I think it's elk. Turkey season doesn't start until December first." Without skipping a beat, she asked, "Do you know about the months of the year?"

I shrugged.

"How did you learn to speak English?"

Her question was inevitable. I considered how much to share. "I know a halvek—erm, a man. He taught me many of your words. I am learning there are plenty more to know."

"Does he have a name?" Tansy gave my leg a playful nudge.

"Dylan."

"Is he good lookin'?"

Why would she question his eyesight strength?

Tansy must have noticed my confusion and added, "Attractive?"

"You are asking a difficult question. I found him physically attractive. But if he had more hair, he might be exceptionally appealing."

"Your voice makes my throat hurt. Is it painful for you to talk?"

I rubbed my neck. "It does not hurt."

"Maybe there's a way we can improve your lung capacity."

What could she mean?

"Have you ever played a recorder? Or any musical instrument for that matter?"

I shook my head.

Tansy rose and opened a drawer in a blue cabinet near the door. She removed a long pipe, similar to the one she had played when I first saw her. After clearing her throat, Tansy placed the mouthpiece against her lips. A sound resonated from the pipe in an ascending pitch until she changed direction to make the sound descend. Tansy handed the instrument to me. Did she expect me to repeat what she had done?

I looked at both ends of the pipe before imitating how she held it to her lips. When I blew into the top, the only thing that came out was spit and a pfttttt.

She held her sides and rocked back to laugh at me. I did not understand how this activity would help my speech and did not appreciate her laugher. I handed her the pipe.

"No, no, no." Tansy pushed the instrument back. "I'll show you how to work it. With your long fingers, you'll master it in no time."

"Tell me about Joe," I whispered to change the subject and placed the instrument on a table next to the bed.

"He's my husband. We've been together for twenty-seven years. We're soul mates. From the first moment I saw him at the diner, I knew we were destined to spend our lives together." Tansy stared off toward the wall and smiled. "It's not only our physical attraction. We were lovers in previous lives and are bonded throughout time."

I blinked, willing for her to continue the story and hoping she would not ask whether I understood or agreed with her fantasy.

"I can't imagine life without him." She leaned forward. "Do Sasquatches mate once in a lifetime?"

"Not always." I thought of my parents, who would never separate or seek a new mate. "But many stay together for their entire lives. I am surprised halveks have committed relationships. I assumed you might mate with whoever is convenient. Like other lower animals."

Tansy burst out laughing. "I'm going to assume Dylan didn't teach you perfect English because the word is *human*, and I can't imagine you're categorizing me as a lower animal." She poked my rib. "There's nothing higher than humans, right?"

I nodded to avoid a conversation she would never comprehend.

"I could talk with you all day. But if I did, who would finish my chores?" She laid a hand on my shoulder. "I'd ask you to lock yourself in, but you shouldn't walk on that cast for a couple days. Give your ankle a chance to mend." She glanced at the door. "I don't trust Lucas. He'd be the type to come around in the middle of the night to snoop. So I'm going to lock your door from the outside."

I understood her logic but grew concerned about being trapped in a structure. This was precisely why our leaders told transferees never to enter buildings. I scanned the room for a sharp object to facilitate my escape if needed but saw nothing.

Tansy must have noticed my anxiety. She pulled a knife from her coat pocket and laid it on a table next to my bed. "If anyone breaks through that door, use my knife to cut your way out of the yurt. We've patched it before, and it'll be mended again."

She left, and my stomach clenched at the sound of a metal lock closing outside the door.

Chapter 15

On an uncharacteristically sunny morning, Dylan pulled Augie's burgundy sedan to the curb. "Feels funny to be in Jamesville and know Destiny and Trip aren't here."

"They're in Salida," Augie injected.

"It was only a month ago when you and I came to visit them." Dylan rubbed the steering wheel with both hands. "So much has happened since then."

"I'm glad they live in Salida again. They didn't belong in Oregon."

Dylan opened the door and quickly closed it as a rush of cold air whooshed inside. He reached across the seatback to grab a fleece jacket before trying again. "Damn, it's freezing here. I'm getting used to the dry air in Salida."

"Humidity sucks," Augie added, and Dylan grinned.

"Bundle up and grab your drawings. The real estate agent said she'd meet us in a few minutes. I want to walk around the house and compare what we see to your sketches before she gets here."

The pair stood on the sidewalk and stared at the For Sale or Rent sign. Dylan asked, "Is this how you saw the sign in your dream?"

Augie nodded.

"Did you see it in color or black and white? Not that it matters, I only wonder. Kalev sent me a transmission of how things look to him at night. He has amazing night vision."

"I saw Destiny's house at night." Augie squinted as if recalling the memory. "I could see colors. Whenever you and me came to Destiny's house in the dark, I couldn't see the details." He turned to look directly at Dylan. "In my dreams, I can see everything."

"That's the same experience I had with Kalev. I'm sure Kati sent the transmission." Dylan gave Augie's arm a soft punch. "I'm grateful you intercepted her message."

"They seem like dreams, and they only come when I sleep at night."

Dylan motioned for Augie to take the lead on the flagstone path to the house. They stopped before reaching the porch, and Augie pointed to the upstairs window. "That boarded-up window wasn't there before."

"It wasn't there when Destiny lived here either. Let's see what your drawing looks like."

Augie opened his notebook to the page with the house's front and tapped a finger on the upstairs window. "There's no boards."

Dylan leaned over Augie's shoulder to see the details. "What are these?" He asked as he ran a fingernail across the glass panes. Broad strokes from a pencil's flat side had shaded the other windows. Augie had etched the upper one with faint erratic lines.

"This one is broken," Augie answered as he moved the notebook close to his face.

"Did you notice that when you drew them?"

"No. I draw what I see in here." Augie pointed to his temple.

Augie had an innate ability to capture subtle emotions within people's portraits. Small details transferred from Augie's memory to his pencil without pausing for evaluation.

They both turned when a vehicle approached and parked behind Augie's sedan. A woman bundled in a quilted knee-length coat bounded from her car.

"Are you Dylan?" she asked with a broad, sales-appropriate grin.

After greetings and introductions, Dylan confessed. "I'm not here to buy this house or rent it. I'm friends with your last tenant and wanted some information about a person who might have come here looking for me within the last few days."

"Did that someone break in three nights ago?" The agent pressed her lips together.

"We noticed the broken upstairs window. But someone actually went inside?" Kati would never enter a building. But based on Augie's dream, it had to be her.

"Somebody hurled a rock through that second-story window. You should have seen the rock." The agent placed her hands together and mimicked holding something bowling ball-sized. "It must have weighed ten pounds." She pointed toward the boarded-up frame. "It wasn't just the window. They smashed the handle off the backdoor and walked around inside, too."

"My gosh. Was anything damaged?" If Kati was taking risks, she must be nervous or desperate.

"Only the door handle and the window. We had a new knob installed right away, and our window man will be here later today." She adjusted the scarf at her throat. "If you know who might have done this, I'd appreciate you letting me or the police know. At a minimum, I'd like restitution for our expenses."

"I don't want to implicate someone without being certain. If it's who I think it might be, they're a bit naive about laws." Dylan pulled out his wallet and handed her a stack of bills. "I'm happy to reimburse you for the repair costs."

"Teens can be hard to control." She nodded and slipped the money into her purse. "Is this a relative?"

"No. The person I'm thinking of is a close family friend."

"He must be quite strong. Probably a brute of a guy." She stared hard at Dylan's face. "He broke that handle clean off the door. Besides, you'd need a powerful arm to hurl a mini-boulder through a second-story window. My friend in the police department found a few latent prints on a window next to the door. But they could have been from anyone, and there were no hits from their search."

Dylan gave her his most engaging smile. "If I had proof, I'd let you know more, but right now, it's only a suspicion. I'll talk with them to be sure it won't happen again. Now that you're whole on the repair costs, I'm hoping we can forget about it."

Kati would be amused to find out she'd become part of law enforcement's fingerprint database.

The agent shoved her hands deeper into her pockets. "It's funny this house has never caused me any problems. Each time a tenant moved out, it would take a few days to find a new one. This time, it's getting a lot of my attention."

Dylan's curiosity piqued. "How so?"

"Yesterday, I had a long conversation with a woman asking a ton of questions about the house and whether anything unusual had happened since Ms. Kusik moved out."

"Did she give you her name?"

"I don't recall." The agent scrunched her eyes as if thinking. "She kept probing about the break-in and asked if we brought in a forensic team to search for hair and fibers." The agent waved a dismissive hand. "Like we'd insist on an in-depth investigation for a few hundred dollars in repairs? This guy didn't burn the place down. He broke in to look around."

"Anything you can remember about the caller?"

"Yeah. She had a strong east coast accent—maybe New York City."

Cynthia is already a step ahead of us.

Chapter 16

DETROIT LAKE, OREGON
LUCAS EDWARDS

Before Lucas released the dogs, he reinforced their objective by reintroducing them to the spot along the highway where the Sasquatch had left the road and headed north. For added motivation, he gave them a whiff of the bag containing hairs he'd plucked from the fence in Jamesville. Instead of allowing them to retrace the scent to the meadow, Lucas kept them locked in their crates and drove them over seldom used backroads to the far end of Joe and Tansy's homestead.

Lucas parked the car a short distance from Joe Palmer's property line and turned on his hand-held GPS. The screen identified both public and private lands in color-coded blocks. Lucas took care to be sure he'd parked on public property.

He walked the dogs the nearly two-mile perimeter, looking for any sign that his Sasquatch had left the Palmer land. Signs of big game surfaced along their walk. While elk and deer scat littered the ground, the dogs paid no mind to those scents. They knew their task and stayed on point. Unless tracks or scat screamed Sasquatch, other significant mammal traces did not exist.

On the far end of their circular route and near the meadow, the dogs quickly reconfirmed the Sasquatch's tracks—where she had crossed into the Palmer land two nights earlier. But they found no signs of his Sasquatch leaving the property. Either she had left the way she came, or she was still there. Lucas had to find a way to scout the place without raising alarms with Joe or his meddlesome wife.

While they closed the loop, Lucas stopped several times and retraced his steps to give the dogs time to scour the ground for hints of her movements. Twice they were reprimanded by territorial critters. A squirrel chirped at them from above eye level in a leafless tree. The varmint intended to either ward off a predator or to warn other squirrels of danger.

"We're not after you," Lucas called to him. But the squirrel continued chattering until they moved on.

A woodpecker drummed high above their heads. When Lucas called out to the bird, it hesitated for a moment and then resumed its drilling—oblivious to their search.

Back at the truck, Lucas secured the dogs and retrieved his rifle. He slapped on a camo cap and backpack full of hunting gear. Before heading to the property line, he removed a pair of binoculars from the custom-made pouch in the console and draped the cord around his neck.

Lucas's common bond with Joe as a hunter should provide a foundation for dialogue. Once they'd established rapport, Lucas would find a way to gain access. He came prepared with both money and a story. Surely Joe would be interested in one or the other.

Lucas crept to the perimeter, cautious not to breach the private property line on his GPS. But he did not need a high-tech border confirmation because Joe had posted regular NO TRESPASSING warnings. Shiny, new signs and others nearly faded from time and weather were secured to trees and waist-high metal stakes.

Using field glasses to see beyond the border, Lucas peered onto Palmer's place. Dense trees and bushy undergrowth obscured his view as he searched for artificial structures. When he saw no signs of a camp or hunting blind, Lucas moved a few feet farther and repeated the process.

Lucas had nearly circled the property when he spotted it. Supported by two lodgepole pines and two four-by-four posts, a rustic treehouse nestled in the branches. A ten-foot ladder connected the structure to the ground.

Besides some wind movement in the trees and an occasional bird call, Lucas heard no sounds from the blind. Lucas sniffed but detected no hint of cooked food or fire. But a lack of human movement or scents did not mean Joe Palmer had abandoned the structure. He could be inside, waiting or resting. If Joe were a veteran hunter, he would know not to promote human odors near his blind.

While a direct approach was a long shot, Lucas tried anyway. Standing a full three feet behind a NO TRESPASSING sign, he called out, "I'm looking for Joe Palmer."

Lucas pulled up his binoculars to scan the blind. No response and no movement.

"My name is Lucas Johnson. I'm on a hunting trip in these parts and hope to speak with you about someone we have in common. His name is Mike Johnson, and I'm pretty sure you worked with him in Alaska in the '70s."

Lucas heard a faint shuffling from somewhere near the blind. It could have come from inside. But just as likely, a small animal may have rustled the fallen leaves. He could not be sure. Something told him Joe was up there and did not want company.

"I don't want to interrupt your hunt." Lucas looked toward the setting sun. "I know we're getting into the prime time of day. So I'll leave you alone. I might try again tomorrow, closer to midday, to see if you have time to talk."

Lucas returned to his truck, realizing another man might feel defeated. But Lucas understood minor setbacks preceded every successful hunt. He'd found Joe and initiated contact.

Joe would appreciate Lucas's sensitivity about avoiding undue noise when game were most active. Despite no direct engagement, Lucas had made forward progress.

He tapped his GPS to review the areas he'd explored and the blind's location. Lucas would not need the waypoints when he returned the next day. He'd perfected his sense of direction long ago and would find the spot again without a map or other device.

Chapter 17

KATI

Moments earlier, Tansy had lit the room to combat afternoon sunset. She clasped her hands in front of her chest while she listened to my scales on the recorder.

"Stop." Tansy interrupted my playing. "Your memory and sense of timing are incredible. I wish I'd picked up the recorder as fast as you have."

Praise from a halvek should not have pleased me, but it did—especially from this one. Dylan had complimented me for my flawless memory, precise logic, and beauty. At the time, I felt his praise hollow, coming from such an imperfect animal. Naturally, anything a Sasquatch might do or communicate would impress him. Our minds evolved over a longer time, and our lives were not focused on survival and greed. Of course, he was impressed.

Tansy's joy over my accomplishment was contagious. No other Sasquatch had touched a musical instrument, much less played one. As I performed, Tansy hummed along with me. Her tones formed a perfect accompaniment to the recorder.

I stopped and asked her to take a turn so that I could mimic her. Tansy took the instrument. She closed her eyes and played something so intricate and beautiful that I forgot to hum. She hesitated and opened one eye.

"Again," I whispered. "I'll do it this time."

She began, and I let the music carry me away. The melody moved in waves with a new and unfamiliar string of notes followed by repeated ones. It was too complex to anticipate the next sounds. After a few breaths that yielded a cacophony of tones, I gave up with a shrug.

"I'll play something shorter and easier." Tansy chewed her lip as she thought. "We can try "Mary Had a Little Lamb." That one has a repeating melody."

These tunes have names? I rolled my eyes at their lack of sophistication. Halveks named everything. But it was no wonder. Without total recall and telecommunication, they identified everything with tags, living or not. Each halvek, other low animals, plants, and every type of domicile, vehicle, and invention had an identifier—both in their slow verbal language and written form.

What a waste of time and effort.

"Mary had a little lamb," I repeated. I knew what a lamb looked like. If I could, I would have sent her a vision of the Porgu-based creature to confirm my knowledge. She probably assumed I understood nothing about the plants and animals in her world. I recognized them all by sight and knew a few with words. But Dylan's lessons were woefully incomplete. If I ever found him in Salida, I would admonish him for keeping words from me and insist he teach me more.

"Are you ready?" Without waiting for my response, Tansy put the instrument to her lips. The new tune was less intricate than the earlier one. Tansy emphasized each note and lingered when the melody changed. She played it through once. "Do you have it?"

"Yes." I'd memorized the music as well as where she'd placed her fingers for each note.

When she started over, I brought breath from my chest, into my throat, and out my nose to copy how I'd visualized Tansy humming. "Thonk." My attempt sounded like a squawking bird, and we both burst out laughing.

She placed the recorder on the floor and lunged at me. With a start, I drew back.

Tansy froze, and her eyebrows swished together. "Don't you all hug each other?"

"We do. We are compassionate and touch frequently."

Tansy sat on my bed and slowly leaned into me with a full embrace. The intimacy made my eyes fill with tears, and I choked back a sob. This halvek kept me safe from a predator, fed me to prevent starvation, and gave me an appreciation for halvek music. Before meeting Dylan and her, I'd never have imagined a Porgu lifeform could trigger emotion in a Sasquatch—at least not pleasant ones.

The halvek males I'd killed on my prior visit prompted abject anger. Maybe feeling a range of emotions for these beings should not have surprised me. But who could have anticipated their complexity?

Tansy rubbed my back. "You're the funniest thing. I know you'll only be here for as long as you want. I'll miss you when it's time for you to go." I returned her hug and stroked the long braid at the back of her neck. This action commonly occurred among Sasquatches. Before that day, I would have never imagined doing it with a halvek—besides Dylan.

Our lesson continued with Tansy trading off with me to play the recorder. When she stopped to explain the piece or how it differed from the one we'd shared earlier, Tansy touched my shoulder or leg. When Sasquatches did these actions, they would send personal transmissions filled with feelings. Tansy showed her emotions through touch, facial expressions, and sounds—not with visions. Our growing relationship was pleasantly tactile.

Her mannerisms made me wonder what I missed from Dylan. If our time together was in Porgu rather than Reval, I might have seen his actions through different eyes. When he told me of his love on our last night together, I automatically dismissed his emotion. What did halveks know about deep-rooted feelings? But Tansy made me think they might be as capable of emotional depth as the Sasquatch.

"Hey," Tansy interrupted my thoughts. "If you've finished with today's recorder lesson, I'd like to help you with some grooming."

What did she have in mind? She had no idea that cleanliness was of utmost importance in Reval. But without cleansing pools, we succumbed to the filth in Porgu.

Tansy left the yurt and returned a few minutes later with a small basin filled with bubbly water and a narrow purse, barely bigger than her hand. She set the tub on a stool next to my bed and reached for my wrist.

The halvek watched my eyes for a reaction as she placed my fingers in the water. It felt warm and pleasant. While the bubbles were slippery and unnatural, I rubbed my fingers together and imagined the sludgy restorative liquid in our pools back in Reval. I sniffed the tub and recognized scents from Porgu's flowers and berries—different from home's subtler fragrances but not wholly unpleasant.

When Tansy opened the purse, I saw a collection of metal tools—some flat and others with hinges and points. I yanked my hand from the tub in shock.

What did she plan to do with those implements?

After a low giggle, Tansy's fingers gently encircled my wrist and drew my hand back to the basin. The halvek smiled at me, but I was unclear if she was taking advantage of my ignorance and trust. Irrespective of my misgivings, I allowed her to place my fingers back into the liquid.

"Don't worry." She patted the fur on my arm. "We're going to give you a manicure."

Chapter 18

Dylan picked at the corner of his menu. Had he expected Kati to be waiting in the bushes at Destiny's rental?

The break-in happened a full three nights earlier. Kati could be a hundred miles from Jamesville or spying on him from behind a tree across the diner's parking lot. Either scenario seemed equally plausible.

Dylan's stomach growled loud enough for both Augie and the server to hear it. "Bring me a black coffee and a slice of pie, please. I'm not very hungry."

"Cherry?" she asked, with a pen poised over a green and white pad.

"What's your favorite?"

"Apple."

"Then why did you recommend the cherry?" Dylan leaned toward her and gave his impish grin.

"We have more cherry than apple."

"Saving apple for your favorite customers?"

"Something like that." She returned his smile. "But for you, I'll make an exception. Do you want the apple?"

"Only if you don't get fired for selling me the wrong pie."

She tapped the pad with her pen. "I'll see what I can do." The server turned to Augie and raised a brow.

Augie looked at Dylan as if wanting to take a signal on what to order.

"Order anything you want," Dylan suggested. "I saw our gal delivering a mean burger to a booth down the line. It's your favorite."

After Augie placed his order and the server left, he moved his hands under the table. His heels bounced on the linoleum floor.

Dylan recognized Augie's angst. "Are you thinking about what we should do next?"

"I want to help you find Kati. But I don't know how."

"You've already done a lot. Your sketches brought us back to Jamesville and confirmed Kati visited Destiny's old place."

"Somebody broke into her house." Augie shook his head. "We don't know if it was Kati."

"You're right." Dylan's shoulders sagged. "But since you had a vision with that broken window before we saw it, I'm assuming you picked up a transmission from Kati."

"Why don't you have dreams from Kati? You used to talk with the Sasquatches."

Dylan scanned the other tables and booths, checking for eavesdroppers. All the other diners seemed otherwise occupied. "Kalev taught me how to communicate telepathically before we went to Reval. When I first got there, my skills were pretty rough. But by the end of the month, I could transmit and receive messages with everyone I met." Dylan considered his limited interactions in Reval. "Well, I guess that's not very many—only Kalev, Alevide, Tiina, and Kati. But Kati and I would go back and forth with complex topics like comparing political structures in both Reval and Porgu."

"All with pictures?"

"No. I'd get stuck and have to throw in some English. But that helped Kati pick up our language."

"Do you think all my dreams are from Kati?"

"You said you could tell when they were from Kalev or a new Sasquatch." Dylan winked at Augie. "Are your Sasquatch dreams different from ones you have about not studying for a final exam or running naked through a park?"

"What?" Augie cocked his head.

"I'm pulling your leg." Dylan laughed. "Do you remember regular dreams—the ones that don't come from Sasquatches?"

"I dream every night."

"The same dreams?"

"No. Some are about people I know, and some are places I've been."

"But are the ones from Kalev and Kati different from your normal dreams?"

Augie took a napkin from the holder and folded it into a square. He slipped it under his fork. "They don't seem different at first. But if I think hard about them, they're with things or places I never saw before." Augie smoothed the napkin. "Or they're different from how I remember them."

"Do you think you've had another dream from Kati?" Any new visions might give clues about where Kati went after Jamesville.

"Maybe."

Dylan took out a pen and pushed it across the table along with a clean napkin.

Augie smiled and moved them back toward Dylan. "I can't draw with these. My pencils are in the car."

"Do you want to get them?" Dylan jiggled the car keys at Augie. "Or should I go?"

"Me." After putting on his jacket and buttoning his coat all the way to the top, Augie took the keys and left.

Moments later, Dylan felt a draft from the diner's door across the back of his neck. He straightened, assuming Augie would slide into the booth. Instead, Cynthia's signature scent—something cloying and sensual—triggered a gag. Dylan tensed, anticipating her unwelcome advance.

Cynthia placed a knuckle on the laminated top and leaned over the table. She looked Dylan in the eye. "Hi sailor, have you missed me?"

"What the hell are you doing here?"

"I heard you were planning a trip back to Oregon. I thought I'd follow along and see if you've considered my offer to memorialize your story."

Cynthia had proven time and again that her investigative skills far exceeded his. Yet he was the detective and she a journalist. To diffuse his anxiety, Dylan flexed his fingers.

"Augie and I are here to pick up some things Destiny left behind. There's nothing mysterious about our trip."

"Oh, yeah?" Cynthia smirked. "My new real estate agent friend had a different story to tell. She didn't mention anything about Destiny's belongings."

"Really?" Flex, unflex. "What did she tell you?"

"Only that you had a lot of questions about the break-in and might know who committed that crime."

"You talked to her again today?"

"Why wouldn't I? I knew she met with you this morning, and I wanted to know how that went."

"You've missed your calling. You should give classes on how to become a master detective."

"I don't know if I deserve your praise." Cynthia straightened her shoulders, forcing her breasts to jiggle. Dylan turned away with a wince. "I'm only doing my job. You know I'd work as hard on your book. It would come across any way you want. It would be more of a collaboration than me telling your story." She tilted her head and leaned farther forward. "What do you say?"

The server approached with Dylan's coffee and Augie's fountain drink.

Cynthia moved aside, leaving only enough space for the delivery. She moved back when the server retreated.

Dylan stirred cream into his cup. "I'm still deciding."

After another breeze, Augie slid into the booth, giving Cynthia an exaggeratedly wide berth. He would not want to contact any part of her.

"Hi, Augie." She ignored Augie's slight.

He nodded at her and placed his notebook on the table. Augie tightly clasped his hands over the cover.

In one swift movement, Cynthia grabbed the corner and pulled it away. "I've heard you're a great artist. Let me see your work." She started to flip through his sketches.

Augie yanked it back. "That's private."

Dylan chuckled at their tête-à-tête. *Augie's never stopped anyone from looking at his work. I guess when it comes to sharing with Cynthia, he has boundaries.*

"Augie and I are having a private conversation. I hope you don't mind leaving us. Maybe we'll see you around town in the next day or two?"

Cynthia bristled. "I'm happy to give you some space." She slid a business card from her shoulder bag to the table. "In case you've forgotten my cell number, here's my card. You can call anytime." With swaying hips, Cynthia made a grand exit.

"She's going to be a pain in our asses." Dylan tapped the table. "Show me what you saw in your dream."

Augie drew a series of long sweeping lines and filled in details with minute strokes and shading from the side of his pencil.

While Augie sketched, Dylan stewed about not keeping a closer eye on Cynthia at the cabin. If only he'd delayed talking about his plans until she left. She would not be tailing them in Oregon. How could he thwart her efforts? Dylan craned around in the booth to look out the window. But night fell quickly in this part of the country, and he could not see a thing.

Dylan rose and walked outside. Shivering, he stood in the cold drizzle and rubbed his hands against his arms to stay warm. Dylan walked from one end of the lot to the other, looking for signs of Cynthia. If he could identify her car, they would know when she was around. But Dylan was too late.

Faced with the same circumstances, Cynthia would have come out right away and not missed an opportunity to gain information about an opponent. Disgusted with himself, Dylan stomped back into the diner. He slumped into the booth, defeat weighing his shoulders.

The server brought their food as Augie uncurled from over the pages. He spun the notebook for Dylan. The sketch seemed incomplete—without the precise details that made Augie's drawings look like photos. But the initial outlines included a partially frozen, nearly evaporated lake surrounded by craggy low peaks—some with snow and all dotted with evergreens. In the foreground, a small wooden sign clearly stated WELCOME TO DETROIT LAKE.

"Augie, this image had to come from Kati." Dylan fished out his cell phone to check the lake's location.

"She's only sixty miles away." A broad grin creased Dylan's face. "We'll head there at first light."

Chapter 19

Despite the misty morning rain cloaking the mountain tops, the sign welcoming Dylan and Augie to Detroit Lake looked identical to Augie's sketch.

"Now what?" asked Augie.

"We need to find some locals." Dylan stared at the tiny idyllic town with board-covered sidewalks. A café across the street had a sign touting giant cinnamon rolls. Based on his experiences in Salida, Dylan knew restaurants and coffee shops held the heartbeat of any small town. "Let's start with that diner."

Smaller than the previous night's establishment, the restaurant had only a few booths. Shiny, red vinyl-covered stools lined a long counter. The scent from freshly baked cinnamon rolls confirmed the sign outside and made Dylan's mouth water. A sole camo-dressed customer sat at the counter, drinking from a thick ceramic coffee mug.

Augie slipped into a booth, and Dylan raised a wait-a-minute finger before strolling to greet the patron.

The man poked intently on his phone with a well-manicured thumb. Dylan patiently waited until he looked up.

"May I help you?" the man asked.

"Sorry to bother you while you're working. My friend and I are new around here and wondered if you might help us with some local information."

"Not from around here." He glanced at Augie and then Dylan. "I probably can't help you."

"Looks like you might have been hunting." Dylan pointed at the man's jacket. "What's in season?"

The man tilted his head, likely to consider the question. "That's the local information you needed?"

"Actually, no." Dylan chuckled. "That was my attempt at small talk."

"If you have a specific question about this area, I suggest you talk with the waitstaff or find someone else who might be able to help you." He nodded at his device. "I've got a full day planned and should respond to a few customers while I finish my coffee."

"No worries." Dylan raised his hands in surrender. "Sorry to interrupt."

I must be losing my touch or my confidence. A year ago, that guy would have become my lifelong buddy.

As Dylan slunk to Augie's table, two men jostled through the front door. The beefier one greeted the fellow at the counter. "Lucas, did you have any luck yesterday catching up with Joe Palmer?"

Dylan sat opposite Augie in the booth. He had a full-on view of Lucas and the two new customers.

Almost imperceptibly, Lucas glanced at Dylan before answering the question. Dylan caught the look, but did the questioner notice? "I found his camp, just at the wrong time. It was dusk, probably right when the elk would browse at the stream under his blind. He didn't respond to me, but I'm sure he was there. As soon as I finish my coffee, I'll head back. Once the sun's up in earnest, Joe won't see any game until late this afternoon."

"I saw your dually parked outside, but no dogs today." The man punched Lucas on the arm as he and his compatriot walked to a booth against the far wall. "You on a manhunt?"

"Something like that." Lucas shrugged and went back to swiping his phone.

Dylan glanced between Lucas and the pair, deciding whether to approach them about where to buy hiking maps or whether they had heard any out-of-the-ordinary stories—not specifically about Sasquatches but reports of disturbed trash. After several days in Porgu, Kati would need food.

The newcomers huddled over menus. After a bit of back and forth with Lucas to lament the rain, they turned to a private discussion about recent football standings. Dylan turned his attention to Augie, who was oblivious to the chatter and engrossed in a new drawing filled with trees and mountain scenery. Dylan would speak with the men after Lucas left.

"Is this a place we passed in the car or from another dream?"

Augie looked at Dylan and pushed his glasses up along the bridge of his nose. "I don't know. But it's not from today."

A bell tinkled when the door opened.

Augie ignored the interruption.

Dylan cranked around to see who came in. Before he could acknowledge her aloud, Cynthia slid into the booth next to Augie. He stopped drawing, slammed shut his notebook, and moved it farther inside of the table—well out of her reach.

"Would you please sit somewhere else?" Augie stiffened, his hands balled firmly in front.

"I don't deserve that." Cynthia huffed. "When have I ever done anything rude to you?"

"I'm not rude, just honest. There's a difference."

"Okay, I appreciate your candor. Why don't you like me?"

"Nate hurt Destiny, and you were friends with Nate. So I don't like you."

Dylan failed miserably at trying to suppress a smile. "Augie's logic is spot on."

"Nate's dead." Cynthia released a dramatic sigh. "He might have gotten what he deserved. But I never did anything to Destiny."

"Except sleep with her husband." Dylan countered.

"They were separated when Nate and I had our fling. I don't make it a practice to chase after men who aren't available."

Unconvinced about her allegiance to social standards, Dylan let the discussion drop. There were more important issues to address. "How did you know we'd be here?"

"Augie's car is outside."

A simple and accurate assessment. "But how did you know to come here from Jamesville? I assume you stayed there last night, too."

"I followed you here."

Would she be the type to search Jamesville for Augie's sedan, sleep out all night to stake them out and show up at the café fifteen minutes after they arrived? No way.

Dylan slid around in his seat as a car passed the plate glass front door. "Did you put a tracker on Augie's car?" He turned to stare at Cynthia. "Don't lie to me."

"It made it easier to follow you." She laid a hand on the table and looked at Dylan with pleading eyes. "Don't fault me for wanting to see where you were going. I'm desperate to work on your story."

"It's not going to happen." Dylan drew himself up and smirked.

"I've already talked with my publisher. She'd love to have the story. But if I write it without you and your experiences, it will sit on the shelf with other Bigfoot books in the mythology section." Cynthia looked down at the tabletop and ran a scarlet nail in a crack at the edge. "To make the maximum impact, this book needs to be squarely in the nonfiction section. And I need your help to put it there."

"I don't want to have this conversation with you." Dylan stood. "You and I are going outside right now, and you're taking that tracker off our car."

"Okay." Cynthia's pursed lips accentuated her pout. "I'll show you."

Dylan followed Cynthia to the car. She bent over the front fender and reached into the wheel well to extract a small disk.

"Here." She showed him the muddy tracker.

"Is this the only one?"

"Yes." Cynthia raised her chin. "But if you don't believe me, you should take Augie's car to a mechanic and have them put it on a lift. You can check for yourself."

Once back in the restaurant, Dylan noticed Augie's breakfast growing cold as he huddled over the notebook, drawing.

Cynthia looked like she intended to slide into Augie's side. But Dylan intervened. "We're planning to discuss a private matter over breakfast. If you're going to order something, we'd like you to find a space somewhere else in the restaurant."

After adjusting the straps of her oversized tote, she pulled out a business card.

"I already have several and don't need anymore." Dylan held up both hands to indicate he had no intention of taking another card.

As Cynthia sashayed to the counter, she called over her shoulder.

"Don't even think about giving someone else our story."

"I won't." Dylan motioned for the server to warm up his coffee.

Cynthia wasted no time and sidled up next to Lucas. She stumbled into his shoulder and quickly apologized, intermittently touching his arm and shoulder. He gave her a once over and motioned to an adjacent seat. Cynthia made a grand display of organizing her coat and bag before she jumped up on the stool and set her décolletage to shudder.

Lucas is having a hard time focusing above her neck.

Before Dylan dove into his breakfast, he asked Augie, "Don't you want to eat before finishing your drawing? Your food is getting cold."

Augie spun the notebook around for Dylan to see the drawing. Thick woods filled most of the page with tall pines, firs, and undergrowth from late-season grasses. A barbed-wire fence stood in the foreground made with a mixture of metal poles and six-inch wooden posts. Off to the side, a large sign warded off trespassers with YOU'RE STANDING ON PRIVATE PROPERTY—EXIT HERE. NOW!

Dylan tapped the picture. "Kati must have been inside this fence to read that sign. Do you have any idea where it might be?"

Augie shrugged. "Nope."

"Seems like we should ask more locals. They may know who around here is super sensitive about their privacy."

Dylan glanced at Cynthia and Lucas. They huddled together like long-lost friends. Now and again, Cynthia giggled and patted Lucas's thigh or shoulder bumped him. While he did not return her touches, he did not recoil. Lucas claimed not to be a local. What was Cynthia getting from him?

While Dylan scraped the last bite of omelet from his plate, Lucas and Cynthia stood to gather their belongings and bundled into their coats. After a conspiratorial nod, they approached Dylan's booth on their way to the door. Cynthia stopped, but Lucas continued on without a word.

"What are your plans for the day?" she asked.

Dylan slapped Augie's notebook shut and pushed it to the side.

"We may stay here and drink coffee all day. It's pretty miserable outside in the rain."

"Listen." Cynthia laid a hand on the table and leaned toward Dylan. "I know you're looking for one of your Sasquatch pals. I suspect you spent a month with them when you disappeared. I want to help you find him again. Take me with you. I'll leave my car here and work the locals with you."

Cynthia found her way to Destiny's house and Detroit Lake without a misstep. She must have charmed Lucas after Dylan failed miserably. She might be helpful, but at what price?

"No," Dylan said with conviction.

"Have it your way." Cynthia shrugged. "You have my number if you change your mind."

After she left, Dylan turned to Augie. "I can't believe Cynthia gave up so quickly. Do you know what just happened?"

Augie nodded. "Yep."

"Fill me in."

"When Cynthia talked with us, I watched her friend."

"And?"

"He put something by our tire."

Dylan craned his body to look outside, but both Lucas and Cynthia were gone. She must have passed the tracker to Lucas, and he reattached it to their car. Had Cynthia convinced Lucas to work with her to follow them?

"Damn. I forgot to look at what kind of car she was driving." How could Dylan even call himself a detective?

"Her car is still outside," Augie suggested.

"Why?"

"Cynthia got in a big white pickup with the man in hunting clothes."

What could Lucas do to help Cynthia track down Kati?

Chapter 20

LUCAS EDWARDS

Lucas stood outside his truck, holding the passenger door open. But Cynthia did not get out. Rain plopped on his cap and ran down the brim until he tipped it up with a thumb. Lucas had agreed to give Cynthia a ride from the restaurant to her hotel, not partner up for the day.

"I'm going with you," she declared and ground both feet firmly on the floor mat.

Grabbing her by the arm and pulling her out would land him in a lawsuit. But he had a schedule to keep and wanted to get to Joe Palmer's blind before the guy decided to take a nap or finish his hunting expedition and go home. Lucas tried a gentle approach. "I'm meeting someone and need to go alone."

"I told you why I'm here." Cynthia stared straight ahead out the windshield. "You agreed to keep me in the loop."

"I never said you could tag along." He shook his head. "Look, I'm meeting someone who can move us forward. I'd be shocked if he took me to search anywhere today. I'm only making contact to smooth my way onto his property. He's reclusive and from what I've learned around town, approaching him man-to-man is my best option."

"What makes you think I can't charm him?" Cynthia's lip curled into a sly smile.

"I'm certain you can, but you can show me your investigative techniques another time." He opened the door wider and motioned to the ground. "Let me do this one solo. If I can find a way to access the property,

I'll come back to get you."

"Okay, but I expect to hear from you in the next couple of hours." Cynthia swiveled in the seat but did not step out of his truck. "If he allows you to search the property, I want to be there."

"Of course." Lucas gave her a customer-is-always-right smile. "In the meantime, why don't you keep an eye on your buddy Dylan's car. I'd like to know if he manages to narrow his search to the Palmer property." He rubbed his stubbly chin, unused to the itch but knowing a grizzled façade might soften mountain man Joe Palmer. "I expect people in town will start to wonder about an influx of nonhunters in town. This time of year, if you're not hunting, you're headed south for better weather."

Cynthia grabbed her tote from the floor and slid it high on her shoulder. "Come closer."

When he complied, she placed a hand on his shoulder and leveraged herself to the ground. Brushing against him on her way seemed an obvious ploy for attention, but he ignored the maneuver. He figured she would use whatever assets she had to gain his loyalty.

Cynthia's unwavering commitment to finding Dylan's Sasquatch might come in handy. He'd decide later whether to join forces with her. For the time being, she was out of his truck.

As Lucas pulled from the lot, he watched Cynthia in his rearview mirror. She strutted to a motel room door with confidence and indifference. He expected her to watch him drive away, a look of disappointment or longing on her face.

Something was not right.

A few blocks from the motel, Lucas pulled to the shoulder and jumped from the truck. He circled to the passenger side and opened the door.

He ran his fingers under the glove box to feel anything foreign— nothing but wires and plastic placed by an assembly plant. Lucas flattened a hand and shoved it under the seat. There it was.

Lucas pulled out the tracker disk. It looked identical to the one he'd put back on Dylan's car—minus the mud. Lucas shook his head and smiled.

She's a tricky one—a journalist with a mission.

He tossed the tracker to the dirt and crushed it with his heel. If she stayed out of his way until he made an inroad onto Joe Palmer's property, Lucas would consider teaming up. But if Joe proved to be a more vital ally, she was on her own.

Lucas bumped along the rutted dirt road, thinking.

According to Cynthia, she'd followed Dylan and Augie from Colorado because they had Sasquatch tracking skills and a lead on one in this part of Oregon.

She'd given Lucas some bullshit line about Dylan gaining intel from Sasquatch sightings. But Lucas had looked at dozens of sites and found unhelpful stories—mostly about catching a glimpse of one in headlights or a peek on the edge of someone's property. Accounts of blurred footprints and unidentifiable scat or hairs also permeated the reports, but none remotely compared to catching one looking into his cabin window. When Lucas had pressed for more details about Dylan's leads, Cynthia changed the conversation.

Cynthia's hiding something. She refers to Dylan's Sasquatch as male, but the one I chased onto Joe's property is definitely female. There can't be more than one, right?

Lucas drew a sharp breath. Perhaps a mated pair had separated. With Cynthia's help, he might find them both.

Lucas parked in the same wide spot as the day before. This time, he left his rifle in the car to appear less aggressive. Besides giving a submissive first impression, leaving his rifle in the truck would save time later. The steady but light rain would undoubtedly moisten everything and force him to clean the firearm with a complete teardown.

He grabbed his backpack from under a tarp in the back and walked to the spot where he could see Joe's hunting blind. Lucas scanned the site with his binoculars. Everything seemed as it was before, with not a scrap of human rubbish.

"Joe Palmer?" Lucas called. "It's me, Lucas Johnson. I was here yesterday. Hopefully, I didn't compromise your hunt."

No response.

"I won't take much of your time. I'd like to talk with you about my dad, Mike Johnson."

Lucas spotted movement in the blind, maybe an outline from a camouflage cap. Not much, but enough to tell Lucas someone was inside.

"My dad died a few months ago, and I have regrets about our relationship. He was a very private man, and I don't know much about his youth." Lucas paused for effect. "I'm taking time away from my job and family to reconnect with my dad's past. He talked about a Joe Palmer who worked with him on the pipeline. I'm hoping you might be him."

A grizzled head slowly appeared above a partially boarded side of the blind. In an instant, it disappeared again. "I don't know anyone named Mike Johnson." The gruff voice reflected brevity and decisiveness. "Please leave my property."

"I saw your signs and have been careful to stay outside your boundary. If you would give me a few minutes, I'd share Dad's stories. Maybe that would trigger memories from when you guys worked together."

Joe climbed down the ladder with the speed and agility of a young man. He rested a hunting rifle against his shoulder and walked to the property line. Without offering an invitation or salutation, Joe looked Lucas up and down. "You must not take after your father. I've never met anyone who looks remotely like you."

"Everyone says I inherited my mom's features." Lucas offered a hand but did not step toward the line. Joe would insist on maintaining control.

"What do you want to know?" Joe gave Lucas a suspicious stare and ignored the hand.

"Do you remember working with my dad? Mike Johnson?"

"Why do you think I worked the pipeline?"

"I found clues on the internet and hope you're the guy who knew my father."

"Internet," Joe muttered. "Nothing's private anymore."

"Well?" Lucas tipped his cap with a thumb. "Did you know him?"

"What can you tell me about him?"

Joe's not making this easy.

"He told me stories about working in Alaska from '75 to '77." Lucas drew from his research. "Your name came up a few times."

"How so?"

"Seems like you might have worked the same stretch for a time?"

"What camps did he stay in?"

"Fairbanks?" Lucas gave an uneducated stab.

"That would have been Wainwright. But none of the workers stayed there long. He must have been other places."

"I don't have any notes with me. But I can mail you copies of what I have later."

"That's all you got?" Joe shot Lucas a stern look.

"Seems like there might have been some card playing—for lack of other entertainment."

"I recall a few nights of poker. Lost my share and won some, too." Finally, Joe smiled and moved his rifle from his shoulder to rest the butt on the ground. "Not much to do when we weren't working besides sleep. It took days for any news to make it up there. Not that I cared. Most of us were there for the paychecks."

"It was a lucrative deal." Lucas nodded, encouraged by Joe's newfound openness. "My dad came back home with enough dough to pay for his college education and attract my mom."

"You got a photo of him?" Joe wiped his nose with the back of his hand. "Maybe I'd recognize him if I could see what he looked like."

"Everything I brought with me is back at my motel. Would you mind if I came by the house to show you? I could come at your convenience— when you've finished hunting."

"I've been out for a couple of nights." Joe glanced at the blind. "Looking forward to a hot shower and a real meal. I was packing up my gear when you called just now."

"Can I give you a lift?"

"Nope." Joe picked up his rifle. "After sitting around these past days, I need to walk. Then I want time with my wife." Joe held out his palm. "Do you have a card or something with your number? I'll call when I'm ready to talk."

Lucas walked back to his truck and found a scrap of paper. He wrote his cell number and returned to the property line to hand it off.

When Joe took the slip, Lucas could smell victory. Joe was intrigued by a voice from the past and would call to reminisce. Lucas and Joe would bond over a shared history and might search the property together.

As Lucas turned and stepped toward his truck, Joe called to him. "Was he part of the 798?"

Lucas felt the hair on the back of his neck stand on end—the same way he felt when bowhunting a black panther in Asia. That cat's pelt had a place of honor near his mantel, but the hunt could have ended differently. What could 798 mean? "I don't remember that number from my notes. Can you help me out?"

"What type of work did your dad do?"

"Welding."

"Teamsters?"

"I think so."

"Yeah." Joe tucked the paper into his jacket's chest pocket. "Maybe we ran across each other back then."

Joe's words held an unmistakable hint of sarcasm, and Lucas's final steps to the truck lasted forever. He felt Joe's stare burning a hole in his back. Lucas did not know how he'd failed the test but knew he had.

After changing into his car slippers and stowing his boots, Lucas turned the key in the ignition. One glance at the property told him Joe was securely back in the blind.

"Ugh." Lucas smacked the steering wheel with a palm.

Teamsters—trucking and transportation and not welders. Damn it. What was I thinking? What are the odds he'll call now?

Chapter 21

KATI

When I heard the lock click, I tensed and stared at the yurt entrance. Each time the door opened, Tansy came through. But I still worried that someone else might invade my secure space. Keeping a Sasquatch contained was not natural. Any halvek might find a way into the yurt—Tansy's Joe or, worse yet, Lucas the dog-master.

"Lunch is ready."

I sighed in relief at Tansy's voice. She came inside, carrying the eggs I longed for. It took all my resolve to wait until she set the pan on a multi-colored mat lying on a table.

"You look terrific." Tansy started her ramble. "Especially your nails. Maybe we can do your feet today. I could bring in all my colors, and I'll let you pick ten—a different one for each toe." She glanced at my plaster-coated foot. "Well, I'd do your left one and the exposed toes of your right." Tansy leaned and inspected her handiwork. "Seems like I got carried away with the plaster to make sure the cast stays together once you start stepping on it. I've heard the term walking cast. But I don't know what that means or how to create one." She glanced toward the door. "Joe's got a medical journal, but I didn't think to look it up. I hope this one will hold you for as long as you need it."

"Thank you," I whispered. My two words barely slowed her verbal onslaught.

"My pleasure." Tansy grinned and tapped each exposed toe poking from the opening. "I only see three on your right foot. I'll bring in the whole shoebox of polish. But we'll only need eight different ones."

"I am available."

"That you are." With a giggle, Tansy straightened the pan and motioned to it with an open palm. "Your lunch is served. Can you make it to the table without my help?"

I rose from the bed and tested my encased foot. I tried to move my ankle, but the plaster kept it immobile. The pressure led to a dull ache, forcing a grimace. But the pain did not increase.

"Thank you for lunch." I sat in the chair and tried to imitate Tansy's posture with knees under the table. But when I slid the chair forward, I bumped the table's underside, and everything on top jolted. Whoever designed this furniture did not have my height in mind.

Tansy grabbed a teetering glass before it toppled. "If you stay awhile, I'll have Joe make us a taller table and chairs. Our pea-sized stuff doesn't work for you." She pointed toward my bed. "Even the cot's a few feet short. Good thing you aren't a fussy guest."

"You have helped me. I am grateful."

"Maybe it's my imagination, but I think your voice is getting stronger. You should keep playing the recorder. Either it's increasing your breath or strengthening your vocal cords. Either way, one day, your voice might be loud enough to have a regular back and forth conversation."

I licked my greasy fingers as my thoughts drifted to Dylan. He might be impressed at my stronger voice, but my new language skills and appreciation for halvek music would not matter in the long run. The High Council would arrange my death when I returned to Reval after the next full moon in three weeks plus two days. I had no intention of transferring memories from my first or second Porgu trip to the other Sasquatches. My recollections of killing halveks on my first passage and learning how to play a musical instrument on the second would vanish with me.

Tansy poured herself a glass of water. "I haven't heard anything from your stalker-buddy Lucas. He hasn't called, and I didn't see hide nor hair of him or his dogs when I took a walk to the meadow late last night. It was too wet to stay outside for long. Got soaked through before getting back to the house." She glanced up at the ceiling. "Was it noisy in here last night? The rain hitting the canvas top must have sounded like a rock band's drummer. I used to love going to concerts before I hooked up with Joe.

Even thought about following the Dead or becoming a roadie." She took a long drink. "Did you manage to get any sleep at all?"

I understood some of what Tansy said—something about not hearing from Lucas and questioning whether the rain sounded noisy.

"I rested well." Leaning over the pan, I grasped another clump of eggs and transferred it into my mouth.

Tansy nodded. "Joe's been out hunting for a couple of nights. He usually doesn't stay away longer than three or four. His timing depends on how long it takes him to find game. If he can down something in the first afternoon, I'll see him the next day. But his luck could be bad, and I won't see him for a few nights. Regardless of what he catches, he's never out for a full week." She tipped her head forward with a knowing glance. "Either my cooking or our bed will lure him home. I expect him tonight or, at the latest, in the morning." Tansy's brows creased as she inspected my face. "We've never kept secrets. I'm not sure how much to tell him about you."

"I can leave today." Standing, I pushed the pan away.

"I'm not suggesting that." Tansy smiled and slid it back toward me. She patted the tabletop. "Joe will want to meet you."

I tensed. Dylan was the only halvek male I trusted. While he did not understand my superiority, I allowed him to assume we were equals.

"Will Joe want to capture me?"

"Not if I talk with him first. From what you told me about Lucas, he hunts for trophies and acclaim. Joe's a hunter, too. But he respects animals and only hunts for food. We use most of every animal he kills, and what we can't use, we leave out for the other animals in the woods. Joe would never decorate our home with animal parts. They gave their lives to feed us."

"Why do you eat meat?" The question had confounded Sasquatches for thousands of years—maybe Tansy would enlighten me.

"That's a great question. I don't eat meat anymore, and Joe only eats vegetables and whatever he kills. I'm fine with cooking meat for him. I'd never judge his choices." Tansy ran her thumb along the rim of the glass. "Our lives are so entwined—sometimes I don't know where my wishes end and his start. When I met Joe, I was only seventeen. My folks died earlier that year, and social services wanted to put me in foster care." Tansy noticed my blank stare and backtracked. "When parents die and their kids are young, our government arranges for the children to be raised by other adults. The change is traumatic for the kids. I was very independent and did not want to live with strangers. So I ran away."

Familiar with running and being chased, I asked, "How did you know where to run?"

"I didn't know where to go. I just knew I needed to leave Pennsylvania. I hitchhiked west." She smiled and clarified. "Hitchhiking is when a person stands in the road and signals they will take a ride with anyone passing. You might get a trip to the next town or halfway across the country. With each one, you're moving in the right direction. I mostly got rides from guys driving big trucks. They liked the company, and I felt safe with them. My last one dropped me off in Marion Forks, about fifteen or twenty miles from here. The trucker bought me breakfast at the diner and told me he was only going as far west as Salem. He planned to go north into Washington—that's the state north of Oregon, where you are now. I wanted to go straight west and see the ocean, and he told me I'd need to go the rest of the way on my own."

"You made independent decisions to change your circumstances at a young age." Sasquatches made decisions about sexual partners and their role in society at a much earlier age. But her story about halvek independence surprised me. I scraped the remaining eggs from the pan and chewed.

"Well, I didn't stay independent for very long. The trucker left, and I was sitting at the counter finishing my coffee when in walked Joe Palmer. The rest is history."

"History?"

"He was a lot older than me, mid-thirties, but he was gorgeous with a thick black beard and long hair pulled into a ponytail. He grabbed a newspaper from a rack and went to sit alone in a booth. I followed him. We talked for hours." She grinned. "If truth be told, he sat and listened while I told him about where I came from, how my folks had died, and my trip across the country."

"What did he share with you?" One-sided communication in Reval was rare. Everyone revealed what they knew to reinforce our shared knowledge.

"Absolutely nothing. Joe just looked at me with his dreamy eyes. While

I poured out my soul, he captured my heart. I asked him if I could work for him—cooking, building, anything to earn money to make it the rest of the way to the ocean. He tried to give me some cash, but I wouldn't take it. I wanted to earn what he gave me. He agreed to keep me on for a few days and drove me to his property."

"Where we are now?"

"Yes, but it didn't look like this back then. Obviously, we didn't have the yurt, and the house was only the trailer." Tansy pulled the empty pan to her side of the table and ran her thumb across the edge. "I started cooking and cleaning for him. It just felt natural. He never asked me to leave, and I never wanted to."

"Are you lovers?" An automatic consequence for cohabitating Sasquatches, but I knew little of halvek coupling practices. We assumed they rutted when convenient or when asserting dominance.

Tansy's laugh exploded through the yurt. "What a question! Of course we are. I would have started all that a lot earlier, but Joe kept pushing me away."

When I had asked Dylan to couple with me, he was reluctant. Were most male halveks generally averse to having sex? I considered the two men I'd killed, who forced themselves on children. Dylan had told me those men sought power and not shared physical pleasure. Sasquatches had physical intimacy whenever willing partners agreed. The halveks' rules and rituals surrounding coupling seemed to promote needless abstinence and sexual aggression. Halveks' barriers certainly stunted their evolution.

The halvek sexual discussion could wait until I understood how risky it was to remain in the yurt when Joe returned. "Will Joe protect me?"

"He will. You can either stay with us permanently or get on your way to Salida after you heal." Tansy patted my leg. "If you feel about Dylan the way I feel about Joe, we will help you find him."

Was my increasing desire to find Dylan based on self-preservation or attraction?

Every hour, I tested my foot by walking around the inside of the yurt. The pain lessened with each test, but my speed would not match my pre-injury pace. The distance between Tansy's land and Salida was great. Based on the pain and needing to haul the plaster cast, I doubted whether I could cover it all before the next full moon.

At midafternoon, heavy boots crunched across the gravel drive. My heart raced. I leaped to my feet and grabbed the knife Tansy left for me. It felt cold and hard in my hand. Like the rifle I had used to kill the pedophiles earlier this year, I sensed the potential for violence in the tool. Did the halveks' lust for power come from the implements they created, or were they innately a violent breed?

As quickly as my encased foot would allow, I shuffled to crouch into the corner where the yurt's sides met the floor. I waited with my knife— poised to cut the fabric or lunge toward an attacker.

I held my breath until the footsteps passed the yurt and pounded up wooden stairs a distance from the yurt, likely to where Tansy lived.

Since I'd heard no vehicle sounds, whoever stood on the porch had come by foot. Who could it be? Lucas might have returned. But he would face Tansy's wrath for a repeated trespassing offense. More likely, the foot-traveler was Joe coming home from his hunt.

Too nervous to wait in the locked yurt and curious to hear how their conversation would evolve, I slid the knife into the fabric. The blade forced an opening large enough to wriggle through feet first.

When my shoulders and head were free, I knelt on the ground and inhaled great gulps of moist cold air. The difference in temperature inside and outside the yurt was dramatic. The interior heater must have been efficient.

I released a haughty huff. If halveks stopped relying on devices to warm their domiciles, they might better withstand the natural climate.

After further consideration, I realized my assumption's error. Reval's constant moderate temperatures made the Sasquatches' lives uncomplicated. We did not require shelters or heaters. Over thousands of years, halveks had continually modernized their domiciles because Porgu's harsh climate forced them to be innovative. Who was I to judge?

The sun had set, and low fog filled the yard to mask the partial moon and stars. As I'd been in pain and exhausted when Tansy led me into the yurt, I recalled little of the outdoor surroundings.

How long had it been since I tried to send a broadcast transmission? I examined the structures and the nearby objects, deciding whether a vision of Tansy's yard would be meaningful to anyone who had never seen it.

Weeds grew between parked vehicles as if they had not moved for a long time. My consolidated Sasquatch memories included images with halveks driving similar devices. In the years before they created them, I recalled other, less noisy machines pulled by harnessed animals.

Halveks forever sought to move more quickly. I did not understand why and decided to ask Dylan when I found him. Or perhaps Tansy could explain this odd compulsion. Sasquatches were imminently satisfied with however fast our bodies could carry us.

Lights spilled out of the windows to make the vehicles look shiny and slick. After bracing hands on my thighs, I stared at the disused halvek cars and trucks—concentrating and focusing. I tried to keep the vision discrete. But when I tried to push the image from my mind, it dissipated. My head throbbed, and I rubbed my temples to ease the sensation.

Surely this transmission failed—like the others I'd tried to send since Dylan and I separated.

Voices inside the structure caught my attention. I crept closer to see Tansy talking with a male halvek. Silently, I inched above the window ledge to watch and listen to their conversation.

As typical when she was with me, Tansy did most of the talking. "I can't believe this Lucas dude approached you after I told him to stay away from our property. I took his number and told him you'd call if and when you wanted to talk." She poked a finger at Joe's chest. "He's got a lot of nerve tracking you down when you were out hunting. You put food on our table. You aren't out there having fun or looking for trophies. Do you think you got skunked because he came out there with his noisy truck and yelled your name?"

"I don't get an elk every time I'm at the blind. Maybe it just wasn't my turn."

"Well, you're awfully kind. I think you would have gotten an elk if Lucas hadn't bothered you. He and his dogs might have disturbed our whole property when they roamed around the first night I saw him. Any elk would have skedaddled after hearing him make all that racket." She drew a quick breath. "What did he say to you?"

"Not much. Just bullshit about a dead father who might have worked with me up in Alaska." Joe sat on a wide chair and poured foamy, yellow liquid from a brown bottle into a glass. Tansy had only offered me water in those glasses. Saliva flooded into my mouth. What might Joe's beverage be, and how did it taste?

"He told me the same story. You worked the pipeline for years. How could you remember every guy from up there? Did you know someone named Mike Johnson? Sounds like a made-up name—as common as can be."

"I remember three Mikes. But Lucas doesn't look like any of them. One was black, one had a long Polish-sounding last name, and the other was a welder from the 798—same as me from Tulsa."

"What's 798?"

"Pipeliners Local Union 798. I asked Lucas if his dad was one of us, but he claimed his father was a Teamster. That's when I knew his story was bogus. Teamsters and Pipefitters aren't the same. Anyway, anyone who welded the pipeline knew about the 798."

"Maybe he got it mixed up, or his father never mentioned it?"

"Nope." Joe grinned. "Now you're giving him too much credit. I don't believe it."

Tansy picked up his empty bottle and walked to where I could not see her. I heard her voice from a nearby room. "Far be it from me to defend him. He's a pushy bastard, and I don't trust him."

"We're going to need a plan to keep him away. He's come here every day—invited or not." Joe rubbed a thumb along the glass's rim—a motion I'd seen Tansy do when she was thinking. "Why does he want to search our land?"

"I need to tell you about that." Tansy returned to sit on the arm of Joe's chair and play with his hair. I marveled at her intimate mannerisms. Sasquatches stroked each other's head hair as well.

"Here it comes." Joe pulled back to smile at her. "What have you been up to?"

"Lucas claims to have chased a Sasquatch onto our property."

"You're joking, right?" Joe set down his drink and stared at her as if searching her face for hints at humor.

"No—not kidding. He wants to search our property to find it. He told me he'd split any recognition or money with us if we helped him capture or kill it."

"Well, he's not just a liar—he's crazy." Joe reached a hand to cup Tansy's chin. "Did you feel threatened?"

"He didn't scare me. And when I told him to leave, he did—right away. But that's not the part of the story I want to tell you."

"Well?" Joe cocked his head.

Tansy placed a hand on his shoulder. "Actually, he did chase one onto our property. She had a hurt ankle and was starving. So I set her ankle in a cast. I've been feeding her scrambled eggs to help get her strength up."

Joe gave Tansy's shoulder a soft shove. "You almost had me." He laughed. "Scrambled eggs? Why not bacon?"

"She doesn't eat meat. I'd call her an ovo-vegetarian."

"What have you been smoking while I was gone?" Joe took a long drink.

"It's all true." Tansy sighed.

"Okay. Okay. I'll play along." Joe stood. "Take me to see this wild woman of the woods." He looked around the room as if searching for something.

"Only if you promise not to harm her. I told her we'd only keep her here until she's strong enough to continue on her journey." Tansy shifted her weight. "Her name's Kati."

"You call her Kati, and she's on a journey." Joe's eyes creased in the corners.

"I didn't name her. I call her Kati because that's her name. She's on her way to Colorado to be with the man she loves. His name is Dylan Cox."

A smile crept across Joe's face. "I assume this woman isn't in the back bedroom?"

"No. Kati's been staying in the yurt."

"I'm dying to meet her."

"Do you promise not to hurt Kati and only help her until it's time for her to leave?"

"Yes." Joe raised a hand. "I promise."

By the time they put on coats and walked to the yurt, I had moved to the slit. Still unsure whether to trust Joe, I waited to hear more of their conversation.

"Well, where is this mystery woman?" Joe's voice echoed from inside.

"You can see I made up the cot for her. The covers are all messed up from where she's slept. We've been sitting at the table and talking, too."

I heard someone pull out a chair as the legs scraped against the floor. "Come and sit with me, Tansy. Was Kati some homeless gal who Lucas is chasing?"

"No!" The thin pitch of Tansy's voice conveyed her anxiety. "I'm telling you, Kati is a Sasquatch who needs our help. Lucas is after her, and we *must* help her get away from him and meet up with Dylan in Colorado. He can protect her." I heard her voice catch, perhaps from a sob. "Promise me you'll help her."

The chair scraped again. I imagined Joe embracing Tansy and stroking her back to comfort her because that is what a Sasquatch would have done to calm a distraught mate. Joe's voice changed to a whisper. "Of course I'll help you. If this is important for you, you know it's important to me, too."

I walked around to the yurt's front, pushed open the door, and lowered my head to clear the entrance.

They both turned to me. Tansy raised her tear-streaked face and smiled. Joe's jaw dropped.

A man of few words, Joe said, "Holy shit!"

Chapter 22

NOVEMBER 26
LUCAS EDWARDS

The server refilled Lucas's coffee mug. He gave her a thank-you smile and tapped his earbud to secure it better. Lucas focused on his client rambling about bond yields and the recently released national housing start figures. Most of his job centered on glad-handing new customers and keeping the rest calm.

His phone vibrated, and Lucas pulled it close to see who was interrupting his call. When he recognized the number, Lucas straightened. "Jason, you're my number one client, but number two is on the line. He's incredibly high maintenance. Can I call you back in about fifteen?" After Jason laughed and agreed to the interruption, Lucas switched calls.

"Joe, I was hoping to hear from you." Lucas waited for Joe to initiate further dialogue. Anything might trigger Joe to end the call preemptively.

"I thought about what you said," Joe started.

"Uh-huh." *And you figured out I was full of crap or didn't notice my mistake?*

"Tansy told me you came by and talked with her, too." Joe's voice was even and measured.

"I did." Lucas struggled to come up with something appropriate. "Your wife is charming."

Joe chuckled. "Charming, yes. But she's not my wife."

"Sorry, I just assumed."

"Everyone does. She adopted my last name." The line went silent.

Had Joe disconnected the call? Lucas's phone screen said otherwise.

After a few more nerve-wracking seconds, Joe continued. "I hear you want to look for something on my property."

"Only with your permission." Lucas's pulse quickened. "Like I told Tansy, I'm happy to share credit for the discovery."

"I wouldn't have it any other way." After another pause. "We'll comb every inch of my land until we find her."

"Joe, you and I are going to make history today." Lucas stifled a laugh, suppressing his excitement. "Should I come right away?"

"Can you stop by around eleven?"

Desperately wanting to jump in and accept the invitation before Joe changed his mind, Lucas took a breath. Being overly eager might prompt a reversal. After all, Joe could search without him and steal Lucas's trophy. Lucas needed to play this right. "Eleven works for me. I'm hoping you'll allow me to bring the dogs. They know her scent."

"Nope. We've still got rut activity going on, and I don't want to disturb that with your dogs. Looking for your creature is one thing—spoiling my elk season is another."

"Understood." Too bad about the dogs. They would track her down in a heartbeat.

What about inviting Cynthia? Based on what he'd seen from Tansy, Joe seemed partial to chatty women. Cynthia might soften him up and give them more time to search the property.

Should he ask whether to bring Cynthia along?

No. Better to introduce them on the spot than to give Joe an opening to decline Cynthia like he had the dogs.

Lucas wanted any advantage—against both the Palmers and the Sasquatch. Cynthia could charm Joe.

After a half-hour of slogging through dense undergrowth on the Palmer property, Lucas expected Cynthia to whine about the misty rain or her sore feet. But she uttered no complaints.

Despite her bright-colored, fitness-center-appropriate footwear, Cynthia kept up with Joe's unrelenting pace. She stuck to him like a spider wrapping its prey. Not literally clinging to him but occasionally touching his arm, ostensibly to steady her footing.

While Joe never rebuffed her touch, he shushed her several times with a finger to his lips—mostly when she asked questions about the land or tracking techniques.

Cynthia knows how to work men to her advantage. It's easier to spot her technique when she's got someone else in her sights.

When they reached the meadow where Tansy had played her recorder four nights earlier, Lucas pointed to the opening where he and the dogs clashed with her. "I know the Sasquatch came near this clearing. My dogs nearly climbed out of their skins when we got here."

"Is this where Tansy plays the recorder?" Cynthia asked.

Without waiting for a response, Cynthia walked up to Tansy's low, flat rock. With dramatic fervor, she laid both palms on the top and leaned over the stone.

As Cynthia's back end propped in the air, Lucas forced himself not to laugh out loud. Was she channeling Tansy's energy from that night? Lucas looked over at Joe and expected to see a smile, but Joe remained stoic and watched Cynthia's theatrics with indifference.

Shortly after the rock incident, Cynthia sidled back up to Joe and followed him around the clearing's perimeter with Lucas a few steps behind.

Joe stopped on occasion to point out hints of footprints or a broken branch. When Lucas paused to look, he discovered nothing significant. Time, weather, and animal feet had obliterated partial prints. The broken limbs seemed too evenly spaced and not random.

Suddenly Joe froze and raised both arms out to his sides. Cynthia and Lucas stopped behind him. Despite Lucas's growing mistrust of Joe, his senses heightened—colors intensified, and the scent from decaying leaves tickled his nose.

Joe turned toward Cynthia and crooked a finger at her, indicating for her to come ahead.

She complied with tiny exaggerated steps.

When Joe pointed to a bare shrub, Cynthia gasped and raised both hands to cover her cheeks.

Now what? Lucas squeezed between the huddled pair to see what they'd found.

Joe pulled a bundle of fine hairs from a branch's knobby tip with the care of someone dismantling a bomb.

The back of Lucas's neck tingled like a breeze had penetrated his thick collar and scarf.

Finally, Joe's found something.

Lucas unzipped a breast pocket to remove his bag of Sasquatch fur from the Jamesville alley and slowly handed the bag to Joe.

Am I giving up my sole connection to the Sasquatch?

"Here, compare them to these."

"You didn't tell me you'd collected his fur," Cynthia's accusatory tone was unmistakable.

"Well, now you know." Lucas leaned in to watch Joe pull threads from the bag and lay them on top of the hairs he'd freed from the bush.

"Looks the same to me." Joe crushed them into a single wad and handed them to Lucas. "What do you think?"

Lucas bit his tongue.

In a frenzy, Lucas pulled the wad apart, searching for any with different textures or colors. But they all looked the same. Lucas shook his head and huffed. He hoped the dogs would not get confused if he used them again. Anyone versed in nose training would not have introduced new smells into the scent article. What was Joe thinking?

Not wanting to alienate Joe or cut short their search, Lucas shook the tension from his shoulders. "Yeah, it seems like the same fur. We must be close."

More than an hour later, they approached the trailer complex, wet and chilled. Only Cynthia lacked a dulled spirit. After seeing no other trace of the Sasquatch on Joe's land, Lucas assumed she had escaped—perhaps days ago.

Lucas jammed his hands into his jacket pockets—angry with himself for being complacent.

I talked myself into believing she stayed here. The dogs must have lost her scent, and I drew a hasty and erroneous conclusion that she holed up. How will I find her now?

Before Lucas could castigate himself further, a burgundy sedan pulled into the drive. Two men were in front—Dylan Cox sat behind the wheel, and his sidekick from the diner was beside him. How did the detective find out about Joe's place? Maybe he had more smarts than Cynthia gave him credit.

Dylan jumped from the car and dashed up to Cynthia. He grabbed her hand and slapped a tracking device in her palm. "I just found out your buddy Lucas has been asking everyone in town about Joe Palmer. You didn't need to track me—you got here first."

"How could I know you might want to visit Joe?" Cynthia's eyes grew wide. "My friend Lucas invited me to come along."

"Are you two teamed up now?"

Lucas took a few steps back to distance himself from Dylan's outburst. The guy sounded eminently frustrated—not surprising since he was several steps behind Cynthia.

"At the restaurant, you told me you're not interested in sharing your experiences from last month. But I want to keep forward momentum on this story, and Lucas has some leads for a sighting in this area. I've agreed to work with him." She leaned into Dylan. Her head tilted seductively upward, and her lips parted. "But I'm happy to talk with you—just name the time and place."

Lucas did not doubt Cynthia would get her narrative—whether from following the female Sasquatch with him or looking for the male Dylan had supposedly spent a month tracking. Lucas glanced at Joe, standing stock still and watching the back and forth between Dylan and Cynthia.

Why wasn't Joe getting all riled up about two more trespassers on his property? It almost seemed like Joe appreciated having conflict in his front yard. That made no sense. Why the switch?

Something had changed.

"Will we see Tansy while we're here?" Lucas asked Joe.

"Nope." Joe's gaze never left Dylan and Cynthia while they accused each other of spying and invading privacy.

"That's disappointing." Lucas stepped in front of Joe's view of the arguing pair. "I was hoping to introduce her to Cynthia."

"I can't understand why." Joe looked past Lucas, and his jaw set, not inviting further discussion.

Lucas could not imagine Tansy missing an opportunity to take center stage when visitors called. Her absence seemed suspicious, especially since they were in the yard right outside her front door.

"Is Tansy inside, or did she leave to take care of something in town?"

Lucas asked, not expecting a response.

"Not sure that's any of your business."

Lucas scanned the yard, looking at the collection of cars and trucks in various stages of rust and disrepair. What was different?

Lucas started at one end of the yard and recalled the vehicles he'd seen before. The International Scouts, in a variety of colors, stood doorhandle to doorhandle. The Willys came next. But where was the hippy van?

"From the last time I stopped by, I thought you had more vintage cars and trucks. It's quite a collection." Lucas placed a hand on Joe's arm to draw him away from Cynthia and Dylan. "Are they for sale, or are you a collector?"

"I've driven them all, at one time or another. They're not for sale." Joe glanced at the row of vehicles. Was he trying to avoid eye contact?

In a burst of realization, all the pieces fell together. The van was missing. Roomy and innocuous, the vehicle was the perfect getaway car. Tansy had driven off with the Sasquatch, and Joe was distracting them to give her time.

Lucas hastened to Cynthia and muscled Dylan out of the way. "We should leave, now."

She glanced at Joe. "Why? Did you say something to offend Joe?"

"No. He's been the perfect host." He grabbed her arm and pulled her toward his truck. "Either you're coming with me now, or you can catch a ride with your buddy Dylan."

"What's happening?" she whispered.

Lucas glanced back at Joe. A smile crept across the man's face. Joe had done his job. Lucas leaned to Cynthia's ear. "Our Sasquatch has been traveling southeast since I first spotted it. I'm guessing Tansy's giving it a head start in that direction."

"The Sasquatch left Salida on October 20th to come up here. Maybe it's going back."

"What?" Lucas's eyes narrowed. "I can't believe you kept that tidbit from me."

Cynthia's creature had traveled from Colorado to Oregon—it made sense the beast would repeat the journey. All sorts of animals migrated. Why not Sasquatches?

Before changing into his car slippers, Lucas pulled a plastic bag from his breast pocket and pressed it into Cynthia's hand. "Put your muddy shoes in this bag before you get in my truck."

"Okay. But where are we going?"

"We've got to catch up with Tansy's van before Dylan finds out his Sasquatch already left."

Cynthia hopped on one foot, juggling the bag and one shoe while reaching for the door handle. "Are we leaving Dylan here with Joe?"

"We're not bringing him with us," Lucas snorted, "And I don't expect Joe to help him."

Chapter 23

DYLAN COX

Lucas's truck tore out of the driveway, spewing gravel as it accelerated. Why had they left in such a hurry?

Dylan motioned for Augie to come out of the sedan, and he reluctantly complied. Dylan figured Augie had stayed inside to wait until the hostility dissipated.

"You must be Joe Palmer?" Dylan asked with his hand extended.

"Who wants to know?" The man stepped back as if to avoid Dylan's gesture.

"I'm Dylan Cox."

Joe's mouth fell open, but he closed it quickly. "You got some ID?"

Dylan instinctively reached for his wallet. After a thought, he left his hand over his back pocket. "Do you always ask for identification when people call on you?"

"No." Joe held out an open palm, waiting for the plastic card. "But in this case, I want to be sure who I'm talking to."

After extracting his license, Dylan passed it to Joe. "Do you need one from Augie, too?"

"No, just you." Joe looked at the license, Dylan's face, and back. "It's a decent likeness, but you look different without short hair."

"It's a long story." Dylan sighed. "Are you satisfied that I am who I said?"

"Why do you have an Illinois driver's license?"

"What were you expecting?"

"Isn't Salida in Colorado?"

Joe Palmer seemed more peculiar with each question. Cynthia must have mentioned that he and Augie might be trailing them and told Joe they had driven from Salida. "I'm from Chicago." Dylan motioned toward Augie. "But Augie is from Salida. We came here together to look for a friend."

"Does Augie know about your *friend*?"

"Everything there is to know." What was Joe getting at?

"Kati is driving to Salida to meet you."

"You know about Kati?" Dylan swallowed hard. He shook his head, trying to make sense of what Joe said. "Kati was here but left?" Remnant doubts about whether Kati transferred and whose messages Augie intercepted vanished. "Wait. You taught Kati how to drive?"

Without waiting for a response, Dylan moved to the front porch and sat, unsure what to think. Dylan rested his chin on folded hands and stared into the yard. Augie dutifully slid to a spot by his side.

Joe approached and blocked Dylan's view. After effortlessly lowering himself to a squat and looking Dylan eye-to-eye, he pressed his lips together as if gathering his thoughts. "Tansy, my erm…my common-law wife, is driving our van with Kati as a passenger. Your girlfriend seemed smart, but I don't think we could teach her to drive and follow a map in one night."

"Kati told you she was my girlfriend?"

Dylan felt Augie's hand on his shoulder. The action reminded him of what Tom might do to help Dylan focus on the big picture.

"When did they go?" Augie asked Joe.

"They left early this morning—before dawn, around six-thirty. They've been driving for about seven hours. Our van can go close to sixty miles an hour, but I'd be surprised if Tansy would average more than fifty." He looked at where Lucas had pulled away. "I'm sure Lucas realized the van is missing. He and Cynthia left in a hurry. Does Cynthia know about Salida?"

"She does." Dylan nodded.

"Tansy's likely to take a few breaks along the way." Joe glanced at his wristwatch, an oversized model with a black rubber band. "I'm guessing they're close to three-hundred-fifty miles from here." He ran the back of his hand across his lips. "They might be near Jordan Valley by now."

"Can we call them? What's Tansy's cell number?" Dylan pulled out his phone.

"We don't have cell phones. We carry two-way radios for when I'm away from the house hunting. But she's too far for them to work now."

"Let's go, Augie." Dylan rose and turned toward the car. If he and Augie hurried, they might catch the van before it reached Salida. Dylan's feet moved forward as if under their own power. He could not stop if he tried.

"Hold on, cowboy," Joe called.

Dylan jerked to a stop when Joe came forward and grabbed his arm. Joe continued—his voice laced with fatherly empathy. "We're talking about a woman who hasn't driven more than the three miles into town for the past thirty years. Now she's got a Sasquatch for a passenger. Do you think I'd send them out on the Interstates to be stopped by the highway patrol? They're taking the scenic route. I drew it all out for Tansy on maps." Joe rested a gentle hand on Dylan's shoulder. "I'll do the same for you if you want me to."

Dylan nodded, wanting to jump into the car in pursuit but knowing the route details could help. Better to catch up with them than pass them.

Augie stood and pulled his sketchbook from underneath his arm. He flipped the pages to very near the end and opened it to show Dylan a drawing.

"Good catch," Dylan said to Augie before he turned toward Joe. "Is this the van?"

Joe took the notebook and held it close. "How did you draw this picture?" He rubbed the back of his neck as if confused. "Have you been on my property before?"

"I've never been here. I saw your cars in my dream."

When Joe gently cupped Augie's shoulder, Augie did not flinch.

Joe asked, "Do you think Kati sent you this vision?"

"I don't know. I only draw the dreams I see."

"Why did you ask if it came from Kati?" Dylan asked.

"Tansy said something about Kati having telepathic skills. But she hit her head on a rock—right around the time you were separated. There's still some bruising even though it happened more than a week ago." He winced. "She still has headaches."

Dylan pressed a hand to his chest. What could a blow to the head mean to Kati? She was far from the restorative powers of Reval's pools. Dylan did not know whether Sasquatches' bodies were resilient to injuries in Porgu. "Is she okay otherwise?"

"She took a fall when she escaped from Lucas and his dogs. They chased her down a cliff, and she broke her ankle. Tansy's a great medic. She immobilized the injury with a cast. Based on how she applied one for me, Kati's double kit behemoth will protect that ankle and not break apart without dynamite."

"Can you hurry and show me their route?" Dylan fidgeted with the key fob. "Lucas and Cynthia are already on their way to Salida. Between knowing what the van looks like and where they planned to drive, for once we're a step ahead."

Chapter 24

Lucas gripped the steering wheel for more than an hour and a half, giving Cynthia one-word answers and calculating how to pry the whole story from her.

At first, the drive followed curvy tree-lined roads. As they neared Bend, Oregon, the views flattened, and ranch-style houses with unmanicured yards dotted the roadside. His shoulders relaxed as his plan coalesced.

Lucas drew a long breath. "Not that it matters, but why do you keep calling the Sasquatch *him*?"

Cynthia tapped a long nail against her chin.

Easy question, why the delay?

"According to one of my sources, Dylan believed he was chasing a male Sasquatch that he'd named Kalev."

"Dylan gave it a name?" Dylan must have been close enough to see her breasts and curvy hips. Perhaps his and Dylan's Sasquatches were not the same.

Lucas tapped his thumb on the steering wheel. His thoughts raced. What if he'd followed Kalev's mate? Two Sasquatches? A mated pair might mean there were offspring as well.

As far as Lucas knew, his female had covered a great distance between his cabin and Detroit Lake, and she never retraced her course to retrieve hidden young. Lucas and the guy in Jamesville had both seen her solo. Or maybe that guy had seen Kalev. The dude referred to his Sasquatch as *he*. But Lucas assumed he had not gotten a good look at her.

"Well, why not name it?" Cynthia snapped Lucas's attention back into the truck. "People name their pets, and researchers name the large mammals they track. Just because the animal may not know it has a name doesn't mean people don't assign names to them." She gave his shoulder a gentle nudge. "I can see why you wouldn't name one—if you're planning to kill and eat it."

"I don't want to eat the Sasquatch. But I plan to make one hell of a trophy out of its head."

"Let's talk about that. Have you considered using a tranquilizer gun and turning him over to a university or government agency for evaluation?"

"For a New York minute."

"I'll take the reference to my home base as a compliment. So you've considered doping him?"

"No." Lucas snorted. "The Sasquatch is huge and has unfamiliar chemistry. I'd have no idea what type of dosage or dart to use."

"It's unfortunate to be hot on the tail of a live one and need to kill it." She shifted in her seat. "I figure the notoriety would be bigger if we could capture one."

"Sweetheart, whether we capture or kill the creature I don't care, as long as I get my trophy and make the cover of a prestigious hunting magazine."

"But you might make the cover of National Geographic, Time, or Vanity Fair if we capture it."

"That'll be your department. You write the story and sell it to whichever magazine will buy it."

When Lucas gunned the accelerator to pass a white minivan, Cynthia gripped her armrest until they were back in their lane.

"While I appreciate your fast truck, Tansy and the Sasquatch could be hours ahead of us. Besides, we have no idea if Tansy will stick to the Interstates or backroads. I can't imagine we'll catch her." Cynthia looked out the side window. "I wonder what's driving him to Salida?"

She let out a giggle, and Lucas responded with, "Mm-hmm."

"I didn't mean that literally. I know Tansy is driving him. But I wonder if instinct compels him to travel between Salida and Oregon for food or breeding. Dylan met him in Salida more than a month ago and ended up

in Oregon. If Kalev is going back again, this might be a migration route."
Interesting theory.

"Hey." Cynthia straightened. "What if Tansy isn't taking Kalev to Salida? Maybe she and Joe have a second home in the wilderness somewhere, and the Palmers plan to hide him there."

Lucas released a long sigh. Cynthia's constant verbal processing drove him nuts. How long could he put up with her? "Do you think Joe and Tansy would be living in that shit-hole in Detroit Lake if they had a second home?"

"Okay. But how would Tansy know to take Kalev toward Salida?"

She had a point. It's not like the Sasquatch wore a collar tag that said, IF FOUND, RETURN TO DYLAN COX IN SALIDA, COLORADO. Lucas replayed Joe's demeanor from the morning. The man was curiously cool and unemotional—hardly like someone who recently discovered his wife was sheltering a Sasquatch.

"Joe Palmer knows more than he lets on." Lucas resumed his thumb rhythm on the wheel. "He's owned that property for nearly five decades. Joe could have been tracking or working with Sasquatches for years. If his place is along their migration route, Joe might have been feeding them and harboring them long before you started following this story. I wouldn't put it past them to create some kind of safe house for them."

"Hmm." Cynthia slid her tablet out of her bag and tapped a note.

"Planning on coaxing a follow-up interview with the Palmers?" Lucas snickered. "Good luck with that."

"Do you think Joe and Tansy drugged the Sasquatch to transport it?" Cynthia reached over to place a hand on Lucas's thigh. "I can't imagine taking off on a road trip with a wild animal loose in my car."

"The Sasquatch I saw seemed curious—like other primates I've seen in the wild. I've watched chimps and gorillas in the bush, but I'd never load one in my vehicle without first crating it. Any wild animal can turn vicious if threatened or trapped. Based on what I saw, the Sasquatch could weigh more than a couple hundred pounds. I'll bet it's crazy strong."

"Like I said."

"Joe's a savvy hunter." Lucas shook his head. "He wouldn't send Tansy alone in the van unless he knew she'd be safe."

"Good point." She stared out the windshield. "If we assume the

Palmers know about a migration route, I think it's a safe bet they're going to Salida. Dylan met Kalev at a cabin just outside of the town. I can direct you there."

"If Tansy's smart, she'll stick to the less-traveled roads. But we can travel the Interstates and beat them to that cabin."

At the sound of a mechanical tone, Cynthia pulled a computer tablet from her tote. He heard her tapping.

"Looks like Dylan and Augie are on the move again," Cynthia mused. "They're headed our way and are about twenty minutes behind us."

"What?" Lucas gave her a double-take. "I saw Dylan give you the tracker I put back in their wheel well. How do you see where they are?"

"You think the obvious one was the only tracker I put in their car?" Cynthia scoffed. "There's one in the back bumper, but the best is the one I stuffed into their glove box when they were inside the diner in Jamesville. Dylan should be more careful about locking his car—being from Chicago and everything." Cynthia stared at the tablet. "Do you think Dylan might have squeezed any information out of Joe Palmer?"

Lucas shrugged. Dylan had little potential for charming details out of anyone.

"Well, maybe he did, and maybe he didn't." Cynthia glanced at Lucas. "But for now, Dylan's headed the same direction we are."

What were the odds Joe could warn Tansy about their pursuit via cellphone? No—Tansy admitted they did not communicate that way.

If, by some miracle, Dylan squeezed the van's route from Joe, he might catch up and caution Tansy that Lucas and Cynthia were in pursuit. Once warned, Tansy could drop the Sasquatch somewhere other than in Salida. Better to fall back and follow Dylan than to wait at the cabin and end up empty-handed.

When Lucas pulled into a convenience store lot, Cynthia tensed. "What's happening? Are you changing the plan?"

"We should hang here and find out if Dylan plans to take the main or back roads. If he follows a less than direct route, he's got better intel than we do. We'll follow him until we see the van. Once we've got a visual, we can find a way to get Dylan out of the picture and recover the Sasquatch."

Cynthia nodded.

Lucas continued. "It'll be hours before we make up enough time to catch Tansy. But with only one driver, she'll take lots of breaks before the van reaches Salida."

"Glad to see you've got our plan under control." Cynthia's smile deepened. "We make a great team."

Lucas pointed toward the store. "You should make a pit stop and pick up stuff to eat and drink. We're not stopping unless Dylan does."

After tucking the tablet in her bag, Cynthia jumped from the seat and pulled her tote high on her shoulder. She sashayed into the store without a backward glance.

Cynthia was not stupid enough to leave the tablet behind. Lucas chuckled at their mutual distrust as he wiped the passenger seat and dash with an antiseptic wipe.

Chapter 25

**PAST JORDAN VALLEY, OREGON
KATI**

Afternoon shadows from peaks and sparse trees grew long. The farther east we drove, the drier the terrain and air.

If I had accessed other Sasquatches' memories of the territory, I would not have been surprised at the barren landscape. But when Tansy and Joe decided she should drive me to Salida, I chose to ignore my recollections from previous Sasquatch travelers. Confident we had escaped Lucas, I sat belted into my seat and absorbed the *road trip*—a new term from Tansy that suggested excessive snacks, music, and driving.

Features sped by—no Sasquatch had ever traveled so fast.

Tansy provided constant noise. Most of the time, Tansy talked about her hobbies, history, and view of the world. I understood some of what she told me, but many anecdotes were beyond my comprehension. She used words like Democrat and Republican—pontificating her views about these halvek subgroups. Without context, I remained blissfully uninformed.

She told me how to make her favorite foods with specifics about measurements—like cups and teaspoons. She befuddled me with ingredients such as cinnamon, oregano, and cumin.

When Tansy ran out of stories, she turned on the radio and sang along to music. The melodies were different from the tunes she had played on the recorder, and many spoke of relationships, dire circumstances, and lost love.

Tansy called the songs country-western. But the concept was unclear. Were the singers located on the western side of this country, or were they referring to a different country? Once, she convinced me to join her for a repeated verse. My awkward squawk sent us both into laughter.

"Now that we're past Jordan Valley," Tansy said, "we're using back roads to Mountain Home. Joe said it'd take about two hours longer than staying on the Interstate, but we agreed the lesser-traveled roads would be safer." Words like Interstate were indecipherable.

Tansy slid an open map from the window ledge and pointed to the towns without taking her eyes from the road. I memorized the lines and their associated numbers. As I traced the route, I learned town names by the number and shape of the letters. When we passed signs with matching locations, I pointed them out to Tansy. I could not pronounce them, but she seemed pleased I could recognize the symbols.

With a glimmer in her eye, Tansy turned to me. "We'll be crossing the state line in a few seconds. Watch for a sign."

I stared out the window, unsure of what to look for.

"There it is!" Without waiting for me to acknowledge anything, she squirmed in her seat and pointed out the window. "Welcome to Idaho."

"What is significant about crossing into a different state?"

"When I traveled across the country—before I met Joe and settled in Oregon—I cheered at each state line I crossed. Back then, I expected my journey to start in Pennsylvania and end at the ocean on the west coast." Tansy slapped the steering wheel. "I needed to travel across nine states to get there. Each one felt like a weight lifting from my shoulders."

"What were you carrying?"

"Not physical weights." Tansy laughed. "My parents had just died, and the government was trying to tell me where to live. I wanted no part of that. The farther away I got, the better I felt."

"You can defy the rules of your society?"

"There are laws about hurting someone or stealing. But for the most part, we can go where we please and do what we want."

"Same for us," I stretched the truth because she would not understand. Sasquatches made personal decisions, but our society prescribed boundaries. Despite what I did, no one would transfer from Reval to Porgu without permission.

"Now that I think about it, we have laws to restrict young people—like for driving, voting, or marriage. But once people are adults, they're responsible for what they do."

"Same for us," I said to avoid embarrassing her. Regardless of their age, Sasquatches needed approval before having children or moving from one tribe to another. Halveks' unrestrained independence likely resulted in chaos and actions that detracted from an orderly society.

"We have penalties for lawbreakers—like jail or fines."

"Same for us," I said, finally being honest but assuming she would not understand the severity of our punishments. How could a halvek comprehend how a banishment sentence might forever impact a Sasquatch? Isolation could be far worse than accepting euthanasia.

"Like what?" Tansy shrugged.

She cannot possibly understand, but she asked. So I will tell her.

"When I return home," I began, "I will sacrifice my life for crimes I committed when I was here the first time."

"They will kill you?"

"No. I will submit myself to be euthanized."

"That sounds like suicide."

"Does it?" According to Dylan, suicide means killing oneself, and in our euthanasia process, a willing Sasquatch allowed others to take their life. The concepts were not dissimilar. "Suicide seems consistent."

"Well, that's just wrong." Tansy's finger tapped the wheel. "My father died from a drug overdose, and my mother committed suicide a day later."

"Was your mother's grief so severe that she could not live without your father?"

"That's not the point." Tansy sighed. "They left me alone to deal with social services and a family who wanted to steal my parents' belongings. My parents didn't have much, but relatives I'd never met before wanted to take everything—the house, a car, furniture—everything except me."

"I understand." *Halveks are forever fighting over their belongings.* "You must have been angry with them for wanting your possessions."

"My relatives?" Tansy scoffed. "No. They were out for themselves, but I don't blame them. We were all poor."

"Then why were you angry?"

"I was angry with my parents."

"But they were dead." *Tansy's logic is primitive and confusing.*

"I was angry that they killed themselves. Their actions, both dad taking drugs and my mom's suicide, were incredibly selfish. They only thought of themselves and not their kid."

Sasquatch families would never abandon an orphaned child. I turned to stare out the window.

In Reval, I independently requested euthanasia from the Council. At the time, a conversation with my parents seemed superfluous. My entire family would be better off living without the stigma of my crimes, and telling them the specifics would force them to block my memories from the collective for their remaining years. I would never place such a burden on them.

"You considered your parents' actions as selfish?" I asked.

"Yes." Tansy gestured wildly with a hand. "People shouldn't make unilateral decisions without considering how it might affect others."

"What if your mother believed she could not be a good parent while she grieved?"

"Really?" She smirked. "She didn't even try. If she'd talked with me, I would have told her we could get through it together. She never gave me that chance."

A knot formed in my stomach.

Am I selfish for not conversing with my family before petitioning the Council?

Dylan knew all the details of my crimes and continually asked me to reconsider my decision. I assumed his suggestion reflected his self-serving halvek desire to keep me alive, but maybe he was correct. Making unilateral decisions was not a sign of sophistication—it was prideful.

If or when I return to Reval, I will discuss the matter with my family.

"Do you communicate with your other family in Pennsylvania?" I asked.

"Not a chance. I'm not sure they know where I am, and I'm happy to leave things the way they are. Joe is my family now. We have each other."

"Families are not easy to dismiss where I come from. The bonds between parents and their children are irrevocable."

Unless the child was born with defects—Sasquatch parents discarded hairless children. While traumatic, sending a flawed baby for euthanasia or to Porgu was best for the child and society.

I did not want to reveal Sasquatch norms, and if I were

telecommunicating with another Sasquatch, I would have automatically censored my thoughts. But I was not used to verbal discourse. Before I realized it, I said, "However, Dylan's parents abandoned him when he was born. That's how he came to live here."

Tansy's gasped. "Dylan is part Sasquatch?"

"No." *Not exactly a lie—Tiina and Alevide are both Sasquatch, so Dylan is entirely Sasquatch. He knows the truth. But he is the only one, and I have no intention of telling Tansy.*

I continued, choosing my words carefully. "I am referring to the story Dylan told me about his birth. His parents left him to be raised by those who understood the extent of his capabilities."

"What's wrong with him?" Tansy's voice was laden with suspicion.

"He could be hairier?" I gave her a thin smile.

"You said that before. You seem to judge a person's value by their looks." She laughed to herself. "Now that I think about it, humans do that, too. I guess we're the same in some respects."

"Also, very different," I said, knowingly.

In the month I had come to know Dylan in Reval, he changed, maybe even evolved. While his development was stunted from more than twenty years of neglect in Porgu, he learned how to telecommunicate. Much to our surprise, Dylan took nourishment in pools—a feat we assumed impossible for a halvek.

After meeting Tansy and Joe, I wondered if Sasquatches were wrong about halvek capabilities. Perhaps halveks had emotions and intellects well beyond our understanding. I probably misjudged Dylan as well and focused too much on the pleasure he gave me—and not enough on how much I appreciated his humor, logic, loyalty, and sensitivity. After all, these were all traits I would have looked for in a Sasquatch mate.

Again without stopping to filter my words, I said, "I hope Dylan will be in Salida when we arrive."

Tansy straightened. "You said he was *in* Salida. That's why we're driving there."

"We were separated when we arrived in Oregon. Salida is the logical place for him to return. But he could as easily still be at my home."

"I assumed you're from Oregon." Tansy glanced at me and raised a brow.

Half tempted to explain the difference between Porgu and Reval, I considered the ramifications of making Tansy the second halvek to know the truth. One that Sasquatches had kept secret for thousands of Porgu years.

Telling her might not matter. No one would believe her. But better not to burden her with reality. "Not far from Jamesville." *Again, not wholly a lie.* "I will know more when I arrive in Salida. If he is not there, I will travel to my home and find him."

"I'm glad to help. If Dylan's not there and you need a ride back to Oregon, I'm happy to drive you."

"You are very kind. But I would prefer to hitchhike."

I turned to the window so Tansy would not see my smile before looking back.

"You?" She looked from the road to me and back. As my attempt at humor sunk in, a wide grin crept across her face, and she released a snort.

The snort turned into a giggle, which escalated into a belly laugh. It became infectious, and I joined in until hiccups stopped me from breathing.

When the van started to shimmy, I thrust a hand onto the wheel to help hold our course. Whether from the insanity of my hitchhiking statement or the idea I could help drive the van, my laugh deepened until my sides ached.

The van slowed, and Tansy steered to the roadside, where we stayed until our composure returned.

"I'm serious." Tansy cleared her throat. "If we don't connect with Dylan, I'll bring you home with me. We can find another way to find him."

"Okay."

The engine roared when she accelerated, and the van returned to the highway.

"Thank you for your friendship." I swiped my moist eye with the back of my hand.

"I know you'd help me if I were lost." Tansy cleared her throat. "I think Joe is a better person than me. He put together a backpack for you." Tansy indicated with her thumb to the back seat. I cranked around to see a cloth bag. "Go ahead," she said. "Open it."

I reached behind and drew the bulky bag onto my lap. The closures were strange, with stubs and metal teeth to hold the seams together. I clasped a tab but dropped it again.

Sasquatches do not have possessions. What could I possibly need that Joe-The-Halvek would give me?

"I added a few necessities, but mostly it was Joe. Don't be shy." She nodded. "Look at what's inside."

The tabs were ingenious. When I moved them across the metal teeth, an opening formed to give access to the interior. How long had it taken the halveks to figure out this type of closure? I swiped the tab back and forth to open and reseal the bag.

"It's just a zipper." Tansy laughed at me. "I know we have another thirteen hours before we get to Salida, but open it."

I reached a hand inside. The first object was a clear bag with small pieces of wood. Carefully releasing the closure to avoid tearing the bag, I opened the package and smelled. The bark's distinct odor triggered memories from the past—not my own but from other Sasquatches who had traveled in the northern reaches of this landmass.

"That's aspen bark," Tansy said. "While you were in the yurt, I made tea for you with it. It has loads of great medicinal properties. It helps with pain relief. But it's also known for treating burns and swollen joints. If your foot starts to hurt, we can stop at the side of the road, and I'll make you some tea. It would also work if you chewed the bark."

I sealed the bag and set it aside. Next, I took out the knife Tansy had given me in the yurt. I placed it carefully on top of the bark. After some cloth Tansy said could be used for many things, like a bandage for a wound or a hat if I became cold, I pulled out a bottle and a bag filled with yellow powder.

"The bottle's filled with water from our well. You're not going to find any cleaner. But I can refill it when we stop for fuel at a gas station."

I dropped the bag into my lap and unscrewed the bottle top to take a sip. "What is the powder?"

"That's dehydrated eggs." Tansy giggled. "Your favorite food."

After replacing the cap and propping the bottle next to my feet, I picked up the clear bag with dry yellow power. "This does not look like eggs."

"No. It doesn't. When we stop for a break, I'll add some water and heat it on our camp stove. Believe me—it will look the same as what I've given you before."

I held the bag to the waning light outside the window. How could this dry fluffy stuff turn into the halvek food I had grown to love? While I wanted to believe Tansy, I shook my head and placed the bag on top of the other items. I would need to see the metamorphosis before accepting her story.

I reached a hand deep inside the bag and recognized the final treasure before lifting it out. "Joe gave me a recorder?"

"No." Tansy beamed. "The recorder was my idea. I thought you'd like to keep up with your music lessons. Your voice is still quiet and hard to hear, but I think it's gotten louder. Anyway, you know dozens of tunes now. I'm sure Dylan would love to hear you play."

My stomach fluttered as I thought about Dylan. Tansy held unfailing optimism for my reconnection with him.

I blew into the mouthpiece and ran my fingers over the holes to play the scales Tansy taught me. Once warmed up, I started one of my favorites—Tchaikovsky's Dance of the Reed Pipes.

When I finished, Tansy pounded a hand on the steering wheel. "That was wonderful! Who knew the Sasquatch were talented musicians?"

"I assure you I am the first." As I returned the articles to the bag, I added up my other firsts. First Sasquatch to befriend a halvek, first to couple with a halvek in Reval, and first to own possessions. I straightened—and first to eat scrambled eggs.

"You know," Tansy started, "I wish there was some way we could warn Dylan that we're coming to meet him in Salida. He must be worried sick about you. You've been apart for over a week. I can't imagine being away from Joe for that long. The only time we're separated is when he goes off to hunt." She sighed. "If I want to see him, I walk to the other end of our property and surprise him in the blind." She winked at me. "He's never turned me away when I slip into his sleeping bag to make love."

Tansy and Joe's coupling sounded more intimate than I imagined for halvek copulation.

She waved a hand and continued. "I know it hurts for you to send messages, but have you tried again recently?"

"Not since before we left your home." I assumed my transmissions were flying into the noisy Porgu atmosphere—never to be received by

Dylan or anyone else looking for me.

"Try once more. You never know how your actions affect others in our universe. Maybe one small transmission can make all the difference. In the movies, people with amnesia have their memories come back in an instant. Your injury could fix itself, too."

I concentrated on what I could see outside. In the fading light, I could make out occasional homes with lights on inside. Most were far from the road. I listened carefully to hear beyond the noise of the engine and our tires against the pavement. A dog barked, and halvek children played in yards—some bounced balls, and others talked in groups.

Nothing seemed distinctive enough to include in a message. Finally, I saw it—a road sign with the words GIVENS HOT SPRINGS. I closed my eyes and imagined every detail about the sign. The pain started at the base of my neck and spread quickly through my skull until my whole head ached.

I hope Tansy is right about my transmissions getting through. I would like to believe Dylan knows I am coming to find him in Salida.

Chapter 26

NEAR GLENN'S FERRY, IDAHO

Blue and white flashing lights pierced the night and strobed into the van.

"Son of a bitch!" Tansy shouted as the engine slowed down. "Joe said to stay off the Interstates, and I didn't listen. We can't have been on I-84 for more than twenty miles, and it's after eight. Not much traffic besides semis out here. What dumb luck."

"Why are we stopping?" Tansy's heightened anxiety made my heart beat faster. We were in trouble.

"Stay down but crawl between the seats and get into the box under the mattress. There's a flashlight and hook latches inside. Be sure you secure the lid so nobody can open it."

I had seen Tansy in her *take-charge* mode when she dealt with Lucas in the meadow. But I had not seen this side of her since. Her no-nonsense demeanor sent me scrambling and into the back of the van to find the bed.

With a leg inside the wooden box and the mattress raised in one hand, I asked, "What is happening?"

"The State Patrol is stopping us. I don't know why. I've kept my speed below the limit, and Joe made sure the van's lights were all working perfectly before we left."

I assumed Tansy meant someone with authority was stopping us, but she was unclear about why. I tucked my legs inside the box and slowly brought down the lid. Before closing the top, I ensured none of the bedding had slipped inside—trapped fabric could betray the enclosure. To avoid detection, we Sasquatches were ever mindful about leaving tracks or evidence.

I ran my trembling fingers along the interior walls. While my night vision excelled, I needed a bit of light to see, and the box was sealed tight. A flashlight, like the ones Tansy had shown me how to use, was stuck to the side with grippy material. It pulled away easily. With help from the light, I found the latches and maneuvered them into place. But they were made of thin metal and barely attached. If someone forced the top open, the latches would give way. Once I shut off the light, I readied myself to greet any intruder with force.

The tires threw gravel onto the van's underside when I felt it move to the roadside and shudder to a stop. Tansy made no noise, and I assumed she waited for a halvek to approach. My heart thundered in my chest.

Footsteps plodded along the side of the van. From the sound, the halvek was large and a slow walker.

"Good evening, Ma'am." Definitely a male.

"How can I help you, Officer?" Tansy's voice sounded calm and devoid of tension. How could she be relaxed with my discovery imminent?

"License and registration, please."

"Certainly." I heard Tansy rifling around in the van. "Here they are, Sir. My goodness. You have the most remarkable hands. I'm a palm reader and have seen hundreds, but nothing like yours. Your finger length is incredible. You must be a musician. What do you play?"

"Uhm." The halvek cleared his throat. "I don't."

"Well, you should take up an instrument. It's a shame to let any natural talent go to waste." A tapping vibrated the van, like Tansy patting the door frame in a rhythmic pulse. "I'm confident I wasn't speeding. I don't think this van can even go the speed limit without shaking to bits. Is there anything wrong, Officer?"

"No, Ma'am. If you could just wait in the vehicle, I'll be right back." His footsteps crunched gravel.

"Take as long as you'd like, Sir. I'm in no hurry."

The retreating footsteps faded. I wanted to raise the lid or call out to Tansy with questions about licenses, registrations, and what she expected from this halvek who had the authority to stop us. Despite my curiosity, I willed myself to stay silent and secure in the box.

Minutes passed before he came back to speak with her. "I need you to step outside the vehicle and walk with me."

"Certainly, Officer. May I ask what this is about?"

"Just follow me out here."

I heard the door open and shut. "Brr," Tansy said. "It's freezing outside. Would it be better if we could sit inside your nice warm squad car?"

"Can you tell me where you're coming from?"

"Sure. I'm traveling from Detroit Lake, Oregon to Denver, Colorado. My sister lives in Denver, and she's having an operation this week. I'm headed there to help out with her kids until she's back on her feet."

I had no idea that halveks had the ability and propensity to lie. Does the Officer find her story convincing? Or, if all halveks lied, is he suspicious?

"You left Detriot Lake today?"

"I did indeed, Sir. It must have been just after six this morning. I've driven straight through and only took a break for gas." She let loose a subtle giggle. "Well, I also stopped to pee, but that would be natural with all the herbal tea I've been drinking. I made it myself this morning and filled a jug to drink along the way. The convenience store drinks have too much sugar and caffeine. If you think I talk a lot now, you'd be shocked at what a little caffeine will do to me. My husband Joe can't get me to shut up if I drink a half cup of coffee. I'm so envious of him. He can drink two cups with dinner and sleep like a log. But not me—I'd be up all night."

"I'd like to see that thermos of tea if you don't mind."

"Of course. If I had another cup, I'd give you some. I mix it myself."

I heard them return along the driver's side. The door opened, and something rattled before Tansy said, "Here, I'll open the top for you, Officer. Doesn't it smell nice? I'm a big fan of cinnamon and orange peel—that's what gives it a spice flavor."

"Have you stopped for meals or consumed any alcohol on your trip?"

"Absolutely not." She gasped. "I have a long way to go. I'd never drink and drive. Why all these questions?"

"I'll tell you because I don't think you're the person we're looking for. The State Patrol received a tip that a retro eastbound Volkswagen van was driving erratically. We're stopping anyone that fits that description."

"Did you stop me because of my van or because I was driving erratically? I don't even recall changing lanes since I got on the Interstate. Everyone drives so much faster than me. I'm a very careful driver."

"I only stopped you because of your van. I can see that you are a good driver. Sorry if I've caused you any inconvenience."

"Well, you've been very respectful." She giggled, and I imagined her placing a friendly hand on the halvek's arm. "Besides nearly giving me a heart attack when you turned on your lights, it's been very nice to meet you."

"Here's your documents, Ma'am. You have a good evening and a safe drive down to Denver."

The van jostled as Tansy returned to her seat and the door closed. After the halvek's footsteps faded, Tansy started the van, and it moved forward. Only then did I let out a huge breath and relax onto the base of the box.

"You can come out now," Tansy directed.

I unlatched the hooks and replaced the flashlight. Tansy had worked a miracle to diffuse a potential confrontation with the halvek. Once out of the box, I straightened the covers before slipping into the front seat.

I gripped my hands together to stop them from shaking. "I don't understand why he stopped us."

"I'm guessing our friend Lucas figured out we left the property and is tailing us." Tansy scoffed. "He must have notified the State Patrol with a bogus story. If he can get them to slow us down, he might catch up."

Chapter 27

NEAR MOUNTAIN HOME, IDAHO
DYLAN COX

A half-hour out of Boise, Dylan glanced at the gas gauge. They were driving on fumes. If they did not stop soon, Augie's sedan would be sitting on the side of the road, and they'd be hitchhiking while Tansy's van barreled its way toward Salida.

Dylan looked toward Augie, sound asleep with his head propped on a pillow against the window. They had agreed to take turns napping and driving to avoid losing time by pulling over to sleep.

"Hey, buddy," Dylan called as he reached over to give Augie's shoulder a nudge.

Augie straightened and stretched. "What time is it?"

"Close to ten. You've slept for a couple of hours."

"I like my bed better." He rubbed the back of his collar. "My neck hurts."

"If all goes well, you'll be home tomorrow afternoon."

"Will Kati stay with us in my trailer or with Destiny and Tom?"

"I hadn't thought that far ahead," Dylan mused. "Someone might see her if we keep her in the town. It seems like we should take her somewhere more remote. Would it be okay if I stay with her at your cabin?"

"Tom's not finished fixing it yet."

"You're right. But the well works, the power is on, and there's a roof overhead. It would be better than camping this time of year."

"You can stay there any time." Augie reached behind the seat to place his pillow in the back—precisely at the seat's center. "Now that Kalev is gone, you'll be safe at the cabin."

"I'm glad I went to Reval and met Kati, but I wouldn't have followed Kalev if I'd known what he was capable of."

"He's a bad Sasquatch."

Simple but accurate. Dylan rubbed his tired eyes.

"I'm pulling over for gas somewhere in Mountain Home. We can take a stretch break and pick up snacks. I'd like to change drivers, too—if that's okay with you."

"Sure." Augie reached for the book bag at his feet. "Do I have time for a drawing?"

"Did you have another dream?"

"I think so."

Augie pulled out his sketchbook, a fresh pencil, and a headlamp while Dylan scoped the sides of the road for a station.

A few miles farther, they approached one with blinding lights and diesel truck pumps. Another less conspicuous station sat across the highway.

"Gas is cheaper across the road. We'll go there. Take a break from your picture while I maneuver the car. I don't want to spoil your sketch." Augie lifted his pencil from the pad as Dylan pulled into the station and up to a pump.

When Dylan stepped outside, Augie was already back to drawing.

Dylan stood next to the pump as the tank filled. He rubbed his hands over his arms to counter the crisp air. A steady breeze brought diesel fumes across the highway from eighteen-wheelers pulling into the other station.

When Dylan finished outside, he opened the door to find Augie had not moved from his spot hunching over the notebook.

"I'm pulling closer to the building so we can go inside. Are you going to take a break?"

"I'm almost finished."

As Dylan drove nearer to the door, Augie added stokes of lead from the side of his pencil. "Here's what I saw."

Dylan took the pad and turned on the overhead light to inspect the drawing. When he saw the road sign, Dylan pulled out his phone to find a location for Givens Hot Springs. "If this came from Kati, they passed this sign a while ago. Could you tell whether it was still light outside?"

Augie took the notebook and added a few more lines to accentuate the shadows. "Not in the night. More like late afternoon."

"According to Joe's directions, they were taking the slow route between Jordan Valley and here. I figured we might gain on them if we get on the Interstate, and I was right." Dylan reached for the door handle. "Let's make this a quick stop. We might catch up before they reach Salida."

A cold breeze shot into the car and ruffled the pages in Augie's notebook. Dylan hurried outside and closed the door.

As Dylan waited for Augie to store his art supplies, a half dozen semi-trucks with trailers jockeyed for a pump position or eased on the highway from across the road. Nearly hidden by the truck ballet, a white dually pickup truck sat idle at the far end of the lot beyond the glaring overhead lights.

When Augie came out of the car, Dylan pointed. "Do you see that white truck across the highway?"

"Yes." Augie moved to stand beside Dylan. "It looks like Lucas's truck."

"Can you see anyone inside?"

"It's dark." Augie squinted. "It has Oregon license plates, and we are in Idaho."

Dylan pounded an open hand against the car roof. "They left ahead of us, and Joe figured they were racing toward Salida. How did they end up behind us?"

"Cynthia must be a good detective."

"Don't remind me," Dylan said, only half-joking. He bent to check near the tires. "Help me look into the other two wheel wells. They must have put another tracker on our car."

After a thorough search, they stood looking at the car with their muddy hands held out front to avoid dirtying their clothes.

"My fingers are numb." Augie wriggled them.

"Go ahead inside and clean up. There's got to be another tracker here, and I'm not stopping until I find it."

Dylan gave the wheel wells another once over before he ran a hand inside the bumpers. "Aha!" he cried when he felt the disk hidden near the trunk. Dylan yanked it from its hiding spot in a grand display and threw it on the pavement. He ground a heel into the plastic cover with all his weight until the tracker looked like he'd taken a hammer to it. Dylan picked up the bits and threw them into the trash can beside the entrance.

Just try and follow us now.

But it was a hollow victory. Cynthia would know Augie's sedan was headed to Salida, and there were few alternative routes to get there from Mountain Home.

After Dylan visited the store, he and Augie stood next to the car—both staring at Lucas's truck.

"Let's get going," Dylan suggested.

Before they could open their doors, Lucas's headlights came on as the truck pulled onto the highway. It rolled past the entrance of Dylan's station, and someone switched on the dome light. Lucas stared, and Cynthia leaned around Lucas to smirk at them.

"They're ahead of us now," Augie said with a sigh.

His simple message sent a shiver down Dylan's spine. Lucas's truck had a more powerful engine and fuel capacity to outrun them all.

What will Lucas do to stop Tansy's van, and what will happen to Kati when he finds them?

Chapter 28

Tansy tipped her head toward each shoulder. "I'm gonna need to stop and catch a nap soon. We've been on the road for more than seventeen hours, and I don't trust myself to stay awake."

"Do you think I should drive?" I asked, knowing the intelligent answer was *no*.

"We could try." Tansy shot me a grin. "We're on the I-84 now. But we're going back on a side road soon. Driving on the state and county highways would be too complicated for you. I can't imagine sleeping with you at the wheel negotiating traffic lights, stop signs, and cars pulling in front of us. But staying on the Interstate with you at the wheel is risky. We can't risk another police stop." She giggled. "That would be tough to explain."

"Because I don't have a driver's license?" Tansy had described the concepts of licenses and registrations, along with numerous other driving requirements and the van's operating features, during the past seven hours since the State Patrol stopped us.

"Well, there's that. But mostly, it would be hard to explain why a beautiful Sasquatch was at the wheel."

"You think I'm beautiful?" I had always figured my features were average, and many males from my tribe preferred darker-haired, taller mates.

"Honey, folks would kill for your high cheekbones and narrow nose."

"They would kill me and cut off my face?" The halveks' brutality never ceased to amaze me. Lucas likely had similar plans for carving me up and creating a display of my parts for his cabin.

"Not literally." Tansy laughed. "It's an expression to say people would like to have the same features you have."

Dylan had spoken of his attraction, but I assumed he found our time together desirable and was not speaking of my physical appeal. He had shared images of Jen, his previous mate. She had light hair, what there was of it, but she was short—everywhere.

I released a chuckle and recalled an earlier assumption about halveks. Sasquatches always assumed halveks copulated at random to produce unplanned offspring, sometimes forming family groups and other times not. We never considered they might have complex courting rituals and evaluate physical attributes when choosing a mate. That level of higher intellect was beyond their comprehension.

I should have paid closer attention to Dylan—he gave me hints about halvek cognitive abilities. At the time, I believed he was far more advanced than the others.

"Shit. Somebody's coming up fast." Tansy straightened and stared at her rearview mirror. Lights from the approaching vehicle reflected from the mirror onto her face.

After a few moments of squinting and adjusting the mirror, Tansy lowered her window. Frigid air whooshed through the van and ruffled my fur.

With only a thin long-sleeved shirt covering Tansy's arms, she must have been cold. Despite any discomfort, Tansy stuck her hand out the window and motioned for our follower to come around.

"Damn it. Why don't they pass us if they're in such a hurry? It's not like this van's going to speed up any time soon." She motioned again. "Come on. Pass us."

Tansy let off the gas and tapped the brakes—a technique I would not have understood without her driving instructions across Oregon, Idaho, and Utah. The engine downshifted, and our speed reduced.

"Nobody's out here." After one more wave, Tansy closed the window and huffed. "Pass me if you want to get around."

I craned to look over my shoulder and through the opaque rear windows. I could see an intense glow. They were following closely, and I could not make out the individual lights. The beams flickered between dim and bright.

"What do they want? Is it another State Patrol car?" I asked.

"No." Tansy gripped the wheel. Her voice came out high and thin. "Just an asshole who wants me to speed up." Earlier, Tansy had explained the meaning of asshole and other words to reference undesirable halveks or frustrations.

She braked suddenly.

I jerked forward until my restraint straps stopped me from crashing into the dash. Before I could catch my breath, Tansy slammed on the gas. The van lurched ahead and pressed me back into the seat.

"Is the van able to withstand these movements?" I braced both hands on the dash. Tansy's actions seemed aggressive and dangerous. What if the other vehicle could not compensate for her erratic movements?

"The van's over fifty years old. I'm sure she's got lots of life in her yet." The engine raced, and Tansy's attention flicked between the mirror and the road ahead.

"Are we in danger?"

Tansy glanced at me. Her brows creased. "I'm sorry if I've scared you." She backed off the accelerator, and the engine slowed to the level I'd heard for most of our journey. "We'll be fine. If I keep a constant speed, he'll pass eventually."

I pondered over her sudden mood shift. Sasquatches understood the potential of calm, sensible behaviors. When Tansy accepted the driver's aggression, she became rational. If Tansy could stifle her anger, other halveks might have this capability as well.

Tansy's breathing slowed, and her grip on the wheel slackened. Of course, halveks were continually challenged to remain calm—they faced ongoing trials with the weather, predatory animals, and each other. Nevertheless, they deserved admiration for subduing anger and aggression.

A white truck roared past in a flash, shocking me out of my thoughts. A female halvek with a mass of red hair stared at us through the passenger window. I leaned back into the seat despite knowing that her subquality halvek eyesight was insufficient to see me.

"Finally." Tansy made a sweeping arm gesture with her center finger held aloft. The red taillights grew small as the truck faded into the distance and around a curve.

I wriggled in my seat to regain comfort, staring at the dark road ahead. The aggressive truck's engine noises seemed familiar, more of a clacking than the rumble from Tansy's van. I scanned my memories over the past few days until I recalled a similar sound.

When I released a yelp, Tansy shot me a glance.

"What?" she asked.

"Did that vehicle look like Lucas's truck?" I asked.

"I thought so." Tansy chewed her lip. "But I didn't want to say anything. How could he have caught up with us or even know where we're going?"

"Joe is the only person who knew." My jaw set. "Would he tell Lucas?"

"No way. Joe invited Lucas to our property to distract him and give us time to escape."

"If Lucas has a truck like the one we saw, it can go very fast." I talked slowly to help Tansy understand my logic. "If he left after us, how could he be here?"

"We were hours ahead of him." Tansy's shoulders slumped. "But the van's top speed is pretty slow. I guess it could have been him." She swiped her nose with the back of her hand. "Why did he want us to see him? It seems like he should have followed until we had to stop for gas."

Her question was logical. But without fully understanding halvek cunning and what Porgu-specific advantages Lucas might use, I was at a loss to suggest his motives. "Tell me your ideas."

"For one thing, maybe it wasn't Lucas. It could have been some other asshole in a white, extended cab dually."

I liked her idea but wanted to prepare for worse. "What else?"

"Assuming it was him, maybe he doesn't want to meet up with us in a crowded place. For instance, if we recognized him and pulled off to go to a police station, I could accuse him of stalking me. While I dealt with the cops, you could hide in the box under the bed. Lucas would be in big trouble with the police, and we could get away."

"Anything else?" Her ability to work out potential scenarios astounded me.

"Okay. If we were running low on gas and needed to stop, Lucas could follow us into the station and pressure me into allowing him to search the van."

"How could we prevent that?"

"If we picked a station with lots of people, he'd have a hard time muscling his way into the van with all those witnesses." She smiled. "And I know how to attract attention. Somebody would help us."

"I understand why Lucas might not follow us. Now tell me what he might do if he is ahead of us."

"Well, I'm not sure." Tansy rubbed the top of the steering wheel with both hands. "All I know is that Joe wouldn't have told him we were going to Salida."

"How did he know where to find us? We went from Oregon to Idaho to Utah." I tapped a map with a finger. "These are crossed with roads. When we left your home, we could drive in any direction." I pulled the Utah one from the pile and waved it at Tansy. "He followed us here."

"Oh, my God." Tansy gasped. "What if they tortured Joe into telling them?"

My heart sank. I imagined Lucas with his dogs, rifle, and the knife attached to his belt. If Lucas and his red-head accomplice hurt Joe, he would be alone and suffering. "We must return to Oregon."

"Not yet. We've been on the road for nearly eighteen hours. I'm not starting the return trip without trying to see if Joe's okay."

Tansy had no telepathic powers, and the distance between them was great. How could she communicate with him?

When the next exit came into view, Tansy jerked the wheel to turn off the highway.

"Explain how you will contact Joe," I demanded.

"We're stopping at the next station and find a payphone." She glanced at me. "I'll show you how it works when we find one."

As we entered the small dark town, Tansy's nostrils flared. Her breath came in short, measured bursts.

"I'll kill Lucas if he hurt Joe."

Halveks continually demonstrated their primitive predisposition for violence, but Tansy's reaction hit me with a jolt.

Was her protective outburst similar to my response before I murdered the male halveks preying on young girls?

Chapter 29

LUCAS EDWARDS

Cynthia squirmed in the seat like a teenager just elected prom queen. "I can't believe you passed them." She spun and pulled up to look out the back window. "I can't see them anymore. We nearly made contact, and you sped up. Tell me you have a plan."

"Are you finished?" Lucas gave her the voice he'd heard all during his childhood—that *you don't have all the answers* tone.

"I don't appreciate your tenor." Her eyes narrowed. "I partnered with you because I assumed you wanted to catch Kalev as much as I do. We found them, and now you've lost them again."

"Hunters don't always take the shot right away. There are things to consider."

"Like what?"

"Like how far is the animal from the truck and can you make a clean shot to take it down immediately? You don't want to track a wounded animal for miles after a mishit."

"I don't need a field lesson from you. I'm talking about Tansy's van." She rubbed a finger across her forehead. Had his decision given her a headache?

"I can think of three big reasons to take this slow."

"Fill me in." Cynthia shoved her hands under her thighs and stared out the windshield.

"One." Lucas raised his index finger. "Forcing them to stop on the Interstate, with cars passing and potential for the State Patrol to see us, is a risky prospect. I want more time alone with them in case we search the van."

"I'll give you that one."

"Two." He added his middle finger. "I haven't seen you check Dylan's location for a while, and we have no idea how far behind he is. I don't want him interfering in our capture."

Cynthia pulled the tablet from her tote and clicked it to life.

"Three." Lucas lowered his hand and rested a fist on his thigh. "Do you want to hear the rest?"

"Go on." Cynthia tapped the screen. "I can multitask. There's no need for me to wait until you finish your list."

"Three." He held three fingers aloft and snapped them toward her for emphasis. "I don't want Tansy to pull over and then take off as soon as we leave my truck. We need to disable the van."

"Whaaa?" Cynthia's jaw dropped as she gave full attention to Lucas.

"Don't give me that bullshit. You said it yourself. You want to capture the Sasquatch as badly as I do. But I'm not going to force them off the road in a place where they have the upper hand."

"Are you planning to shoot out their tires?"

"You watch too many movies."

"What then?"

"First, find out Dylan's location. Then I'll tell you."

"Fine. That's what I was trying to do a minute ago." Cynthia poked the tablet. "Looks like they're near Brigham City. Depending on how fast they drive, they could be here between forty-five minutes and an hour."

"That should give us enough time. I see an exit ahead for I-80. Can you give me an aerial view on that thing?"

"Yes." Cynthia tapped and manipulated before she handed Lucas the tablet. He glanced between the map and the road to assess the best route.

"I've found the perfect spot." Lucas tossed it back to Cynthia and grasped the wheel with both hands to move the truck into the left lane.

They bounded through the median, across oncoming traffic lanes, and through an open field to a frontage road.

"I love a man with a plan. But where are you taking me?" Cynthia's throaty voice betrayed her excitement. She gripped the dash with one hand and the grab handle in the other. Her curly mop bounced and recoiled as

Lucas steered over low-lying brush.

Branches scraped the truck's underside like nails on a chalkboard. Lucas gritted his teeth, knowing he would spend hours buffing out dings and scratch marks. But the costs were well worth his prize.

After rounding a curve, Lucas found what he was looking for. With few overhead lamps and no traffic, Lucas made his decision and pulled to the shoulder.

"What do you see?" Cynthia asked.

Lucas opened his door. But before he got out, he turned to Cynthia.

"In less than an hour, we'll have our Sasquatch."

"How? Why here?"

"You can come outside and help me set up our trap or stay inside where it's warm."

Cynthia unclasped her seat belt. "No way. I want to see what you have in mind."

"Suit yourself." Lucas jumped into the back and yanked open a toolbox. He removed the top tray filled with hand tools and pushed aside an assortment of chains until the bag at the bottom pulled free. Lucas grabbed the handle with both hands and muscled the case out of the box.

As he lifted it to the edge of the truck bed, Cynthia jumped up and down, ostensibly to see what Lucas was doing. "Ooh. What's inside?"

Lucas leaped from the truck and transferred the bag to his shoulder. He walked onto the highway and checked out the shoulder before putting it on the blacktop. He unzipped the case and pulled out an accordion-designed spike strip made of nylon and hardened steel.

"Who carries something like that with them?" Cynthia stood next to the strip and leaned over to test a spike with a polished fingertip.

Lucas adjusted the strip until its placement was perfectly aligned. After pausing to review his work, he looked up at Cynthia and placed his hands on his hips. "When are you gonna get it?"

"What?" She scoffed.

"Your chances of catching that Sasquatch were nil until you teamed up with me. I'm one of the best—no, probably *the* best hunter on this planet. I always get my target."

Chapter 30

KATI

When Tansy pulled into the station, I slipped into the back of the van and hid inside the box. I lay in the narrow container and pulled a blanket over my body to stifle my trembling nerves.

In the darkness, I imagined I was back in Reval, floating in a relaxation pool, letting the gelatinous fluid fill my ears and block errant sounds. I forced myself to ignore all of Porgu's noise—engine rumbles, humming lights, and Tansy's voice. But to no avail.

My imaginary trip to Reval evaporated as I heard her footsteps approach and then fade away as if she walked in a different direction.

I tensed. Another car was driving on the road. Not like Lucas's truck with its loud rumble, but one of the smaller vehicles. The car stopped, and I heard the whine of a window lowering. Tansy spoke, but I could not decipher her words and understood nothing from the halvek she talked with. The voice sounded male, but it could have been a deepthroated female.

Suddenly, Tansy's voice seemed louder, and the other person did not respond during her pauses. Her voice's rhythm sounded like the cadence she reserved for conversations with Joe. Her high-pitched ramble slowed and eventually stopped. Without telepathy, how could the other driver help her to communicate with Joe? He was a great distance from here.

I snuggled deeper into the box. *How* she managed to communicate with Joe was not the issue. First, Tansy would confirm he was not injured and hear what Lucas had done. Then, Joe could suggest how to proceed. Joe had good ideas. He would know how to escape from Lucas.

"Thank you," Tansy called out as I heard her footsteps return to the van. The other car's engine revved, and it moved away until I no longer heard it. Shortly, Tansy opened the door.

I unclasped the locks and raised the box's lid. "Did you speak with Joe?"

She turned on the ignition and pulled from the lot as I climbed back into my seat.

"It's never easy," she started.

More would come. I waited.

"Since it's the middle of the night, the station is shut. There's no payphone anywhere outside. But I flagged down a guy driving past and asked to borrow his cellphone. I can't believe he let me borrow it. Of course, maybe he felt sorry for me when I told him someone was following us, and I wanted to call my husband."

Most of her chatter was lost on me. But eventually, she would tell me whether she spoke with Joe. So I wriggled in the seat, wanting her to get to the part about Joe.

"He had a nice new phone, and I had no idea how to use it. There weren't any buttons, just a plain flat screen. He helped me to put in our home number, and it rang and rang. It's an hour different there, and Joe was asleep because it's after midnight." She took a long breath. "He's fine."

"Did Lucas try to hurt him?" I clenched my fists.

"No. But Lucas had a woman with him, and she knows Dylan." Tansy stopped at a sign and laid a hand on my arm. I tensed, waiting for what would come next. "Dylan came to our property just before Lucas left."

"Dylan is in Oregon?" I strained against my seatbelt. While relieved Dylan was not stuck in Reval, had I made a mistake to drive with Tansy to Salida?

"He's coming after us. Joe gave him all the information about our route."

"Will we wait for him here?" I looked outside, wondering where we could meet Dylan yet hide from Lucas if he came back.

"Since Dylan planned to either catch up with us or beat us to Salida, I don't know if he'll take all the same roads. What if he takes the Interstate the whole way and passes us while we're stopped on a side road?" Tansy nodded, thinking. "Our best bet is to keep to our original route. If he's behind us, maybe he'll catch up. Otherwise, we'll meet him in Salida."

"How much farther is Salida?"

"I don't know for sure. But it's got to be at least another eight or nine hours."

I leaned forward to scan her face and bloodshot eyes. "You said you needed to sleep. You cannot drive another eight hours without a rest."

"After seeing Lucas ahead of us and knowing Dylan might be behind us, I'm so full of adrenaline I couldn't possibly sleep. If you stay awake and make sure I don't doze off while I'm driving, we should be fine."

We passed a sign saying LEAVING MORGAN before Tansy entered the Interstate.

"Are we going on the fast road for a while?"

"Yeah. I don't think the local roads connect here. We'll get back on the small roads at Henefer."

We passed an interchange marked Croydon when I spotted a white truck on the other side of the divided highway coming from the direction we were going. When it passed, I craned around to see its Oregon license plate.

"Look." I pointed. "Is that Lucas's truck?"

Tansy looked into the rearview mirror. "I can't tell. But I can see brake lights." She squinted. "If they decided to pass us before, why would they come back now?"

"What should we do?" Tansy's instincts about halvek behaviors were robust.

"I'm taking the next exit at Henefer. Maybe Lucas will assume I've stayed on the Interstate and will pass us." She glanced at me. "Just hope that he's not fast enough to see us get off."

Within minutes, we left the Interstate and drove through a sleepy town, crossed under a bridge, and flew down a narrow highway flanked with a hill on one side and a tree-filled ditch on the other.

Lucas's halvek-eyesight was not as sharp as mine. But would he have seen our van from the other side of the divided roadway?

It did not take long for me to find out when his lights blasted through our rear window.

"Shit!" Tansy yelled.

The van's engine roared as Tansy sped up and widened the gap between Lucas's truck and our van.

My heart pounded, and I gripped the seat so hard I feared my newly manicured fingernails would pierce the fabric.

We zoomed past ancillary roads and an access point for the Interstate. A sign marked Speed Limit 40 flew by. One glance at the dials in front of Tansy told me we were going faster. A part of me wished she had not explained about limits and the measurement dials.

"Hold on tight," Tansy called as the van started into a curve. I braced an arm against the door and a hand on the dash. Forces I did not understand pushed me to the side. The van teetered.

When the road straightened, I realized I had been holding my breath. Once the van—and my body—shifted back to center, my restraints loosened.

"He's coming around us." Tansy leaned forward and jammed down the accelerator pedal. "I'm flooring it." The meaning was lost in translation.

Our van's engine revved so loud I feared it might break free. The white truck inched along the side until it was abreast of us.

A redheaded halvek stared at us from inside Lucas's truck. While she would not see me in the dark van, she strained—ostensibly to catch a glimpse. Her eyes grew narrow and cold, and her scarlet lips formed a tight thin line.

Bam. My shoulder collided with the doorframe.

"He hit us!" Tansy's eyes bulged as if she could not believe Lucas's maneuver.

Lucas's truck pressed next to the van. The road in front of us seemed to move to the right. I shook my head to rationalize what I saw. Lucas was pushing us off the road.

The muscles on the back of Tansy's hands tightened as she gripped the wheel and struggled to keep the van moving straight. But to no avail. Their vehicle was bigger and heavier than ours.

They pushed, and we inched farther to the side—over the lane lines until two wheels crossed onto the shoulder.

The tires bumped against the road edge and kicked gravel. Our van vibrated in protest as it continued forward.

"What's in the road?" Tansy yelled, and I squinted ahead.

Something dark lay in front of us like a thick, motionless snake. But this snake had shiny spikes.

When Lucas peeled away to the left, we jerked back onto the road, leaving us on a direct course with whatever lay in our path.

Bang. Tansy fought the wheel as it yanked from her hands, first in one direction and then the other. *Hiss.*

A short distance ahead, Lucas's truck slowed. The tires kicked dirt and gravel as they rolled to a stop.

Our uncontrollable van skidded sideways, across the junction, and into a shallow ditch off the right shoulder.

I willed it to stop, but we bounced forward. Finally, the van smashed into the hillside next to a pillar holding up elevated railroad tracks. In concert, Tansy and I lurched forward before slamming back against the seats.

I gulped air to replace the breath lost in the crash and turned to Tansy. Her forehead lay against the steering wheel, her body unmoving with flaccid arms. I pushed her back against the seat, relieved to see her shallow breathing.

Her eyes were closed. She must have hit her head on the wheel or the windshield—blood trickled from her forehead.

"Tansy?" I gently pressed the flesh on her forearm. She *had* to respond.

"Go." Her voice crackled. But she did not open her eyes. "It'll only be a minute for them to reach us. Take your pack and our maps." With force inconsistent with her condition, she seized my arm. "Run!"

Torn between making certain Tansy was not irreparably damaged and fleeing for safety, I stroked the side of her face. "I cannot leave you."

"Don't be crazy." Her head turned, and her eyes narrowed into slits. "I'll be fine. You need to leave. Now!"

Through the broken window, I heard Lucas's truck engine roar. It grew louder as it clunked into gear. Tansy was right—they were coming for me.

I unclasped my belt and reached for the backpack before trying to open my door. I yanked and tugged. But it did not unlatch.

Red and white lights from Lucas's truck drew nearer.

I rammed a shoulder into the door. Again. And again.

Finally, it gave way.

"Thank you, Tansy. You have taught me many things. But most of all, you are my friend." I longed for her to ramble on about something—anything. Instead, Tansy licked her dry lips. Her shallow breathing reminded me of listening to a Sasquatch's final gasps before succumbing to death.

"Go." She reaffirmed.

I took a second to send another image into the night and ignored the now-familiar stabbing at the back of my neck.

Lucas pulled his truck near the van.

Heart pounding so loud I could hear it in my ears, I yanked the straps from the backpack over my shoulders and ran under the bridges toward the hills.

Lucas's tires kicked gravel as he backed away from the van—another thump as he changed from reverse to forward. Without looking back, I heard his truck follow me under the bridges.

Despite the cast protecting my ankle, I raced across a moist weed-filled gully, past a sign with symbols that said ROAD CLOSED, and to the top of a hillside.

Up and up I ran, taking in great gulps of air. Stones skittered under my feet and clacked as they hurtled downward. The truck's clattering engine faded when I gained momentum. My muscles sought to engage after the long recuperation at Tansy's home.

At the crest, I glanced over my shoulder. Lucas's truck had stopped when it tipped into the gully. The front was buried in the marshy ditch. His engine revved, and mud clumps flew from underneath.

The door opened, and Lucas tumbled out. With each lumbering step up the slope, Lucas huffed to catch his breath.

I turned to look at the terrain ahead of me and smiled, knowing Lucas would not make out details with his stunted vision. For as far as I could see, hills and the barren landscape lay in front of me.

I hitched up the straps on my pack.

Without his truck and lights, Lucas is slow. And I am fast.

Chapter 31

DYLAN COX

Emergency lights strobed the intersection where I-80 broke away from I-84. Dylan reduced his speed.

Probably some trucker fell asleep at the wheel. I hope nobody was hurt.

Augie raised from his pillow and rubbed his eyes. He turned to look out the driver's side window—not at Dylan but past him. Dylan twisted to follow his gaze and then snapped back to the front windshield. What was mesmerizing Augie? High-mast poles stretched nearly a hundred feet into the air to cast an amber glow over the interchange. The blue and white lights flashed from beyond.

"She's there." Augie raised a finger to indicate.

Dylan nearly careened the sedan off the road as he jerked to look where Augie pointed.

It can't be possible. That's an accident. It's not her—Kati's on her way to Salida.

Dylan pried his eyes from the intersection and forced himself to focus forward.

Stay between the lines. You're no use to her if you crash Augie's car.

"Kati?" Dylan gave Augie a sideways glance, trying hard to keep his attention on driving. "How do you know?"

"I had a dream with a crashed van." Augie swallowed hard enough for Dylan to hear. "I can tell she's been here."

"Is she hurt?" Dylan pressed the accelerator and raced for the next exit. "Tell me what you're sensing."

"In Kalev's dreams, I knew how he felt. I can tell Kati is scared."

"Scared about what? Was she hurt in a crash?"

"I don't know." Augie nodded. "We should go there and find out."

"Agreed." When Dylan reached Coalville, he made the exit loop and headed north toward the I-80 interchange.

As he approached the flashing lights, Dylan pulled off an exit—in time to see men maneuvering lines and pulleys to ease Lucas's pickup out of a ditch. Along the road's shoulder, portable light towers floodlit the hillside. Their generators rumbled loud enough to hear them through the car windows. A broad-shouldered man stood next to the ditch, watching the workers.

Lucas. He not only found the van before we did but caused an accident. If someone was injured, let it be him—Cynthia's my second choice.

Three emergency vehicles sat on the other side of the Interstate, and Dylan made his way under two bridges. Tansy's van sat crumpled in a berm adjacent to a concrete pillar.

When Dylan pulled up, emergency crews shut an ambulance door and left in a blaze of lights and sirens.

Dylan's hands shook as he jammed the sedan into park and ran to the van. He wedged his head and shoulders inside the passenger side. Papers, pillows, and clothes were strewn everywhere—but no people.

As he lifted himself on the seat to make a more thorough search, an officer called for him to stop.

"Kati!" Dylan squeezed between the seats into the rear compartment. He slid a mattress from its frame over a plywood box, and his pulse raced as he pounded the top of the box. "Are you in there?"

"Step away from the van." The officer shined a light at Dylan. "Now!"

Dylan slumped to the floor, and the officer opened the side door to repeat his demand.

"Where is she?" Dylan asked.

"The ambulance is taking her to Park City Hospital. Did you know the victim?"

"Did?" Dylan's voice caught. Was the victim Kati or Tansy?

"Sir, I'm sorry." The officer fumbled for words. "I didn't mean to say that in the past tense. I meant to ask *do* you know the victim? She's banged up a bit, but she'll be fine." He reached toward Dylan. "I'm serious about you getting out of the van."

After accepting the officer's help, Dylan walked to the front, where Augie stood. The van's grill and windshield were smashed beyond repair.

Augie, unmoving, stared at the wreckage.

"I know the people who were in this van," Dylan told the officer. "Did the ambulance take them both to Park City?"

Glancing at a piece of paper on his clipboard, the officer shook his head. "There was only one person in the van. Her name is Tansy Palmer."

Augie pointed to the tow truck team inching Lucas's truck out of the ditch. "Where are the people from that truck?"

"There." The officer nodded toward a squad car. "Seems this couple came along and saw the van hit a spike strip along the road. They stopped to call for help. When the fellow thought he saw someone leaving the scene—maybe the person who laid the strips—he drove to the embankment to follow the guy. But he got away."

"How the hell did his truck get stuck?" The minute the words left his lips, Dylan realized he was babbling. He could care less why Lucas drove into a ditch. But he let the officer respond.

"Must have kept driving until the front axle dug into the soft mud. The towing guys have the gear to get it out."

With hands on hips, Dylan eyed the recovery. "I can't believe they came out in the middle of the night with that crew and work lights. It's freezing out here. Seems like they'd want to wait until daylight."

"You must not know the truck's owner." The officer turned to look Dylan in the eye. "Lucas Edwards must have a wallet full of cash to convince the higher-ups not to wait."

As the officer finished, the squad car door opened, and Cynthia emerged. She tightened her faux fur collar against the cold and shook her auburn mane. When she spotted Dylan and Augie, Cynthia smoothed her coat and sashayed toward them.

"Dylan, how did you manage to find us so quickly? I was just planning to call you." Cynthia pulled Dylan out of the officer's earshot. But the deputy did not seem to notice and went back to rifling papers on his clipboard.

"What the hell happened here?" Dylan whispered through his teeth. "The last time I saw you, you were leaving Detroit Lake in a hurry with

Lucas."

"That's not exactly true. We saw each other at a gas stop in Idaho."

"This is not the time to get cute with me." Dylan grasped Cynthia's arm. "I'm betting you and Lucas caused Tansy's crash."

"That's not the story the police have." Her eyes widened with innocence. "According to Tansy and us, somebody blocked the road with a tire-shredding strip. Tansy lost control of the van when she hit the spikes and crashed." Cynthia pointed for emphasis. "Then, Lucas and I happened by to help."

"That's got to be bullshit." Dylan stiffened. "Why would Tansy agree to collaborate with you?"

"Well, for one thing, it's the truth," Cynthia declared with a head tilt. "For another, none of us want the police to know about Tansy's cargo." She gazed through the railroad underpass. "It's a shame he ran off. Lucas tried to catch him, but Kalev was too fast. Man, he sure can run."

He? Kalev?

Cynthia turned to face Dylan. "It was too dark for me to get a photo, but believe me, I tried."

Dylan considered Cynthia's words carefully. Erle must have told her the whole story about how Dylan followed Kalev into the woods. Cynthia did not know she and Lucas had been chasing Kati and not Kalev.

I'm not clearing up her misconception.

"You can let go now." Cynthia looked down at her arm, still clamped with Dylan's hand. He complied. "Where are you headed now? I assume you're going back to Salida."

Disinclined to feed Cynthia too much information, Dylan said, "Augie and I will be going to the hospital in Park City. Tansy should have someone with her until Joe gets here."

"In case you're wondering, I loaned her my cell phone to call him as soon as we found her. If he takes the fastest route, he'll be here in about twelve hours."

Dylan turned away from Cynthia. "Let's get moving to the hospital," he called to Augie.

Augie started toward the car. Suddenly, he jerked toward the hillside and squinted. Could Augie sense Kati nearby? Dylan wanted to ask but could not risk alerting Cynthia to Augie's powers.

Augie slumped and shook his head. "She's gone."

"Come on." Dylan opened his car door and waited for Augie to do the same.

"Wait. *She* who?" Cynthia stamped a foot when Dylan slid into the seat behind the wheel. "Hey! Aren't you sticking around to see if Lucas's truck is drivable? I might need a ride."

Dylan leaned out with the door propped open. "You're resourceful. I'm sure you and Lucas will figure out what to do."

He slammed the door and turned the ignition. Dylan pulled the sedan into a wide circle and headed toward the highway. What was worse—the nausea or the ringing in his ears?

"Kati will be okay." Augie smoothed the top of his slacks with both hands.

"I know she will. There's a lot of wilderness between here and Salida. Kati knows how to keep ahead of Lucas and stay safe." Dylan glanced toward the slope where Lucas's truck was still stuck in the dirt. "For now, we need to be sure Tansy's okay."

"Are we going to the hospital?" Augie's smooth face betrayed no emotion, but his strained voice told of his concern.

"Yes." Dylan stifled his urge to dash to the hilltop and call her name. She'd be long out of earshot. He shrugged at Augie. "We may have to meet Kati in Salida."

Chapter 32

TEN MILES EAST OF ECHO, UTAH
KATI

When the first rays of sun nudged above the horizon, I topped my sixth noteworthy hill. Some peaks lay dusted with snow on the side hidden from daytime sunshine, and all had moderate gains without cliffs or challenging route finding.

In the last few hours, my energy had waned. I needed a place to rest and take nourishment.

I stood at the summit of a bump and looked from where I'd come. There was no evidence of Lucas's truck or his slow halvek body coming after me. Down in the valley below, two small crossroads intersected near a structure with a tall white steeple. I pulled maps from the pack and sat to evaluate my accomplished distance and anticipated direction—for when evening fell again.

Pebbles and cactus pricked at my rear, reminding me of the toll Porgu was taking on my body. Despite Tansy's eggs, my muscles had atrophied in the seven days I'd spent in Porgu.

After flattening the Utah map on the ground and placing stones on the corners to keep the edges flat, I made mental images of the terrain and roads. Echo, the closest town to the accident, was easy to find.

In Tansy's van, I had followed our route since we left her home and understood how to track our journey. As I sat on the hilltop, I accessed memories from other Sasquatches who traveled in these environs. Unfortunately, there were few. But their images of these surrounding hills confirmed my paltry distance since the accident.

Needing to comprehend my overall objective before the next full moon, I nested the Utah and Colorado maps on the ground and placed rocks on the corners.

My jaw dropped. I'd only covered a tiny portion of what I needed to travel in the next twenty-one days.

A stiff wind gusted across the maps. Despite my weights, Colorado lifted into the air. I reached to grab it, but it slipped through my fingers. I scrambled to dump my pack on top of Utah and lunged for the airborne map. Angry with myself for not securing them with heavier rocks, I leaped to my feet to follow Colorado. It fluttered, hitting brush and rocks, staying just beyond my grasp.

Nearly halfway down the slope, it wedged on a bush where I quickly plucked it from between the branches. I folded it as I walked back up the hill.

A familiar truck engine rattle made me freeze. I turned to scan the valley below.

There it was.

When a single vehicle approached the crossroads and slowed to a stop, I gasped. It was a white truck like the one Lucas had used to chase our van.

I dropped to slink behind shrubs. Could I have pushed through the night only to be captured by Lucas after a few hours on my own? I pounded a fist on the dirt.

Confounded halveks and their machines. If Lucas had just his wits and personal strength to rely on, I would have evaded him long ago.

Focus. He does not know you are here. He's only searching.

I peeked between the shaggy branches. Far below, the truck turned in the direction of my hiding spot. From his distance, he could not possibly see me.

Something flapped. A bird?

I'd left my pack on the summit. The bag was small, but the Utah map fluttered underneath it.

I jerked to look back at the truck. Inside with the windows raised, the sound would be muffled by the noisy engine. From down on the road, my eyesight would see the map like a vast waving flag. But a halvek would not detect unnatural movements from that distance.

Thankfully, the terrain between the pack and me was devoid of snow.

I'd not left footprints to attract Lucas's attention.

His truck made its way slowly down the road. I pictured both he and the redheaded female scanning the hillsides, looking for any indication I had crossed nearby.

I closed my eyes and recalled the Utah map with its tiny lines surrounding Echo. I visualized the main highway and connected roads where Lucas could loop around where he lost me.

As his truck rolled closer, it crept past a cluster of farm buildings and came to a complete stop. I held my breath and slunk further behind the bush.

Waiting for him to open a door or pull to the side, I lay still—listening and barely breathing. But soon, he accelerated and disappeared behind a hillside blocking my view. I took a deep breath and noticed my hands were trembling.

Had he been circling this route since I started my eastward journey?

Once confident he was gone and no other halveks were in sight, I hurried up the hill to where I had left my things. After stuffing the maps inside, I shouldered my pack and moved to a drainage on the far side of the hill—without a view of the buildings or road. If I could not see them, they would not see me.

A cluster of trees with low boughs looked inviting. As the sun came up, the soft dark dirt next to the trees would grow warm. I dragged a few lifeless, needleless limbs to block the wind and tucked myself underneath, resting my head on the pack.

The myriad of potential routes and Sasquatch terrain memories rifled through my head, thwarting any possibility for much-needed sleep. I rose to study the maps, and carefully folded them, so only the sections I needed were visible.

I could take a southeast diagonal route to Salida, but massive lakes and high mountain peaks were in my way. A southern route seemed more populated, and the terrain was devoid of vegetation, allowing passersby to see me from greater distances. If I headed due east, trees offered more protection.

When I drew a finger straight across Utah and Colorado, I identified a place with letters that said STEAMBOAT SPRINGS. If I reached that town, I could travel directly south and hit Salida without crossing the highest peaks.

After measuring the previous night's distance between my thumb and index finger, I used the gap to estimate how many days it would take to reach Salida. Since the night had been short, I could double my distance on all subsequent nights. If I maintained a consistent pace, I would be at Dylan's cabin before the next full moon—in twenty-one days. Using the halvek calendar, Dylan would call it December 17.

Once my plan was firmly in place, I fell into a much-needed sleep.

I would not discover my error about the next full moon until much later.

Chapter 33

Dylan and Augie sat, stiff-backed, on vinyl-covered chairs in Tansy's hospital room. A nurse bustled around Tansy's bed, tucking a warm blanket around her legs. All three stayed silent while the nurse checked the monitors flickering with numbers and graphs showing Tansy's vitals.

When the nurse left, Tansy sat up with a wince. "I'll be fine until Joe gets here. I'm sure I'll see him by midafternoon. He's not fond of driving for that long without a break. But when I spoke with him, he seemed anxious to bring me home." She drew a breath, and Dylan marveled at how long she could talk without stopping. "He spends most of the day on our property—walking or hunting. I'm not sure if he's left the state since before I moved in with him. That's been a long time—maybe forty years, give or take." She glanced at the open doorway before adding, "You and Augie should be out looking for Kati."

"You should relax and stop telling us what to do." Dylan rose to pull his chair close to the bed. He gently pressed her shoulder back into the sheets. "With a broken arm and a couple of bruised ribs, you need rest. Besides, I've already told you we're not leaving until Joe gets here."

"Kati could be miles away from here by the time you start looking for her. Even lugging the cast on her foot, she ran faster than Lucas. I wish I could have watched him trying to catch her on that hill. He was stupid to try. What a macho asshole."

Dylan had trailed Kalev in Reval when they logged mile after mile for the Sasquatch Ranger duties. Despite being an avid jogger, Dylan struggled to keep pace with Kalev's long stride. Kati's strong legs would carry her far from Lucas—as long as she stayed away from the highways where Lucas had an advantage with his truck.

"You spent time with Kati and know how smart she is." Dylan sighed. "She'll figure out the best way to keep out of Lucas's reach and meet us in Salida."

"But Joe gave you our route. Why are you waiting here with me?"

"Kati isn't going to follow the same path. She has the maps of Utah and Colorado you gave her. Kati can also access memories from every Sasquatch who ever traveled through these parts."

"How does she know all that without her telepathy?"

"While she probably can't update what she knows with new information, she can draw on what they've seen before. How much could rural Utah and Colorado have changed since we were in Reval? Kati will find the best way based on what she can handle with the cast on her foot, the topography, and how close she wants to come to cities and towns along the way."

"You know her better than I do." Tansy pulled the blanket under her arms and smoothed it over her lap.

"We've got plenty of time before Joe arrives." Dylan reached out to grasp Tansy's hand. "Tell me everything you and Kati did." While desperate to know whether Kati had feelings for him, he would be satisfied to hear the details of what he'd missed.

"We were only together for a few days." Tansy picked at a loose thread at the blanket's edge. "Kati made me realize we don't know diddly about what goes on in anyone's head—human or otherwise. As soon as Joe and I get home, I'll insist we both become vegetarians. Just because we can't communicate with animals doesn't mean we should assume they're here solely for us to exploit." She looked from her lap to Dylan's face. "She's in love with you. Did you know that?"

"No." Dylan stared at the back of his hands. "I was in love with her, but Kati made it abundantly clear that our relationship was more experimental than emotional."

"Uh-huh," Augie chided from the other side of the room. "But Dylan still loves her."

Tansy nodded toward Augie. "I'm sure Augie can read your feelings the same way I could read Kati's. Whenever she talked about you, her eyes lit up. She went on and on about how you taught her how to speak and about human customs."

"I'm not sure I believe you." Dylan touched Tansy's brand new plastic splint. "First off, Kati's voice is a mere whisper. So I'd be surprised if she went on and on about anything. Secondly, she would have called our customs *halvek* and not *human*."

"I heard her use that word. She said it meant *human*. Is that right?"

"Ostensibly." Dylan smiled. "But with a bit of ridicule thrown in."

Tansy broke into a belly laugh but quickly drew a breath and draped an arm across her stomach. "Man, it hurts to do that." She looked at Dylan with watery eyes. "No more jokes."

"I'll try." Dylan offered a weak promise with a sly smile. "Tell me more about Kati."

"Well," Tansy settled into the bed, "she's musically gifted."

"Again, I don't think we're talking about my Kati. She's never seen a musical instrument."

"I taught her to play the recorder. At first I figured it would improve her breathing and give more volume to her speech—and it did that." Tansy inspected the end of her braid. "She can repeat melodies after hearing them only once. Kati memorized my fingerwork and played exactly what she heard. She advanced from children's melodies to complex classical pieces in no time."

"Classical?" Dylan pictured Kati at a symphony and knew she would enjoy every moment of the new experience. Unlike Kalev, who would judge humans' appreciation for music as another time-wasting activity.

"Don't get me wrong." Tansy interrupted Dylan's thoughts. "I love country music—same as Joe—but when I play recorder outside in the moonlight, I want to hear Bach, Mozart, Vivaldi, or Handel before anything modern." She cocked her head. "What type of music do you listen to?"

"Classic rock."

Augie issued another, "Uh-huh."

"When you and Kati get back together, you'll need to negotiate for the radio channels." Tansy nodded toward Augie. "Seems like Augie might appreciate a widening of your repertoire, too."

"Despite what Augie might have you believe, I used to listen to classical music. While my mom played rock in the car and her home office, Dad tuned in to classical music whenever he was home." He scoffed. "Kati and I will find a happy medium."

Saying it aloud made Kati's return feel probable. "You're sure she's planning to come to Salida? I can't help but think she might wait until the next full moon and go back to Reval."

"Where is Reval?" Tansy's head tilted.

Kati must not have shared anything about where Sasquatches live or how they transfer between their world and ours.

Dylan backpedaled. "Sasquatches sometimes live in groups where they isolate themselves from humans. I visited one of these places with Kati and met others like her. They don't name the spots, but I called it Reval. I'd consider it her birthplace or home."

"She never mentioned anything to me about going home. Every time she talked about where she would go when her ankle healed, it was Salida. Or if she couldn't find you there, she planned to come back to Oregon with me until she came up with a better plan on how to find you." Tansy straightened. "Did any of her messages get through to you? She hit her head the night you were separated, and it hurt her to send messages. But she kept trying."

"When we were together in Reval, I could easily hear Kati's transmissions. But I haven't heard any since we left." Dylan pointed toward Augie. "When Augie is sleeping, he can intercept Kati's visions. That's how we tracked you down in Detroit Lake. After that, Augie knew you'd passed through Givens Hot Springs in Idaho and could feel Kati nearby when you crashed near Echo."

Tansy looked from Dylan to Augie. "I wish she knew you could see her messages. She was ready to stop sending them. They give her massive headaches. But I urged her to keep trying."

"Thank you for encouraging her." Dylan turned to Augie. "If Kati keeps them up, maybe we'll find her before she reaches Salida. But if we don't intercept any soon, there's no point in staying in Utah. We'll go home and wait."

Chapter 34

**TWENTY MILES INSIDE THE COLORADO BORDER—
DECEMBER 4
KATI**

I paused on the insubstantial summit to fist pump—a ritual I'd started to honor both Dylan and Tansy. To catch my breath, I slumped to the pebbly ground. As I strained to see a reasonable path for my descent, an icy wind penetrated my fur and started a shiver that shook my body to the core.

The night sky had not yet turned from black to gray. I could have another hour of walking—if I wanted.

In Porgu, the coldest part of the day was immediately before dawn. If I kept moving, I could countermand the early morning chill.

The previous night, with moderate terrain, should have seemed easy after two nights with massive elevation gains and losses. But steep hills were not the only barriers.

Shortly after the middle of the night, I had negotiated an ice-covered canyon bordering a body of water identified as GREEN RIVER. Hunks of slippery rock broke loose in my grip and sent me sliding down the nearly vertical walls. Down in the canyon, I'd twice fallen through the river's not-completely frozen surface and soaked to the bone.

But that was hours ago. I'd had enough frustration and wanted to rest.

I dragged a manicured fingernail across the dirt, musing about the great distances I'd traveled since leaving Echo, Utah. Most of my journey was isolated and the scenery repetitive. I forced a smile, thinking about the joy I felt when I crossed Utah's border into Colorado. While I could not identify the specific point where the halveks demarcated the two states, I knew by comparing my maps and the topography in Colorado. If Tansy were with me, she would have joined my celebration dance near the border.

On that night, the Colorado line seemed like an excellent place to send my final broadcast transmission. Weary of the searing pain they caused and not knowing whether anyone could receive them, I decided to push out one last broadcast.

I had twirled in a circle so my message would include a full panoramic view. Sadly, it looked the same as much of the landscape I had walked through the past eight nights—all low shrubs and never-ending hillsides.

Based on my images, how could Dylan—or any other halvek for that matter—locate where I had been? To them, everything would look identical—endless wilderness with sporadic roads. No halveks occupied these valleys. Who knew why they built motorways and rarely accessed them?

My eyes started to close, and I bobbed forward, too exhausted to care whether I slept in the open or a secluded place.

No. I shook myself awake, knowing I'd appreciate a darker environment once the sun rose in earnest.

I forced myself to stand and snugged my pack.

A dark cave might be a nice change from sleeping beneath shrubs. My few belongings were likely still wet from crossing the GREEN RIVER. If I could lay them out in a cavern, they might dry before nightfall. I had passed a few caves along my route and knew how to find them near the valley floor.

With all the deliberation I could muster, I eased into a drainage choked with bushes and dried grasses. Sharp, brittle limbs tore at the fur on my legs and hips. I rolled my eyes at the inconvenience, not concerned enough to find an easier path.

Before reaching a dry creek bed at the hill's base, I spotted a shallow cave under a rocky overhang and stopped to have a look.

Once inside, I no longer heard the rushing wind. Dry leaves and branches lined the floor.

Hmm—inviting.

After carefully arranging my moist maps and fabric away from the opening, I fluffed the detritus to form a soft bed.

My stomach growled, letting me know to take sustenance before sleeping.

Most of my eggs were gone. I'd eaten them by pouring a bit of the powder into my water bottle and shaking it into a slurry.

I evaluated my remaining egg powder and added only a tiny portion to the water bottle—less and less each day. It would not last much longer, and the diluted nourishment was better than having to stop to look for desiccated berries or bark while I was trying to make forward progress.

After resealing the bag and packing away my precious powder, I slowly sipped my breakfast. With each mouthful, I held it long enough to savor the flavor. Once back in Reval, I would never again eat eggs. I chuckled. Further, I would never tell another Sasquatch that I had eaten them. My kind would disapprove of taking a gift from a halvek.

While other Sasquatches who traveled to Porgu came home to unload every last experience into our shared knowledge, many of my experiences would go no further than me. My peers would never know what they were missing—some practical knowledge and other events quite appalling.

I emptied my bottle, sealed it, and stowed it in my pack. After only a moment to wad leaves for a pillow, I snuggled into the bed and immediately fell asleep.

I jolted upright when a sniffing sound woke me. Gray light spilled through the entrance. It was not yet midday, and I must have only slept a few hours. Was it a dream, or had someone found me?

In my exhausted haze, I cringed. Could Lucas have tracked me here? No. I shook my head. If it were Lucas, I would have heard his firearm's metallic click or his boots on the loose gravel outside the cave.

Another sniff. Something with a nose close to the ground lurked outside—possibly a halvek but more likely a different animal.

I took a long, hard look at my perfect sleep site. Had I stolen someone else's bed?

A low moan followed another series of sniffing. The animal surely smelled me. Would it attack and chase me away or find another place to bed down? I searched my Sasquatch memories about encounters with

Porgu's wild beasts and quickly narrowed my species identification—most likely bear. After accessing memories of this area, I decided a black bear was most probable.

I released a slow breath, grateful it was not an area populated with more violent ones like the aggressive grizzly, who was not as simple to control. A low growl followed—indicating frustration more than anger.

The first time I came to Porgu, I managed large and small animals with ease. But after my head injury, could I encourage the animal to go elsewhere?

My telepathic skills remained impaired. If I sent a misinterpreted message, I might trigger a violent response. Better to wait and see if the bear decided to leave without intervention.

Another moan and then digging sounds. The bear was either rooting around the entrance or sharpening its claws for an attack.

Slowly, I reached into the far end to slip my dried maps into the pack in case I had to flee. While I tried not to make noise, the paper crunched as I refolded

The sounds outside stopped—as if the bear was listening.

As I waited for him to resume any sound, my eyes started to close. I was too exhausted to remain vigilant. While I had not heard the animal shuffle off, perhaps it decided to make its new bed near the opening.

Niggling thoughts kept me from sleeping. What was he doing?

Only one way to find out.

Silently, stealthily, I crept forward on my hands and knees until I could peek outside.

His musky scent stings my nose—Porgu's creatures must be impervious to their horrific odors.

As I lowered my shoulders and emerged to see beyond the overhang, a massive bear lifted its head and stared at me. We locked eyes, mine likely full of dread and his with curiosity about who stole his den.

His body blocked my way. So I sent him a message—nothing loud or insistent, only encouraging him to remain calm. As he looked at me, the bear exhaled with force, fluttering the loose skin near the sides of his mouth.

Sensing something got through but unsure what he would do, I sent it again. His enormous head nodded before he eased his belly to the ground and placed his chin on top of his folded paws.

My control skills worked. Tears welled in my eyes.

When I reached a hesitant hand to rub between his ears, he groaned with a sound I took as appreciation. His body was thick with fat, and his fur dense. He had prepared well for the dozing and starvation of Porgu's winter season.

In a flash, I had an inspiration and backed into the cave. After moving my pack into a crack, I covered it with loose rocks to deter the bear from taking my supplies without notice.

Then I invited him into the cave.

The creature lumbered into the opening with a huff and flopped onto the leaves. He curled into a ball, and within moments I heard his breath grow into a steady rhythm.

After turning my back to him, I snuggled against his bristly fur and had the best sleep since I'd left Tansy's yurt.

Chapter 35

SALIDA, COLORADO—DECEMBER 6
DYLAN COX

Dylan stood to the side of the half-finished fireplace. He watched Tom meticulously attach stone veneer to concrete board on the outside of the new prefabricated masonry.

"How do you know how to do all this stuff?" asked Dylan. Tom took charge of the house projects on their greystone in Chicago, but Dylan had never thought to ask.

"Working construction and rehabbing old homes on Chicago's west side with my uncle." Tom glanced over his shoulder. "Did you think I took summers off from college to hang out at the beach?"

"No—I did not." Dylan smiled at the implication. "I'm sure Augie appreciates your skills. His cabin is going to look fantastic when you're finished."

Dylan's parents paid for his education and encouraged him to spend summers waterskiing and reading at their summer cottage. He and Tom had different experiences growing up, and neither apologized. Their divergent skills made their detective agency successful, or at least good enough to cover the bills.

"Everyone's doing their share. Augie's installing the light fixtures in the back hallway." The corner of Tom's mouth ticced upward. "Except, at the moment, nobody's painting the bedroom."

Hint taken. Dylan moved to the bedroom to refill the paint tray. After adding a layer of paint and tamping down the can's lid, Dylan heard a knock.

Someone's at the front door. Don't let it be Cynthia again.

The door creaked open before either Dylan or Tom had a chance to respond. A bitter cold wind swept through the cabin. Drop cloths ruffled, and instruction sheets skittered off the countertops.

"Shut the door!" called Tom.

"Sorry to interrupt your work." Cynthia's brash New York accent echoed against the cabin's stark walls as the door closed. Dylan's shoulders sagged.

Why didn't I check the lock? Dylan glanced at the exposed paint in his tray. *I hope this is a short visit.*

"We're pretty busy here." Dylan carried the tray to the kitchen island and moved to block her at the entryway, hoping she would leave.

Cynthia gave him a sultry smile that in the distant past would render him vulnerable. After the events out west, her manipulations made him bristle. "You've got a lot of nerve showing up here." He nodded toward the front. "Is Lucas with you?"

"He stayed in the truck." She cocked her head. "I suspected he might not be welcome."

"You called that right." Dylan jabbed a finger toward her. "Tell him to leave the property and take you with him. I don't want to see either of you again."

"Why are you so hostile?"

"You and your new boyfriend nearly killed my friend, and you ask why I'm angry?"

"We did no such thing," Cynthia scoffed. "We slowed Tansy down so we could talk with her."

"Tell that to Tansy. She broke an arm and a couple of ribs when you forced her off the road."

"Lucas has already arranged to cover her medical bills and repair the van." She tapped a finger to her lips. "To be more precise, he offered to buy them a brand new conversion van. But Tansy insisted he repair their old one—that'll take about a hundred calls to junkyards across the county. I've agreed to help Lucas."

"Are you getting anything back for your generosity?" Tansy might be willing to share her experiences about Kati with Cynthia for a price.

"I'm still working on it." Cynthia pulled her shoulders back. "Her exploits with Kalev may be as vital to my book as your stories."

Nope—Tansy hadn't shared anything. Or Cynthia would know it was Kati and not Kalev.

"Since you're here, I'm assuming you've run into some dead ends in Utah. How long did you and Lucas stick around Echo?" Dylan grabbed Cynthia by the elbow and steered her toward the door.

"We drove the roads east of Echo for nearly a week." Cynthia planted her feet and gently pried Dylan's fingers from her arm.

"And?"

"The wind out there was brutal. If there were any footprints or other evidence, I'm sure they were obliterated." She sighed. "I feel like I'm in the same place as when I spoke with you a few weeks ago."

"You pretty much are." Dylan looked at her feet. "Maybe a few inches to the right." He narrowed his eyes. "But aside from that, I haven't changed my mind about talking with you."

"You still agree to give me an exclusive when you decide to open up?" She never quit.

"If—and that's a big if—I ever decide to talk with someone, I'll consider talking with you."

Dylan heard Augie snicker in the back hallway. Dylan walked to the front door, waiting for Cynthia to move. "Goodbye, Cynthia."

She stepped to the door but hesitated when her eyes landed on Augie's notebooks on a table next to the window. "I noticed that you and Augie are very protective of his sketches. Do they have anything to do with your search for Kalev?"

Should I outright lie or tell her it's none of her business? A lie might close the subject.

"Augie's drawings are private. They're abstract, and he doesn't share them with people he doesn't trust."

"May I?" Cynthia reached out a hand and slowly moved toward the notebooks.

"No!" At lightning speed, Augie rounded the corner. He raced to the table and yanked the books before Cynthia had time to react.

"You can trust me." Cynthia laid a hand on Augie's forearm, but he jerked away. "I won't tell anyone about your work or show them to a soul."

"I said, no." Augie stuffed the books under an arm and strode back to the hallway.

"He might need a bit of counseling." Cynthia tipped her head toward Augie as she watched him retreat.

"You could use some professional advice yourself—maybe about how you continually violate boundaries," Dylan countered.

"Boundaries aren't black and white lines." Cynthia gave Dylan a wink. "You'll be a better detective when you learn that."

"Maybe I don't want to be an investigator who breaks laws to gather evidence—and I'm talking about laws in the broadest sense—like the rules of decency."

"Whoa." Cynthia laughed. "Let's see how far you get by putting restrictions on yourself." She strutted to the door and let herself out.

Dylan stood at the window to watch Cynthia climb into Lucas's truck. Cynthia's mouth moved without taking a break for air while Lucas looked at Dylan through the windshield. His piercing glare gave Dylan a chill—Lucas and Cynthia were not finished looking for Kati.

"Speaking of investigations," Tom broke Dylan's concentration, "I have some work for you when you're ready."

This time, I'm not walking away until they're gone. Without turning, Dylan responded. "What do you have?"

"One of your regular clients from Chicago sent me a text. She knows a guy in Vail who could use your services. There's no rush. I told her you'd think about it."

"In Vail?"

"Yeah. It would only take a couple of days, and Vail's not more than two hours from here. I figured you might be interested."

Augie came out from the back hallway with a screwdriver in his hand. "I will go with you. I can be your assistant."

"I thought I was Dylan's assistant." Tom chuckled. "But he never takes me along on jobs. What makes you think you can jump the queue in front of me?"

"I don't want your job." Augie returned Tom's smile. "But Destiny and Trip would miss you."

"You've got a point. If Dylan will have you, I'm okay with you doing a ride-along." Tom raised a dramatic finger toward Augie—the hint of a smile never left his lips. "Only this once. The next time Dylan takes a gig in Vail, I'm the one."

"Hey," Dylan interrupted. "I like how you're both making decisions for me. I haven't agreed to take the job yet." He turned to Augie. "Why do you want me to go to Vail?"

"Kati is coming here, but it will take a while. You should do something to help other people—if you cannot help her." Augie stared at the screwdriver and touched the end with a tentative finger. "You might feel better."

"You're right." Leave it to Augie—always spot on. "Anything to get me out of this mood. For most of my investigations, I sit around and wait for people to misbehave."

"Do you want me to go with you?" Augie asked.

"No." Dylan shook his head. "I appreciate you asking, but I'd rather do this solo. Anyway, Tom's relying on you to help him finish the work in the cabin."

"Okay." Augie nodded. "I promise to call you if I see a dream from Kati." His wide eyes confirmed his conviction.

Except for the featureless landscapes Augie intercepted two days earlier, which could have been ordinary dreams, he had not received a transmission from Kati since the intense visions in Echo.

"I'm counting on you. Call me in the middle of the night if you have to." Dylan stepped back to his tray to see if skin had formed over the top. He touched the wet paint, then stared at his coated finger. After swiping his hand across his speckled shirt, Dylan headed toward the bedroom.

"I hate all this waiting around and doing nothing," Dylan called over his shoulder. "Whatever else happens, we must connect with Kati before Lucas and Cynthia find her."

Chapter 36

NEAR STEAMBOAT SPRINGS, COLORADO—NIGHT OF DECEMBER 8 AND MORNING OF DECEMBER 9
KATI

After the sun set, I sat on a hill's crest to scan the topography, looking for a windblown path to minimize footprints in the snow. After eleven nights on my own, I had grown used to the silent peacefulness.

I typically rose shortly after sunset and walked uninterrupted until dawn. Occasionally, I heard a faraway vehicle or would pass a farmhouse with glowing lights. But generally, my night's walk was a solo event—until I neared STEAMBOAT SPRINGS.

As I approached the town, the sky grew lighter. The amber glow from lamps near the highways was dim compared to the night sky over the city. Traffic and machinery hummed like a life force. Even with my ultra-sensitive hearing, I could barely detect leaves rustling.

I planned a southward turn near this town but considered whether I should backtrack to the west and make a wide loop to avoid coming too close.

Ever curious, I wanted to see what made this area different from the earlier places. Why did halveks flock to STEAMBOAT SPRINGS and avoid central Utah? I decided to stay on course and travel as close as possible without being detected.

In Reval, we had access to food and hydration everywhere. A Sasquatch only needed to prepare a simple sleep site and could live anywhere. But food was not always easy to find in Porgu. Perhaps some areas in Porgu were more desirable because they had plentiful sustenance.

STEAMBOAT SPRINGS must be rife with food and drink.

As I made my way southeast, I came across isolated snow-packed roads. They made traveling easy as I had no worries about leaving tracks.

When I approached the city, I heard a humming—first at a distance, but it grew louder. This racket was different from the thrum from Tansy's van or Lucas's rattling truck. As the high-pitched whine grew close, I jumped to the side of the road and up an embankment to hide behind a dense tree.

Not one but five open vehicles zoomed into view. Their front lights shuddered as they skittered over the road, bringing a suffocating scent that made me gag. The riders were encased from head to toe with shiny suits. My heartbeats quickened as I sensed their aggression and energy.

Would a time ever come when a Sasquatch might feel such exhilaration? Probably not. We appreciated only sophistication, knowledge, and quiet contemplation. The halveks' sports and modes of travel held no appeal for our kind.

When the pack drew immediately below me, the lead driver raised an arm. In unison, they came to a stop and shut off their machines.

The leader pulled off a helmet and shook her long hair in the breeze. Until that moment, I did not know whether the halvek was male or female. They all looked similar in their bulky suits.

"Look what I found." She tromped to where I'd left the road and pointed to my footprints tracking up the slope. "There's been some activity here since we came by earlier. Let's see if we can identify what passed. Maybe it was elk or deer, but what if it was a bear or mountain lion?" She scanned her troupe. "Wouldn't that be amazing?" Her enthusiasm rivaled Tansy's.

From a pocket over her breast, she removed a flashlight—smaller than the one Tansy used, but I recognized it just the same. The leader clicked on the light and bent to examine the disturbed snow. Others joined her and removed their helmets to gain unobstructed views.

I stayed hidden, watching—listening—ready to flee up the slope if they decided to investigate further.

"I can't tell what they are," a woman claimed. "It's freezing. Can't we keep moving?"

The leader remained stooped over my tracks, ignoring the others. "I've never seen anything like this. I see toe impressions." She straightened to look up the slope and scanned her light. I held my breath—sure she would spot me. But her beam stopped short before it returned to the road.

"No one would come out this far at this time of night in bare feet," she mused.

"Mandy, we're not climbing up to see what's there," a man insisted. "This is a snowmobile trip, not a mountain-climbing excursion. Save your tracking lessons for another group. I want to ride."

"Don't worry. We'll be off in a jiffy." She sighed. "Before you mount up, take some photos if you'd like."

Several flashes strobed.

"I know what it's from." A loud voice boomed from an oversized halvek. "Bigfoot has invaded Steamboat Springs."

Laughter burst from the halveks before they scattered and walked back to their respective machines.

"Wait to start your engines until I give the signal." The leader's piercing voice carried over the individual conversations among the group. "We're not far from the shed. Keep your speed slow, and don't crowd each other."

She walked ahead to mount her machine. "Remember." She extended her arm and made a flapping motion with her hand. "When I signal you like this, I want you to slow down. You've been a fantastic group. We've had a wonderful dinner, a great night ride, and a possible Sasquatch sighting. Let's get back to base safely."

The riders who had not already replaced their helmets giggled in unison.

After revving and some jerky starts, the pack sputtered away. The stench from their machines wafted up from the road but dissipated in the stiff night breeze.

I glared down from where I sat. In case the leader returned, I needed to obliterate my tracks. How could I be sure to erase all traces? Dragging broken tree branches might help. The halvek had looked closely and pointed out minute details of my footprints. I wanted them completely gone.

My luck in communicating with the bear made me want to try other large animals. I closed my eyes and focused on the surroundings.

Aha!

From faint ripping sounds, I sensed a group of adult deer stripping bark from a grove just beyond the hillside.

With deft concentration, I drew them to me and envisioned their positive response. Before long, I could hear their snorting breaths and footfalls in the crusty snow. When I opened my eyes, six deer stared at me as if they wanted to know why I had called them.

Staying in the middle of the group, I walked them to the road and back up again. After returning twice more, I released them to scamper away.

Satisfied with my handiwork, I continued along the road—a mass of hard lumps from the machines' tracks.

The rest of my trip circumnavigating STEAMBOAT SPRINGS was less eventful than my encounter with the noisy machines. I skirted a large section of a hill fully illuminated with lights. Halveks with boards affixed to their feet slid down the terrain. I assumed they were engaged in a game but did not understand their objective.

On paths not occupied by any halveks, enormous machines drove up and down the slopes. Again, I did not understand their purpose, but their routes seemed intentional and steady.

When Dylan and I were still in Reval, I attended the annual Sasquatch Festival. A white Sasquatch was scheduled to speak about halvek ice sports. If I ever returned to Reval, I would connect with him to learn more about their games.

That is, if I decide not to be euthanized when returning to Reval.

Long after I left the activities behind, the night grew quiet and the air much colder. Stars speckled the black sky. Eventually, I spotted the rising partial moon. I stopped to admire the crescent.

The moon would grow larger each day until, at its zenith, I would return home to Reval. Part of me wanted that day to come soon, and other parts longed for more Porgu experiences. On my first trip, my only objective was to collect observations. This time, I had a greater purpose—to reconnect with Dylan. My goal was unique from other Sasquatches. I hitched up the straps on my backpack and walked taller.

As I continued southward, the stars disappeared and the sky transformed from black to gray. I glanced at the glowing horizon and noticed a distinct rock formation. Two spires jutted from a platform—like a giant fist with the first and last fingers raised.

I beamed, knowing I'd finally seen something unique and transmission worthy.

Chapter 37

Dylan's breath came out in icy gasps. He wriggled his toes inside his insulated boots. The movement did not help, as he could barely feel them. He'd spent the night perched on the hill behind Dr. Glista's luxury Vail townhome, waiting to take morning shots of Glista's cheating wife.

Hours earlier, Dylan had followed the couple from a bar a block away. The pair had stumbled toward the front door. While she staggered from too many drinks, he maintained the slow precision of a man on a mission. Based on the paramour's official-looking ski jacket, Dylan guessed he might be a ski instructor—or just a man born to win the birth lottery with a chiseled body, symmetric face, and a disposition to attract a wealthy woman on her own for a weekend.

From scoping out the place earlier in the day, Dylan knew the master bedroom was at the rear with a huge picture window facing the ski hill. Once the couple was inside, Dylan dashed to the back and crept up the slope to gain a better view. A bushy blue spruce gave him cover, but he was confident they would not bother to look outside.

As predicted, the lights clicked on, and Dylan captured their frantic scramble to undress each other. Their faces were glued together with kisses that bordered on violence and desperation. Before Glista's wife hastily pulled the blinds, Dylan pressed the shutter release. But his mind was elsewhere.

Had he and Kati experienced moments of unstoppable passion? Their first encounter was awkward, as he overwhelmed her with questions about pleasuring her. But once he understood she was built the same way as any human female, Dylan abandoned thoughts about technique. As they spent time sharing cultures and past secrets, the more passionate their physical relationship became.

Maybe that's the difference between making love to someone you care about and having an affair. There's passion in both. But without respect and familiarity, the craving won't last.

Those initial photos and revelations were from the previous night. At the moment, Dylan sat waiting for the morning shots. Dr. Glista would ask how long the lover had stayed, and Dylan would need an answer.

Finally, a light came on in the bedroom and brightened between the slats. Dylan lifted the camera to his face. He held his breath to avoid frosting the viewfinder.

Last June, Jen had told him the coldest time of day is right before sunrise. Something about the sun coming up to heat the surface air and allowing the colder upper air to sink.

Dylan stared at the blinds, willing them to open as he realized Jen's memories had become more scarce since he'd met Kati. They were both strong-willed and independent, alike in so many ways.

Come on. The dawn is incredible. Look at the view.

Dylan's cell phone vibrated in his down-filled coat.

Not now. Whoever it is can wait.

Dylan's instincts told him Dr. Glista's wife and her lover were awake. He could not miss the shot and have to spend another day or two in Vail. Proof of one overnight stay would be enough evidence for Dr. Glista.

The vibration stopped, and Dylan felt a tremor indicating whoever called had left a message.

Great. I'll deal with you later.

The blinds wavered as if someone started to open them and then stopped. Moments later, they slowly rose to expose Mr. Ski-Instructor— not figuratively but completely. The man's every naked inch stood in front of the full-length window with arms stretched high above his head. Dylan's camera captured the moment, as well as when Dr. Glista's nude wife snuggled behind her lover.

Dylan shut off the camera, knowing his work was finished. As he rubbed his gloves together encouraging blood flow to his frigid fingers,

Dylan recalled when he used to feel guilty about tailing spouses and ratting them out. But he'd come to believe the cheaters deserved unearthing. Perhaps that was why his dating record respected serial monogamy. That and he fell hard for every woman he'd dated.

The camera slid easily inside his jacket as Dylan settled into the snowy bank. He would wait until the lovebirds left their nest before climbing down from his perch behind the spruce.

He chuckled as their awkwardness started to show—they picked up discarded clothing and turned their backs on each other to dress. Words were infrequent, and she checked the wall clock several times as he pulled on his socks and shoes.

How predictable.

Once they left the bedroom, Dylan made his way down the slope, stomping his feet with each step. His toes tingled with intermittent stabbing pains. It would take time before they felt normal again. Years ago, Dylan took a few outdoor winter gigs in Wisconsin, where his feet stayed numb for more than a day.

Dylan rounded the end unit of the block-long townhome complex and nonchalantly walked past the front. Dr. and Ms. Glista's door opened, and Dylan caught a glimpse of the Adonis as he strode down the walk and turned toward the bar—where he'd likely parked his car.

As Dylan crossed the quiet street to his rental, he felt another call vibrating the cell phone.

Shit. What if Augie's had another dream?

Dylan glanced at the screen, and his pulse quickened when he saw Augie's name flash twice. Dylan had missed two of Augie's calls.

Dylan jumped into his car, and Augie answered right away when the call connected. "Augie, I know you wouldn't try to reach me if it wasn't important. Did you have another vision from Kati?"

"Yes. But that is not why I called." Augie's voice trembled.

"What?" Whatever happened, they would face it together. "Tell me what's up."

"My sketchbooks are gone."

"Gone?" How could they be missing? Augie kept them close all the time. "You're going to need to give me more. I don't understand."

"I had a dream in the middle of the night. I went to find my books, and it's gone."

Dylan imagined Augie tapping his heels to countermand his anxiety. "Did you have them last night?"

"I ate dinner at Destiny's with Tom. I didn't bring my books."

"And you didn't sketch last night after you came home from dinner?"

"I draw in the morning and at Max's studio." A long pause. "I don't draw before I sleep."

"Good point." Despite the gravity of the situation, Dylan smiled. "I forgot. Are all of your notebooks missing?"

"Only one."

"Want to let me know which one is gone?"

"The blue one with dreams from Kati." Augie's voice cracked, and a lump grew in Dylan's throat.

"Don't worry about it. I'll be back in Salida before noon, and I can stop and buy you another notebook."

"It is navy blue."

"Got it." Dylan sighed. "You can redraw the pictures. I know you have an amazing memory."

"They won't be the same."

"Maybe not identical, but mostly the same. If you want to start sooner than when I get there, you can pick up some paper on your own. You decide."

"I can wait." Augie's anxious sigh came through the speaker. "There's one you haven't seen."

"That's not important. You can redraw that one first. I'm sorry this happened to you." A tear welled up in Dylan's eye. He had left Augie vulnerable when he took the Vail job. "It was my fault for getting you involved in all this stuff."

"I like helping you to find Kati."

"You're the best."

"I thought Tom was your best friend."

"I can have two best friends, right?"

While he could not see it, Dylan knew Augie smiled before he said, "I don't think so."

"You're right most of the time. But not always. I'll see you as soon as I'm back from Vail. I'll drive fast."

"Be careful."

"I will."

Dylan disconnected the call and pressed the button for Cynthia's number. Anger flushed through his body as he waited for her to answer his call.

Chapter 38

STEAMBOAT SPRINGS, COLORADO
LUCAS EDWARDS

Lucas kept his snowmobile mere feet behind Mandy's as they gunned the throttles and sped along tunnel-like trails nestled between a hill on one side and piled snow on the other. The low, early December sunshine kept the track in perpetual shadow, preserving its rock-hard surface. The machines flew unhindered on the straight snow-covered road.

The faster he pushed, the tighter Cynthia wrapped her arms around his middle to keep from sliding back on the seat. He'd never owned a motorcycle or rented a snowmobile. Still, he imagined the combination of open-air and control over a powerful machine was why men bought bikes to haul around their girlfriends.

The machine's power and a woman's total dependence on his driving skills gave him a semi—even if the woman on the back of his snowmobile was Cynthia. He valued her enthusiasm for the hunt, but Cynthia tended to think fast and jump too quickly.

The night before, Lucas showed her Mandy's posting on a Bigfoot site. Cynthia had lost it. Before they had time to talk about a plan, Cynthia called each snowmobile tour company in Steamboat Springs until she found the one with Mandy as a guide and booked the next open tour.

That's why they had to get up at four in the morning to make the three-plus hour drive from Salida. Registration and suit-up time was seven-thirty—only a few minutes after sunrise.

If Lucas had taken charge, they would have booked an afternoon tour and had time, in daylight, to scope out the area on their own. But here they were, at the crack of dawn, barreling down a snowmobile trail to see if anything remained from possible Sasquatch tracks made two nights ago. Could a few more hours have made any difference?

Mandy raised her arm to signal Lucas to stop, and they pulled to the side. She jumped from her machine with the nimbleness of someone who drives snowmobiles as often as others would their car.

Lucas let Cynthia extract herself first. When she caught the toe of her boot on the edge of the seat, Lucas lunged out to grab her before she faceplanted into a snowbank.

"Whoa," Cynthia called out as she righted herself and wiped her glove-clad hands down the front of her borrowed one-piece suit. In a motion that had become very familiar to Lucas, she tugged her oversized tote higher on her shoulder. The bag seemed out of place on the trail. But Cynthia was *always* prepared, and her most critical investigative tools seemed to emerge from that tote.

Their guide was tall, lean, and a natural in her grimy one-piece snowsuit. On the other hand, Cynthia needed to roll up her cuffs to accommodate her short legs. The tour company's child-size rentals would have never fit her curves. She waddled forward like a penguin. After glancing down the front of his rental suit, Lucas made a mental note—wash every piece of clothing that touched this outfit.

"This is the place I saw them." Mandy pointed to a spot in the snowbank, directly below a massive blue spruce. "I'm sure of it."

"I'm not sure what you saw." Lucas leaned over the jumble of snow. "It looks like something tracked up the hill, but I can't tell what it was."

"Show us the photo again," demanded Cynthia.

Mandy drew out her phone and flipped the screen until she found the image. She handed it to Cynthia.

"The flash washed out the details," Cynthia said as she held a hand over the screen to eliminate glare. "It could be human prints, but I don't see any details from toes."

She gave the phone to Lucas and waited for him to weigh in.

He manipulated the image, trying to zoom in. Cynthia had called it right. The flash obliterated features evident to a naked eye. "You're sure you saw toe prints—like a bare foot?"

"Absolutely." Mandy nodded like a bobblehead doll. "But only for one side. The other seemed more like an ill-defined boot print without a lugged sole."

"How big?" Cynthia injected.

"Definitely more than a foot long for the actual print, but the boot one was bigger." Mandy indicated with her hands, and Lucas estimated eighteen inches. Could Mandy be exaggerating?

"I wish we could have been with you that night," Cynthia mused.

"No kidding." Mandy scoffed. "My group was pretty lukewarm about the whole thing. I don't know why they weren't more excited. Fill tourists full of food and a bit of booze, and all they want to do is head back to base."

"Really?" Cynthia propped her hands on her down-layered hips. "They could have been part of a major sighting. What's wrong with them?"

Curb your enthusiasm, Cynthia. We don't need any more people joining our search. Lucas gently squeezed her arm, hoping she got the hint to stand down.

He turned to Mandy. "Tell us the rest of your story."

"After I dropped my guests at base, I came back up with another guide to show him. By the time we got here, all the prints were gone."

"How could they be gone?" Cynthia attentively leaned toward Mandy as if the answer might prove the meaning of life.

"The first time I saw them, there was one set in one direction—up. But when Jake and I came back, it was riddled with other animal prints—probably deer." She pointed to some of the puncture marks in the snow. "What we saw two nights ago was way more defined. We got a dusting last night. At this time of year, we get a lot of snow. Great for the ski area, but impossible for you to see what was here before."

Lucas scanned the embankment. The private tour and getting up at four may not have been worthwhile. But they'd had few leads of late.

"I wish there was more to show you." Mandy shrugged. "You seemed so interested in my report on the Bigfoot site."

"We're avid searchers." Cynthia laid a hand on Mandy's forearm. "Your post seemed more plausible than others we've seen lately. Plus, we just love this area."

"Are you skiers?"

"We're not, but I'm hoping you might take a look at something else."

Lucas rubbed the back of his neck. *What is Cynthia getting at now?*

Without removing the tote from her shoulder, Cynthia opened the top and reached inside. She pulled out a blue spiral-bound notebook and flipped it open to a page near the back. Thick rubber bands tightly secured the earlier pages. "Take a look at these drawings and see if you recognize anything from around here."

Where had Cynthia found the book, and why was this the first Lucas knew about it?

Lucas rolled his eyes at Cynthia and sidled next to Mandy to look over her shoulder. The first couple pages had sketches of stunning landscapes with vista views and nondescript mountains. Mandy examined each drawing. When she turned to a blank page, she flipped through the remainder of the book. The rest were empty.

Mandy started to remove the bands from the beginning pages, but Cynthia snatched the book away.

"No. I only need you to see the open ones." Cynthia resecured the bands and opened the book to where she'd started before. "Look at these again."

Lucas itched to yank the book from Mandy and see what Cynthia was hiding. He would do just that when they were back in his truck. Apparently uninterested in Cynthia's secrets, Mandy methodically turned each open page after taking in the sketches.

"I know this one." Her eyes lit up as she pointed to a barren landscape with paired rock formations. "This is Rabbit Ears. You must have noticed it when you came into town."

"I did not." Cynthia glanced at Lucas. "But maybe we were talking."

Leave it to Cynthia and her magic bag to get us back on track.

Lucas pulled out the local area map he'd found at the snowmobile base camp. "Show us how to get to Rabbit Ears."

Chapter 39

SALIDA, COLORADO—DECEMBER 12
DYLAN COX

On moving day at the cabin, Dylan rested the back of a scratched leather sofa against his knee while Tom shifted to open the cabin's front door. They tilted the couch to fit through the opening and moved it to the great room's center without confirming instructions. Tom and Dylan had helped enough friends move and had become a well-oiled machine.

Maybe if they dropped a few dishpacks or intentionally scratched furniture, they would not get so many requests to help. For this move, Dylan was happy to assist. Without new leads on how to find Kati, Dylan spent most days in a distracted funk. After the Glista job, Tom had not come up with nearby gigs, and Dylan was reluctant to leave the area.

"We need rugs," Tom declared as he stood next to the sofa with his hands on his hips.

"And a dining set and bed." Dylan scanned the room before focusing on the naked, newly painted walls. "Too bad all of Jen's mother's paintings were destroyed in the fire. They were a special part of this place."

"I hope Kirk Steadman rots in hell for setting it on fire."

Dylan raised a brow. "He can't do that until he's actually dead."

"Before he gets to hell, he can rot in jail." The muscles around Tom's jaw tightened. "I don't know how he manages to let others pay for his crimes."

"By offering evidence against his associates in return for freedom."

"How does he find new partners?" Tom sniffed.

"Come on. You've read about Laurencell and Calvert—neither are the brightest bulbs in the box." Dylan dropped to the couch and propped his legs on a cushion. "One of these days, I should call Sheriff Austin for an update about Steadman's case." Dylan picked at a loose thread on the back of the couch. "Have you heard anything around town or from Destiny about what's going on with him?"

"Sometime last week, the *Salida Sentinel* mentioned the police filed additional charges against Steadman."

"Bigger than the arson charges?"

"Something about his drug activities with Ariel Laurencell and Jason Gray from last June. Maybe they can pin some of that fiasco on him, too."

He was involved with meth manufacturing, selling stolen goods, domestic abuse, and arson. If anyone deserved to be kept away from the good people of Salida, it was Steadman.

"The *Sentinel* published a piece with Steadman's claims about being framed for the arson charge."

Dylan jolted upright. "How did he get that in the paper?"

"One of his buddies posted a letter to the editor. It named us both and implied we might have set the fire to collect insurance and blame him."

"That's libel." Dylan smashed a fist against the seat cushion. "How could they print it?"

"I'm simplifying the message. But the implication was there." Tom shrugged. "Don't get worked up about this. Steadman might be trying to promote local sympathy, but anyone who knows him wouldn't believe a word he says."

Tom was right. Stewing over Steadman's claim was a waste of time. Lately, small things could set Dylan on edge. He took a deep breath and laid back down.

"Don't get too comfortable," Tom urged. "We're picking up the rest of the furniture at Free the Monkey Consignment. Despite what Destiny says about how often the forecasts are wrong, I want the basics here before the big storm hits in a few days."

Mustering hard-to-find energy, Dylan stood. Whether remnant exhaustion from his month in Reval or continued despair over losing Kati, Dylan's lethargy nearly consumed him. He had not jogged since being back. Dylan decided to go for a run after he and Tom finished the move. Anything to start feeling like himself again.

"I heard back from Glista." Tom interrupted Dylan's mental ramblings. "He got your images and thanked you for your work. It was a professional response. He didn't blame you for uncovering his wife's bad behavior."

Dylan knew Tom was trying to encourage him to take more jobs—irrespective of the distance from Salida. But Dylan was not ready to stray too far. What if Kati showed up and he was away?

"It's good to know he appreciated the results. Most of the time, clients already know what's going on. Hiring me only confirms their suspicions." Dylan zipped up his jacket and moved toward the door. "It'll be good to have the place move-in ready before Kati finds me here."

Tom rubbed the stubble on his chin as if measuring what to say. "You know I'll support whatever you decide to do, and I hope she finds this place. But you won't be able to keep her hidden. Cynthia will hound you until she either gets your story or catches up with Kati. From what I've seen and heard of this Lucas character—with his spike strips and highspeed chases—he's borderline psycho. We don't stand a chance to keep Kati safe here at the cabin."

"We'll figure out how to protect her once she gets here. Kati's smart enough to watch for any sign of Lucas or Cynthia. I guarantee we won't know Kati's near the cabin until she's ready to make contact."

As they left, Tom stopped to lock the door. "Have you heard from Cynthia about Augie's sketchbook?"

"No." Dylan shoved his hands into his pockets. "I've sent dozens of texts and messages, but she won't take my calls or respond. She's the only person who had anything to gain by breaking into Augie's place and stealing his drawings."

"How's he coming along with redrawing them?" Tom slipped his keys into his jeans.

"You know Augie." Dylan smiled and shook his head. "He's doing it in the way that's comfortable for him—that's a linear process. First, he's recreating all the scenes he intercepted from Kalev. Augie will get to Kati's transmissions when he's satisfied the earlier ones are identical to what's in the notebook Cynthia stole."

"That could take a long time."

"Arguing won't make a difference to Augie. He needs to manage things in his way."

Chapter 40

NEAR GRANITE, COLORADO—THE NIGHT OF DECEMBER 13 AND MORNING OF DECEMBER 14
KATI

When the sun dropped, I braced myself against the stiff wind and started walking south. Windswept hiking trails led me down to a partially frozen body of water. My map called it TURQUOISE LAKE.

The eastern shore came perilously close to a busy highway—trucks and cars zoomed by at high speeds. The west side of the lake nestled against the base of a long mountain range. Trees and tangled bushes formed a barrier from halfway up the slopes to the water's edge. Choosing the better option, I decided to skirt the western side and pick my way through the woods.

Each time I caught a glimpse of the high peaks, I slowed to admire the thick layers of snow and windblown cornices balancing on the ridge. Memories from Sasquatches, who visited Porgu's most remarkable mountains, included visions with mighty avalanches. What would it take for a slab to break free and send a snow cascade into this valley? I moved with stealth and speed.

Glistening snow blanketed the ground, and hovering specks danced in the frozen air. Once, I stopped on the top of a low hill to stare at the moon.

Seems too early for it to be this round. Maybe the higher altitude distorts the shape.

The full moon would peak in five nights. With only two additional nights of walking to reach Salida, I would have three full days with Dylan before transferring to Reval. Would he be at the cabin when I arrived?

Without telecommunication, how could I contact him? I straightened my pack's shoulder straps and kept walking. I would deal with that challenge after reaching Salida.

A foreign vision flickered and obscured my view. I dropped to the ground, concentrating to define the image. But it dissipated like fluttering wings from a departing bird.

I pounded the frozen ground with a fist, willing it to return. When I had last slept, another vision had flitted into my thoughts—not loud and clear like before my collision with the rock but more like a whisper. This latest one seemed more intense, but it too faded before I could catch its meaning.

In Reval, Dylan sent cryptic messages with a mixture of images and the halvek language. The ones I'd recently intercepted were not like his. These were authentic Sasquatch messages, jammed with fast-moving likenesses and representations only a Sasquatch would understand. Some referred to locations, and others captured emotions. Perhaps I was growing closer to the sender—someone who could help me send a message to Dylan or share their food supply.

My steps felt lighter as I bounded over the next set of ridges and through tree-choked ravines, leaping over felled trees and jumping over frozen creeks. I nearly forgot about my cast as my leg must have grown stronger to compensate. Beyond a ridge, a pair of lakes sat in the distance. My map called them TWIN LAKES.

Down, down, down I loped until I crossed a road and stood on the bank. The flat icy surface covering the lake gleamed so brightly, it seemed like daylight. Smiling, I picked up a rock near the shore and tossed it as far as I could. Smack. It hit the surface and skittered across the ice, tumbling until it stopped at the far shore.

Without warning, my eyesight blurred, and an image of a fat white bird flashed across my vision. I froze. Instead of seeing what was in front of me, a ptarmigan sat on the snow in broad daylight, its feathers nearly camouflaged with its surroundings. A second later, the bird image disappeared, and TWIN LAKES returned.

Slowly, I sat and crossed my legs to rest my elbows on my knees, determined to wait until another broadcast came. I ignored the wind and faint highway noise. The mysterious transmission came again—this time with more details.

A Sasquatch's broadcast defined his mission objectives. He was tracking color changes in nonmigrating birds and animals. The images included ptarmigan and hares in various winter and summer colors. His mission seemed innovative, and tribal leaders in Reval would undoubtedly be pleased.

But loneliness and trauma over Porgu's brutal temperatures laced his message.

Some transferring Sasquatches found the solitude of Porgu unbearable. We were social beings. Exchanges about family life and politics continually floated between the Sasquatches in Reval.

My eyes were drawn to the south, where Dylan waited for me in Salida. But I could not shake the sorrowful call from the solitary Sasquatch.

The night I had spent cuddling with the bear was of great comfort. Even though he was a lower animal, I appreciated the sense of nearness I had not felt since leaving Reval. While I had time to travel for another few miles before stopping, the sky had started to lighten.

The lonely Sasquatch might appreciate company for the day—even if I slept for most of our time together. He would enjoy knowing another being like himself was nearby.

I can make up the distance tomorrow.

Based on his transmission, the Sasquatch had been in Porgu for a while. He might have a snug and comfortable hiding spot—perhaps a dry cave with a bed of leaves and branches he'd gathered in the fall.

I had not sent a transmission since STEAMBOAT SPRINGS. While continually diminishing, would the pain of sending a message still bring me to my knees? Two nights ago, I considered sending one near a massive bridge spanning a river. I'd stared at it long and hard, debating whether to endure the pain, confident the image was sufficiently recognizable. I never sent it, opting to avoid the agony. But who knew? Maybe it transmitted anyway.

These circumstances were different—the Sasquatch's messages had come to me. My earlier attempts were broadcast messages. If I sent the Sasquatch a directed one, the pain might be less.

What to send him? A lone coyote crossed the lake in front of me. I focused on his thick fur and muscular gait and closed my eyes.

As I released the transmission, the back of my neck felt a tug—nothing like the stabbing from before.

The Sasquatch's response was immediate, a message filled with visions of comradery and hopefulness. I repeated my vision and added an image of the surrounding area, including the nearest trees and shrubs.

"Your transmission is weak and not completely clear. But I know where you are. I will meet you," he said, not in Dylan's tongue but in a way I completely understood.

His fast-paced vision's intimacy tugged at my heart. For nearly a month, I had focused myopically on returning to Dylan. While waiting for the Sasquatch, I realized how much I missed the familiar.

I sat in the snow, full of optimism about helping the Sasquatch, and mentally rifled through Dylan's naming conventions. For my kind, places and Sasquatches had no identifiers before Dylan gave them names.

Drawing from Dylan's knowledge of ancient halvek civilizations, I named my new friend Hugo.

Chapter 41

**LEADVILLE, COLORADO
LUCAS EDWARDS**

Each gravel road started to look the same. Lucas found himself forever searching and finding nothing. He gripped the wheel harder.

Perseverance. You'll get her.

From the main highway out of Steamboat Springs, Lucas followed the most direct southerly route. Like exploring a feather's barbs from its shaft, he drove to the west, back to the central highway, and then east. He cruised slowly, staring and hoping to see oversized footprints, a tuft of hair on a barbed-wire fence, or anything to confirm he was on track.

Hour after hour, Lucas squinted, spotted something, got out of the truck, and grew disappointed to find nothing of consequence. He saw scat from deer, elk, moose, bobcat, and unidentified canine—likely some hiker's pet.

Lucas would have settled for human boot prints that stomped up a hill and disappeared. Anything mysterious would break the tedium of dead ends. He wished he'd brought the dogs. They could pick up her scent and lead him to her.

At least the weather had cooperated. Every time Lucas left the truck to take a short sojourn up a hillside, he broke into a sweat. Sun pounded down on him and reflected up from the radiant snowfields. His lungs screamed, trying to take in more thin air. He was a west coast guy and used to walking beaches or hunting in low altitude forests—not slogging around at nine-thousand feet above sea level.

Lucas rolled his eyes when he approached the tiny metropolis of

Leadville that sat two hours south of Steamboat Springs. Road signs tried to make the relic from mining days into something special, but all Lucas saw was mine tailings and denuded hillsides. Old wooden headframes, dilapidated ore houses, and scattered rail tracks whispered of days gone by when down-on-their-luck men risked all to strike it rich in the Colorado hills.

Lucas drove through the labyrinth until he spotted his own tire tracks and figured he'd already seen everything there was to see. He stopped at a wide spot in the road, not that it mattered. He had not seen another car for over an hour.

Rumble, rumble, rumble. The diesel engine lulled Lucas until his eyes nearly closed. In many respects, he appreciated the quiet cab, devoid of Cynthia's constant yammering. She had bailed on him for a few days, making up some excuse about spending more time on the Internet looking for leads like the one from Steamboat Mandy. Cynthia figured if they split their time between scouring the countryside and cyberspace, they could narrow their search from the two-hundred-mile swath between Steamboat Springs and Salida.

His Sasquatch could be anywhere by now. Cynthia had an unshakable idea that the creature would head to Dylan's cabin. But Lucas could not comprehend why a primate might want to reunite with Dylan Cox. Long ago were the days of *Lassie Come Home*. Could Dylan have a strong enough bond with this wild animal for it to seek him? Why did Dylan abandon it in the first place? And was Dylan's animal the same one Lucas had seen?

Despite Lucas's attempts to understand why Cynthia believed the Sasquatch was male, she never wavered and would not expand on her conviction. As far as Lucas knew, Cynthia had not seen the creature, and neither had her source—some police officer named Erle. How would they know whether it was male or female?

Lucas still had not called it *she* in front of Cynthia. Let that tidbit be his secret. Based on the undisclosed sketchbook theft, Cynthia kept stuff from him, too.

He'd asked her why Augie would have drawings from the Sasquatch's route. It's not like Augie had traveled with Dylan and the creature on their way to Oregon. From contacting Augie's employer, Lucas knew that

Augie had worked when Dylan and his Sasquatch went from Salida to Oregon. What was Augie's connection with the creature?

Enough with the questions. Time to start working the west side of Leadville.

After stopping at the Golden Burro Café to refill his thermos, Lucas crossed the highway and found fewer roads.

Must have been less mining activity over here.

He pulled to the side for a view of Turquoise Lake. Despite some spots that did not look completely frozen, tracks crossed the lake—some made by animals and others by humans on snowmobiles.

Lucas opened his thermos and inhaled steam. After pouring a cup, he brought it to his lips, expecting to cool it with his breath before tasting. He tested a sip to discover it was lukewarm. Would the boiling point be lower at higher altitudes?

Something moved, and Lucas nearly dropped his cup. An animal walked on all fours at the other end of the lake.

Lucas jammed the truck into gear. As he drew nearer, the animal stopped to watch who had taken an interest. Up close, the size and shape revealed it was not the animal he sought—just a fox.

I've got another fox. It's standing in my living room—well, really just its hide and head.

After Lucas had shot his fox, the taxidermist recommended stuffing the entire body. After all, the fox's beauty was not found solely in its pointy nose and ears. To pay homage to the creature's life, the fox was posed to accentuate its luxurious fur. The same applied to the Alaskan grisly who stood with fangs and claws exposed next to Lucas's fireplace.

How will I mount my Sasquatch?

Lucas pictured her expression when he surprised her at his window in Oregon. Her head and shoulders would tell the story of how human-like she appeared. But with features so like a person, the tribute might seem a bit barbaric. Perhaps something more like his mountain gorilla hands that captured the animal's intelligence and essence without the complete body or head.

If Cynthia had a say in the matter, she would insist they donate the entire carcass to science. She claimed the public had a right to understand where Sasquatches fit in our evolution theories.

Like I would allow that. It'll be my kill, and I'll decide what happens to the body.

But Cynthia was right in some respects. Public or political pressure may deter him from taking the whole body.

Lucas needed a negotiation strategy. Better to decide what he wanted but ask for more. Everyone wants to deal, and everyone gives up something. If he could settle for less than her entire body, what could he accept for his trophy?

Warmth spread through his body as he decided on the perfect tribute. A metal artist could fashion a half dozen photo frames into an arc with images of Lucas holding her lifeless carcass. Centered within the arch's middle, the artist would create a shelf for her mounted foot. How better to pay tribute to the animal called Bigfoot?

Decision made, Lucas's swiveled his attention back to the fox. Before it slipped into the woods and out of sight, the animal glanced at Lucas's truck as if to say, "You have your space, and I have mine. Why are you here?"

"Every square inch of this planet belongs to us." Lucas flipped off the retreating fox. "We sit at the top of the ladder, and we'll kill you all if we want to."

Chapter 42

I kept telling Hugo I needed rest, but he was too excited to give me any peace. Finally, after spending most of the daylight hours traipsing behind him so he could show me his favorite spots to observe birds and small animals, he suggested we sleep.

Hugo took me to his cave when late afternoon shadows were already growing long. If I were following my regular schedule, I would be waking and looking for bark or cones to eat. But because I decided to make a new friend, my sleep would be short and, in a few hours, I faced a long, arduous night's walk.

"There is plenty of space in here for the two of us." Hugo held an arm wide and invited me inside. "I prepared my winter bed earlier in the year when the juniper limbs were supple and the aspen trees still had leaves."

"It's lovely and welcoming," I responded with visions of my sleep site in Reval to let him understand how he'd made the cave into a unique sanctuary.

"You must know the food in Porgu is sparse, but I have stored more than I will need before spring. I will share some with you." Hugo indicated toward a pile of cones stashed at the back. "Tomorrow, I will show you my favorite high alpine lake. A family of ptarmigan frequents that area, and some of the pica are still active. I am sure we will see them."

"I have told you that I am journeying to a place two days' walk from here." I gave him an encouraging smile. "I only travel at night to avoid the halveks. I must rest for a few hours and then be on my way."

Hugo's dropped chin and trembling lip told of his disappointment before he could transmit his thoughts. I recalled my isolation and misery from my first Porgu trip and sat to reflect on his situation. He had been kind to show me his research and planned to share food and accommodation. Maybe I could delay my journey for another day. The full moon was still four evenings away.

"Let us rest now." I nodded toward his food stash. "After I have had time to recover my strength, we can eat and discuss my plans."

Slowly, he transmitted images suggesting he agreed to my request. Hugo curled on his side on top of the leaf bed. He patted an adjacent spot, and I moved to nest my back against his chest.

Hugo was friendly and attractive. If we were in Reval, I might have asked him to visit a bathing pool, and we might couple. An hour of physical pleasure would not be uncommon among friends or passing travelers. But Porgu was different. Our fur was covered with dirt, and the bed lacked Reval's soft clean features.

In my final transmission about welcoming sleep, I did not send any images to encourage intimacy. Thankfully, neither did Hugo.

I woke alone with the cave completely dark. How long had I slept? Hugo knew I planned to leave after a short nap. Had he decided not to wake me so I would extend my visit?

I crawled to the opening and stuck out my head. Hugo sat with his back against a thick aspen tree, picking needles from a pine twig. While the moon was not visible, night had fallen, and early evening stars dotted the sky.

"Why did you allow me to sleep for so long?" I sat near him and leaned on an adjacent tree.

"I am concerned about you." Hugo avoided my gaze. "You are not on an authorized transfer."

"What?" I straightened. "How do you know that?"

"You injured your head when you came to Porgu. Is that correct?"

"Yes," I transmitted with reluctance, unclear of what to admit and confused about how he would know.

"All of your thoughts are open. Your mind is as exposed as a newborn."

"And you decided to look into my mind?" My fists balled at my sides. "Without asking permission?"

"I did not intend to at first. I believed you were pushing transmissions to me about your recent experiences—sharing what you have discovered about Porgu. But images of you with a halvek in Reval came through as well." Hugo's mouth pulled into a firm line. "You transferred to Porgu with him and had no permission to come here."

"You misinterpreted what you saw. Another Sasquatch brought him to Reval, and he was in danger. That Sasquatch had plans to harm him."

"Sasquatches do not harm halveks." Hugo shook his head. "But according to your memories, you killed two of them on a previous visit to Porgu."

"Again, you have taken these actions out of context. Those males were abusing halvek children. They needed to be stopped."

"By your justice?" Hugo's eyes narrowed. "Halveks are a crude and violent race. They exploit one another. No Sasquatch has meted out punishment for creatures in Porgu before. When we see a hawk toying with its prey before killing it, do we punish the hawk?"

"No," I transmitted as a lump grew in my throat.

"Porgu is rife with animals seeking power over other creatures—at times for food and other times for pleasure or claiming superiority. Your actions are vile—for both this illegal transfer and the crimes you committed on your first visit. I must ensure these infringements are reported to the High Council."

I stood and slung my backpack over a shoulder, preparing to leave. The moon finally started to nudge above the horizon, spreading light over the snow-covered landscape. "If you have reviewed my memories, you must know I asked for the euthanasia ceremony from the High Council, and they accepted my request."

"You did not follow through with your pledge and came to Porgu with your halvek lover." He jumped to his feet and grabbed me by the arm.

"That was a mistake. I had no idea I would transfer with him. He was supposed to transfer to Porgu—that is where he belongs. I was to stay in Reval and accept my sentence." I tried to pull free, but Hugo was more muscular and held firm. "Release me. I will go back to Reval at the next full moon."

"I don't believe you. You have proven your disregard for our rules." He paused his transmission to sneer at me. "Coupling with a lower life form only highlights your indifference toward our morality."

"You have no right to judge the halveks. You spend days watching birds and rabbits with simple minds. If you engaged with a halvek, you would understand they have complex emotions and societal traditions as rich as ours."

Hugo's head tipped back as he laughed. "They are the deformed discards of our breeding—to be exterminated or allowed to root around Porgu if they are strong enough to survive."

"They are as sentient as we," I insisted.

With a surge of strength, I leveraged my foot against a rock and yanked my arm from his grip. I wanted to storm away. Hugo was not worth my time, and Dylan would welcome my return.

I managed two steps forward before my mistake registered. In that instant, my foot broke through a thin mat of leaves and sticks. I tried to catch myself and lean backward. But Hugo shoved my shoulders, and both my feet punched through the trap's meager cover.

My arms and legs flailed as I tumbled through the air—falling, falling.

I collided with sand and rotting plants. While my backpack absorbed most of the impact, I lay still, trying to regain composure. Hugo had lulled me into trusting him, and I felt sorry for him. How could I be so stupid?

"Your thoughts are muddled, but I can still hear you." Hugo transmitted from above.

Ignoring him, I gingerly moved my limbs one at a time to inventory the damage. Nothing seemed broken—except my achy ankle inside my cast.

I scanned my surroundings to find an escape route.

The cavern's floor was oblong with piles of rocks along the base of concave walls. I looked up toward the hole—the only light source in the center of the sloped ceiling.

There is no way to climb out of here on my own. Why did Hugo trap me?

"You have no private thoughts," transmitted Hugo. "I hear everything you are thinking."

"Then tell me why."

"I do not want you to escape until I can discuss with another Sasquatch what should become of you. I expect someone will transfer nearby at the upcoming full moon. We can discuss your crimes and decide whether to force you to transfer to Reval or hold you until my mission here is complete. When I return to Reval, I can report your transgressions to the High Council. They can decide what to do with you."

"What if no other Sasquatch transfers to this area on this moon?" I slumped. Hugo could confine me to this prison for many months, and Dylan would never know I was nearby.

"You should hope someone comes in this cycle or the next. Otherwise, you will stay restrained until someone does."

I slumped and reached for my backpack to dig out Tansy's aspen bark.

What better time than the present to take halvek medicine designed to ease my pain?

Chapter 43

SALIDA, COLORADO—DECEMBER 15
DYLAN COX

Dylan and Tom walked out of the public defenders' offices on an unseasonably warm afternoon after giving their depositions. Dylan slipped on a pair of sunglasses as he strolled to Tom's half-ton pickup.

"Doesn't seem like winter now." Tom draped his jacket over a shoulder. "But they're predicting a blizzard in a few days."

"Fingers crossed it either goes around us or holds off for a while. I'm still hoping Kati makes it here before the next full moon on the seventeenth. If not, she might decide to transfer back to Reval without seeing me."

"I can't imagine she'd travel almost all the way from Oregon and decide to go back without contacting you." Tom reached out and patted Dylan's arm before crossing in front of the truck. "She might decide to stay away from Reval for another month—or if you're lucky, she'll stay for good."

"I'd give anything to see her again." Dylan sighed. "But she made it clear that I had deeper feelings than her. I don't know where her priorities lie."

"If she's on her way, the snow won't stop her."

Dylan could always count on Tom's optimism. Dylan opened the door and pulled himself into the passenger seat. "Who would have imagined you'd be driving something like this when we were living in Chicago?"

"It would have come in handy for all the work I did on your folks' place. We had to pay for delivery on everything. I couldn't carry lumber and drywall on the train."

"You used to be such a city guy. Who knew?"

Tom started the ignition but did not put the truck in gear. "Do you think our depositions will help to keep Kirk Steadman locked up?"

"Hard to tell." Dylan shrugged. "No matter what we say about him being a lifetime criminal, they might not have enough evidence to pin the arson case on him. *We* believe Steadman burned down the cabin, and he had a motive. But where's the proof?"

"I hope the Sheriff has enough to convict." Tom tugged the gear shift out of park and draped an arm over the seat to look out the back window.

The truck inched back but slammed to a stop, pressing Dylan into his seat.

"What the hell?" Dylan turned to see Cynthia's rental blocking their exit.

She jumped from the car and dashed to Dylan's window.

After an unanswered knock, Cynthia motioned for him to roll it down. He opened it part way.

"It's good to see you guys. What have you been up to?" Cynthia's head bobbed.

"I've left you a billion messages." Dylan stabbed a finger at her. "Now *you're* acting like we haven't tried to stay in touch?"

"Messages?" Cynthia gave him a wide-eyed stare.

"Don't give me that crap." He started to close the window. "You've been avoiding me."

Cynthia grabbed the top of the glass before Dylan could close it. Half tempted to crush her fingers, he sighed and lowered the window.

"I haven't been avoiding you." Cynthia tipped her chin. "Lucas and I have been in the hinterlands looking for traces of Kalev. I probably didn't have any cell service when you called." She drummed her fingers on the top of the glass. "You have to believe me. I would never intentionally avoid you."

"Have you found anything?"

"About what?"

Dylan nearly fell into her trap. She wanted him to admit he'd been chasing Kalev, too. If she'd found anything, she would not be standing in this parking lot. Cynthia must be fishing for an angle. Dylan gave her a narrow-eyed squint. "What do you want?"

"I was hoping to find you and give you this." Cynthia opened the top of her tote and pulled out Augie's notebook.

"You have the nerve to steal it and hand it back with no explanation or apology?"

"I didn't steal his sketchbook." Cynthia cocked her head and gave a sly smile. "I just borrowed it."

Dylan grabbed the notebook before Cynthia could change her mind. "How do you justify *borrowing* when the book was missing from *inside* Augie's house."

"I went to see Augie and ask if I could look at them. When I got to his trailer, the door was wide open. Naturally, I wondered if he was okay and went inside. His notebooks were just lying there on the dining table, and he wasn't using them. So I borrowed one."

Plausible, but more likely a full-blown lie.

Dylan flipped through the book from every angle to look for damage or missing pages. "Augie was frantic. You should be ashamed of yourself."

"Well, it's back now. Or at least it will be when you return the book to him. Please, tell him I appreciate the loan, and I think he's a very talented artist." Cynthia straightened, apparently disinclined to offer an apology. "Why were you here at the State Public Defender offices?"

"I don't have to tell you anything." Dylan turned to face the windshield.

"I'd appreciate it if you would move your car." Tom cranked his head and leaned into the steering wheel as he spoke. "We have errands to run."

Oblivious to Tom's request, Cynthia continued. "Anything to do with Kirk Steadman?"

How does she know why we're here? Cynthia's skills are uncanny.

"Why?" Dylan cleared his throat, reluctant to ask for information but believing she had more to divulge. "What do you know about his case?"

"I can't reveal my sources." She gave him a knowing look. "But I've heard a few things that might interest you."

Dylan was close to shutting the window, but her words tempted him to keep listening. "What?"

"While in lockup, Kirk's been on an endless rant about you. Well, mostly about Tom. He claims Tom has it in for him and falsely accused him of starting the fire at Augie's cabin. Kirk also said Tom used illegal means to entrap him when Mike Calvert coerced him to hide stolen goods."

"Coerced?" Dylan's jaw dropped. "Steadman was the one who knew about the cabin. It was probably his idea to have Calvert stash the merchandise up there."

"Steadman was never charged in that case. But I don't know if that's because he was cleared or gave evidence against Calvert."

"Probably the latter," Tom chimed in. "From the photos in my wildlife camera, they were both moving stuff from the box truck into the cabin. It's not like Calvert held Steadman at gunpoint."

Cynthia tapped a long nail against her chin. "That's all well and good, but Kirk Steadman has been telling anyone who will listen that he feels wrongfully accused and will make things right when he gets out."

Dylan's gut clenched. Were Steadman's threats intended to bluster, or were they credible?

Chapter 44

When the chipmunk dropped another seed cone into my prison, I caught the morsel before it hit the ground and thanked the tiny animal. It would have brought me another cone whether I gave appreciation or not. Still, the response seemed appropriate.

My cavern floor had rocks, dirt, and a bit of moss, but nothing for me to eat. Hugo had not come to my hole since he trapped me. I assumed he was disinclined to share his stores. Did he realize I would starve if I did not eat until he decided my fate?

While munching on the seed cone, I decided to give the helpful chipmunk a name. Days ago, I had given one to Hugo. Naming a sentient being seemed fitting. But halveks gave wild animals identifiers as well.

The names mainly applied to groups. They called lions, deer, and snakes by their category and did not give them personal labels like Tiina, Kalev, or Dylan. I searched my memories from Dylan and found few instances where he bestowed a unique name to a lower animal. In those instances, they were pets and lived with Dylan's family.

I decided to give the tiny creature a name to honor one of Dylan's former pets, a tricolored cat.

"Felix." I tried the name aloud and liked it.

The chipmunk chattered above as if reprimanding me for my choice. But I knew the more likely scenario for Felix's reaction. The creature was protecting his territory—someone was approaching the entrance hole.

When Felix grew quiet, I figured Hugo had decided to visit me and silenced him with a thought.

Hugo's shaggy face appeared. "I see you are finding lower animals to do your bidding. I will not need to share my food with you."

What a hollow threat. Hugo had not shared anything for two days. I retreated to a corner and ignored him. Knowing he was eager to start a conversation, I would not give him satisfaction. While he was right to hold me accountable for my actions and keep me from breaking more of our cultural rules, Hugo had made me his prisoner. I did not intend to offer him friendship.

"I hope you have fully recovered from your fall. I chose this particular shaft because the drop was not precariously deep, and you would sustain few injuries."

"How do you expect to release me?" The message came out before I could stop myself. "There is a side entrance, but it is blocked with rocks and dirt. I spent all yesterday and the day before searching for any way to get out. It is impossible."

"I know of a way. But I will not explain it to you until after I can converse with another Sasquatch about what you have done and how to address your indiscretions."

"Tell me about how you plan to get me out of here." When he did not immediately respond, I added, "Tell me so that I have comfort in knowing there is an ultimate plan for my release." Perhaps he would respond with empathy.

Silence.

I could not tell if he had left or did not care to inform me. I continued, "Had you been the one to commit an error in judgment, I would have comforted you." My transmission included acts of tenderness. "It is our way. I am not asking you to release me—simply tell me how you will help me leave this place. You can decide when the time is right."

He sighed. "I have a halvek tool and will use it to retrieve you."

From the images in his transmission, I recognized a rope. Covering my mouth with a hand, I tried to stifle my elation. It must be hidden nearby. If I could convince an animal to help me find it, I might save myself.

Where has he hidden it?

"I'm not going to tell you." Hugo laughed. "You keep forgetting I can hear everything you think."

I needed him to see me as an ally and not a prisoner. Straining to focus my mind exclusively on his mission, I deflected. "Tell me what you've seen today. I want to know about the birds."

Hugo sent me visions of a ptarmigan with its pure white plumage. A short clip from an earlier encounter included the same bird with speckled gray feathers. When it moved, I could see the bird's belly and tail feathers were still brilliant white. "When it changed color during the fall, its metamorphosis was breathtaking. Each day I saw a difference."

"You must be grateful that you selected a mission objective about natural wonders."

"Others have followed their migratory patterns, but I wanted to analyze their color changes." His transmission paused for emphasis. "These are the other species I have followed closely." Hugo's message included a snowshoe hare with some visions in complete white and others in various mottled brown and beige stages.

I let Hugo go on for a while with periodic messages to encourage his transmissions and compliment his work. When I could no longer resist, I transmitted, "Please free me. We can discuss your work and my actions at length. You will grow to understand why I acted as I did and how I could develop a relationship with my halvek friend Dylan."

"You are fine where you are." My shoulders slumped as he continued. "After tonight's full moon, I will broadcast a message and see if a new transferee is nearby. If so, I will let you know when we should expect them."

"Tonight?" Hugo must be mistaken. The full moon was not until the following evening.

"Yes. Tonight. I have kept careful track of each full moon. It is tonight."

"But that is not possible. I have been in Porgu for twenty-eight days. The full moon is tomorrow."

"I assure you it is tonight."

I flipped back through time to inspect my memories since arriving in Porgu. I accounted for each day before falling into Hugo's trap. After filing through my recollections of Colorado and Utah, I recalled every detail in Tansy's van going through Oregon, Idaho, and Utah. Each night in the yurt came back to me. Finally, I remembered being chased by

Lucas's dogs and the frantic search for Destiny's domicile. Then my memories grew cloudy.

Soon after we transferred from Reval, I had lost Dylan and tried to return to Reval but to no avail. I'd smashed my head on the rock as I collapsed in an explosion of lightning sparks. Could I have lain next to the tree and the blood-stained rock for more than a few hours? My memories included brushing snow off my shoulders and thighs. The falling flakes had stopped, but several inches lay on the ground.

Maybe I had been unconscious for two entire nights. That would answer why I had lost a day.

I looked up at the hole. Unless—Hugo might be trying to trick me. But what would he gain by misleading me? I was stuck in the cavern until he decided to release me.

I succumbed to the obvious. Most likely—I had missed a day.

With a hard sigh, I closed my eyes and collapsed on the dirt floor. A whole month had passed. Despite my daring work and sacrifice, I was no better off than when I struck my head on the rock in Oregon. Inside this cavity, I had no access to the moon's powers to transfer back to Reval and face the High Council.

With Hugo standing guard and another Sasquatch potentially coming to judge me, I would never be able to continue my journey to find Dylan. Worse yet, Hugo and the new Sasquatch might decide to stop me from tainting the Sasquatch collective by covering the hole and leaving me to rot.

Would anyone find me as I died a slow death from starvation and loneliness?

Chapter 45

Dylan lifted his stocking foot from the floor and placed it on Augie's coffee table without thinking. The sock was recently laundered, and Dylan's foot was clean—he had just finished showering after installing the new outdoor lighting at the cabin with Tom.

"Ooh," was Augie's not-so-subtle response.

"Sorry, sorry, sorry." Dylan jerked his foot off the table and placed it firmly on the floor where it belonged.

How could Augie see my foot when he's at the dining table making his second set of sketches?

No matter. Augie set the rules in his home, and Dylan would graciously obey.

"How're your drawings coming along?" Despite recovering the notebook from Cynthia, Augie was determined to continue his project to make a duplicate. Suggesting Augie change directions mid-stream would prove fruitless.

"I'm almost finished. Two more to go."

Dylan rose from the sofa to look over Augie's shoulder. "Why don't you use the old book as a guide to be sure you don't omit any of them?"

Augie lifted his pencil from the paper and let it hang suspended in midair while he looked at Dylan. "I need to draw them from the dreams. Otherwise, I won't know if I missed one."

"Logical approach. May I look at the original?"

"Yes." Augie slid the closed notebook toward Dylan.

After flipping the pages, Dylan opened it to the final drawing of a windswept landscape. "Do you recall if this is the last one you drew?"

Augie pursed his lips into a line. "I need to do this my way."

"Okay." Dylan moved back into the living room as his phone started to vibrate. "I'll leave you alone."

Dylan looked at the readout—Cynthia Waters. "Ugh. I'm not sure I want to talk to her."

"I will work faster if you go outside."

Dylan grabbed his coat and left the trailer. He answered and offered a gruff, "What?"

"You've been friendlier to me."

"This is the best I've got for you right now."

"I have some news. I don't want to upset you, but you should know." Cynthia's pregnant pause made Dylan grimace, waiting for the gut punch. "They released Kirk Steadman this afternoon."

"What?" Dylan's weak legs would not hold him. He dropped to sit on the wrought-iron steps. The cold metal immediately penetrated the back of his jeans, and he yanked down his jacket to cover his behind. "How could they release him? He burned down Augie's cabin. This case was cut and dried."

"You're a detective. You know no case is simple. I've heard he agreed to give further testimony against some lowlifes, and they're releasing him on a lesser charge with time served."

"Isn't he ever going to have to pay for the trouble he causes?" Dylan stared at the chipped sidewalk.

"That's not something I know how to answer." Cynthia scoffed. "Do you believe in karma?"

"I did until I met Kirk Steadman."

"Well, there's that. I'm sure he'll get what's coming to him someday."

"Not soon enough." Dylan sighed. "Did you call to suggest I avoid him? I can assure you that neither Tom nor I had plans to take him out for a liberation dinner."

"The other day I told you he was mouthing off about wanting revenge on you and Tom."

"You think that was a credible threat?"

"How you perceive his threat is not up to me. I only wanted to warn you. I don't have Tom's number. You might let him know."

"Augie and I are meeting Destiny and Tom for dinner tonight. I'll mention it to him."

Maybe Tom will consider investing in a firearm to keep at the cabin.

"Good idea to let him know." She hesitated. "And good luck."

After Cynthia disconnected, Dylan sat on the steps despite the cold, musing about Cynthia's motivation for the call.

Probably trying to get back in my good graces if her partnership with Lucas Edwards peters out.

Dylan slipped the phone into his jacket and jammed his hands into the pockets to keep them warm. The temperature had dropped about twenty degrees, and the air felt humid—not like the recent days with bone dry air. Maybe Tom was right about the blizzard.

The previous night's clear skies had added to Dylan's discouragement. The full moon had shone so brightly that Dylan imagined someone was shining car headlamps into Augie's guest room. The penetrating light kept him awake, ruminating about Kati. Had she left for Reval without sending him a transmission or even saying goodbye?

While in Reval, he observed strong relationships among Sasquatches. His parents had a loving bond until the day his father died. On that day, Dylan watched them stroking each other's fur and sending transmissions until his father drew his last breath.

Thinking back, Kati also loved to touch. She and Dylan always held hands or caressed while floating in the pools. Dylan closed his eyes and could feel her fingers caressing his cheek and ears while he taught her how to speak aloud. But his opportunity for more intimate moments with Kati came crashing to an end with the accident in Echo. Dylan cringed when memories of that night flooded back—the flashing lights, crunched van, and the empty passenger seat where Kati had once sat. If only he had reached her before Lucas and Cynthia.

"I am almost finished," Augie called as he opened the front door and jolted Dylan's attention. "You can come inside."

"Thank you." Dylan stood and brushed the back of his jeans. "I'm sure both sets are perfect."

As Dylan took off his coat and hung it on the wooden rack, Augie motioned for him to approach the table. "One is missing."

"Cynthia took one of your sketches?"

Augie nodded and pointed to the final drawing in the new notebook. "This one used to be in my book, but it is not there now."

Dylan looked at Augie's recent pencil sketch of a hillside with two prominent outcroppings. He picked up the original book and could not find anything similar. After bringing the spine to his eye to inspect it more closely, he discovered no remnant paper bits hidden in the coil. Cynthia must have carefully removed any trace of the page.

"Do you know this place?" Dylan asked.

"Nope."

If Kati sent the message with these distinctive bluffs after all the nondescript landscapes in Utah and western Colorado, the location might be close.

"Since last night was the full moon, she's probably already back in Reval." Dylan braced both palms on the tabletop. "But what if she isn't? What if she's still here in Colorado? She could be hurt and is hoping I come and look for her."

"Maybe Destiny knows this place." Augie offered.

Dylan scooped all the notebooks into a bundle and handed them to Augie. "We're going to the gallery to talk with Destiny now."

Chapter 46

NEAR GRANITE, COLORADO
KATI

All day long Felix brought me cones every time I asked. I ate them right away, trying to build strength. When darkness fell, I would have a more complicated task for him and a few of his friends. Anxiously, I waited until the light from my portal grew dim and finally dark.

If my plan worked, I could reach Dylan and figure out a way to stay in Porgu. The scheme was complex and required several steps. But I had broken them into straightforward tasks for the chipmunks' simple minds.

I waited for time to pass before I called Felix and his pals to my hole. I wanted to be sure Hugo was sound asleep when I made my escape.

When the rodents started to chirp at one another, a typical reaction for animals not used to working in concert, I compelled them to silence and sent them to perform the first job.

Despite making every effort to sit quietly in the center of the cavern, I felt my heartbeats throb. I needed to escape before Hugo found a like-minded conspirator. My plan was sound, and it would succeed.

After a time, I rose and moved to the edge where I had found the water trickle. I pressed my lips against the crack between the rocks to access the scanty flow. The water directly from the gap tasted cleaner than the little collection pool at the wall's base. So I slurped from the wall.

Finally, I heard Felix's shrill chirp and a dozen minuscule footfalls from him and his friends. I listened intently and could detect something dragging along the ground outside—like a thick snake pushing dried grasses and leaves from its path.

I concentrated hard to form my next command—a barrage of images from other Sasquatches who observed life in Porgu. A wolf spider dragged an insect into its hole. An eagle dropped a fish into its nest to feed her young. Halveks tossed debris into a cave. I hoped Felix would understand my suggestion.

When the tip of the rope dangled from the hole, I breathed a heavy sigh. My chipmunk squadron had found it. I offered positive transmissions to encourage them.

Slowly, the tip snaked closer. I was afraid to jump up and grab the end. What if one of the chipmunks got tangled up, and I accidentally pulled it in with the rope?

On tiptoe, I stretched an arm above my head. Teetering and grasping, it was just out of my reach.

I slumped for a moment to catch my breath before stretching again.

Come on.

Once in hand, I would pull the rope inside my cave. After knotting the end into a loop, I'd throw that end back to the surface. My chipmunks would drag the circle over any stout rock near the entrance. When I was sure it could hold my weight, I would use it to climb out of the cavern. Simple.

Closer, closer it came. I strained until the muscles along my sides were tight. Almost there.

It stopped.

Much to my horror, it retracted. Drawing ever higher, the rope receded far beyond my reach until it disappeared out of the hole.

"No!" Hugo's transmission blasted down to me. "Did you think I would not see them taking the tool from my cave?" His message included faces of angry Sasquatches with flaring nostrils and bulging eyes.

"Do not be angry." I stifled my frustration. "You knew I would try to escape. If you contact a newly transferred Sasquatch to decide my fate— who knows what you will decide?"

The chipmunks chittered furiously at Hugo. I could tell some had moved farther away as their chirps persisted but grew fainter. I directed them to flee.

"No, you don't!" Hugo transmitted as a broadcast. A sharp squeak cut through the silence before a small bundle of striped fur flew through the entrance hole.

I lunged forward and skidded across the earthen floor on my stomach, desperate to catch the tiny animal before it hit the ground.

Mercifully, the creature plopped into my cupped hands before it splatted to the floor. Carefully cradling him, I sat upright and cringed at Hugo's callousness.

I pressed my tiny comrade to my cheek and heard its faint heartbeat. Felix was alive but just barely.

"You nearly killed him," I transmitted to Hugo. "Why would you harm a lower Porgu animal? We are here to observe and not interfere."

"A hollow message coming from you." Laughter at the irony blasted through his transmission. "You have already tragically altered this animal by coercing it to bring you food and the halvek tool. You have lost your ability to follow our traditions. Everything you do is tainted with self-interest. *This* is what compels me to report your actions and hold you accountable."

Again, he was correct. When had I lost my perspective? Sasquatches are honorable and operate within long-understood rules. We do not interact with halveks or compel Porgu's animals to assist us. Sasquatches direct lower animals only in cases where we are in danger. Even then, we only direct them to be calm and leave. Asking Felix to gather food and fetch the rope was unconscionable.

I stroked the soft fur on Felix's back, wanting to apologize for my actions. The chipmunk's breath came in shallow gasps. Tears welled in my eyes, and I choked back a sob. Hugo was not to blame—I and I alone had risked Felix's life.

"You might be interested to know—a Sasquatch transferred last night." Hugo's transmission thundered from above, full of self-confidence.

I bowed my head. *Could my predicament get any worse?*

"We have exchanged communications. He rested today to recover from the transfer. But he will start his journey this evening. He wants to travel exclusively at night to avoid halveks and should arrive late tomorrow night or the next morning."

I straightened. "He is two nights' journey from here?"
From which direction?

"Do I need to keep telling you that I can hear all of your thoughts? He arrived on a mountain top." Hugo's transmission included a cleared summit with halvek-made disks. A fast-motion scene showed the sun rising in the southeast and setting in the southwest. It glimpsed to a town far below with glistening lights. Beyond the buildings, an illuminated letter S blinked on a hillside. Dylan had shown this town to me—Salida.

"When I sent an image of you, he was most delighted. It seems he knows you."

"Send me an image of this Sasquatch," I demanded.

Hugo taunted me by sending a blurry likeness of the Sasquatch looking into a rippling stream on Porgu and a moving shot with a quick glimpse in a halvek's window.

"This is not his first time to Porgu," I responded. "If he knows me, I must have seen him before as well. Show me an image with his face."

Hugo's initial visions were from the other Sasquatch's memories in Porgu. Either the new Sasquatch had transferred long ago, or this was not his first time in Porgu.

I recalled colleagues with whom I had trained for my first transfer. They all knew me and had been to Porgu. None of them would have traveled here—their transfer points were beyond oceans and large landmasses. Further, their coloring did not match the blurry images from the mysterious Sasquatch.

Who was this new Sasquatch, and was he intent on judging me?

"When I explained how you had interacted with several halveks, he agreed to abandon his mission and meet me directly."

"I've told you already. I do not want the actions from my first visit to Porgu to join our collective knowledge." I trembled—partly in anger but mostly in fear of what they would decide to do with me. "It is not fair to taint my family's standing with my crimes. They may want to have other children and encourage them to transfer. What if the High Council denied future petitions for my family based on my actions?"

"Why would they do that?"

"The Council encourages parents not to produce new offspring if the first is born deformed. Following that logic, my parent's future offspring would likely be as rebellious as their first. Therefore, the Council would discourage new offspring."

Before responding, Hugo sent images of Sasquatches consoling one another, ostensibly to tell me he understood my position. "I have not told him any details about activities from your first Porgu transfer, your coupling with a halvek in Reval, or engagements with halveks during this transfer. I did not even mention that you are here through an illegal transfer."

"Then what did you tell him?" Tears of gratitude welled in my eyes.

"Only that you have directly contacted halveks, and I sent your image."

I stroked Felix's fur and focused on its texture and color to mask my mind from Hugo.

Maybe I had jumped to an unfounded conclusion about why this Sasquatch wanted to meet with Hugo. Perhaps he knew me from my youth and was coming to my aid. If he was a friend, he and I could convince Hugo to release me. It was only two nights' journey from Salida. Dylan could keep me safe until the next full moon in twenty-six days.

"What are you doing?" Hugo's message included visions depicting curiosity and not demands. "I cannot detect your thoughts."

Pleased with my ability to mask some thoughts from Hugo, I released my concentration on Felix. "Please, send me an image of this Sasquatch. He might be a friend, and I would like to know who he is before he arrives. It will give me something to look forward to in the next two days while I am stuck in this hole."

"Very well." Hugo forwarded images sent from the other Sasquatch. The transmissions showed the newcomer's hands and legs, and I gained a sense of his height and coloring but needed more to place him. Finally, Hugo sent a clear image of the Sasquatch staring at his reflection in a mirror hanging in a halvek's yard.

I gasped. The face was disturbingly familiar. My hopes of someone coming to rescue me and taking a stand against Hugo were dashed.

His sky-blue eyes were distinctive and cold. I had no doubt—Kalev, the Sasquatch who wanted to exploit Dylan and orchestrated his own brother's death, was coming to meet Hugo and decide my fate.

Chapter 47

**NEAR RABBIT EARS PASS, COLORADO—DECEMBER 19
DYLAN COX**

Biting wind whipped their jackets as Augie and Dylan stood by the roadside and stared at the outcropping, barely visible in the building storm. Thin clouds scurried past the pinnacles. Wispy snow flurries alternatively veiled and unveiled the view.

"Destiny told us it would be here." Augie squinted at Dylan and held his Rockies cap firmly on his head. "Now what?"

Ice pellets spattered against Dylan's face, and he pulled up his hood. "Let's get back inside the car."

Once behind the wheel of Augie's sedan, Dylan cranked the heater to full blast and rubbed his chilled hands in front of a vent. "When we were in Echo, you felt like Kati was close. Do you feel that now?"

Augie turned to gaze out his window and up toward the iconic pass. After a few minutes, he looked back at Dylan and shrugged. "Nope."

"Do you think you'd recognize that sensation if it happened again?"

"I never felt it before." Augie shoved his hand under his thighs. His heels tapped the floor mats.

"But if it happened again, would you recognize it?"

"Maybe." The tapping increased speed.

"Don't be nervous. There's no right or wrong answer—I only want to know what you think." Dylan reached across the seat to touch Augie's leg with a single finger. Not too invasive, but a connection nonetheless. "You didn't have any similar dreams or feelings while we drove here. Did you?"

Augie adamantly shook his head. "Nope."

Dylan thought back on when they passed through the intersection in Echo. Augie had been sleeping before he sensed Kati's presence.

"I think we should drive slowly back to Salida and stop every few miles for you to check for that feeling. Try to relax and even take a nap. Maybe it will help us figure out where she might be."

"I can't relax." Augie pressed his lips together and exhaled a huge breath through his nose. "There's a big storm coming."

Dylan turned on the wipers to swipe away the snow dusting the windshield. "Tom's been telling me about the storm. I was hoping we could beat it." Dylan swiveled in the seat to look at Augie straight on. "It's your car. Would you rather drive?"

"Nope." Augie snorted, and the tapping stopped. "I trust your driving."

"Okay. I'll be careful." Dylan turned on the lights, pulled the car in a circle across the highway, and headed back to Salida.

Nearly three hours later, Dylan drove with a white-knuckled grip and struggled to see any part of the road where the snow had blown off. He glanced at Augie, sitting straight-backed with his hands balled into fists next to his thighs.

"I'm sorry I brought you out in this mess." Dylan raked a hand through his hair but quickly replaced it on the wheel. "We'll reach I-70 soon. That's about halfway home."

"Do you think we'll make it?" Augie asked without deviating his eyes from the windshield.

"I do." Dylan wished he felt as convinced as he sounded.

When they took the exit from I-70 toward Minturn, the tires lost their grip.

The car fishtailed.

Heart pounding, Dylan turned the wheel to correct for the skid.

After giving a high-pitched squeal, Augie lunged forward to grab the dash with both hands.

Dylan clenched the wheel as the car's backend edged to the right, then the left.

Before they reached the ramp's end, the car straightened.

They slid to a near stop before sliding slowly past the yield sign and onto U.S. Highway 24.

Augie jerked his head in both directions and gasped.

"Don't worry. Nobody's coming." *That was close. But everyone with half a brain is at home.*

The fluttery feeling in Dylan's stomach dissipated as they crawled through the tiny town of Minturn. Despite being early evening, all the touristy shop windows and restaurants were dark. The owners must have decided to close early before the storm hit.

As they left the town, Dylan kept his speed slow around never-ending switchbacks. After a turnoff for Red Cliff, they entered a cantilevered steel arch bridge spanning a railroad and the Eagle River. Dylan had noticed it on their clear drive to Steamboat only hours ago.

"Stop." Augie's command startled Dylan.

"Right here?" Dylan felt hesitant to put on the brakes until after they had crossed the bridge. Were not bridges notorious for ice?

Augie pointed ahead. "There."

Dylan tapped the brakes, slowing the car to a stop in several inches of snow beyond the bridge.

"Do you feel something?" Dylan turned on the dome light to see Augie's face more clearly.

"Nope." Augie pulled a notebook from his backpack lying near his feet. He flashed through the pages until he reached one after the Rabbit Ears formation. "Look."

Augie handed the book to Dylan and his heels rat-a-tat-tatted on the floor. "All I see is a deep rock cleft and scattered trees. What are you seeing?"

When Augie indicated to the top corner of the page, Dylan stared hard to understand what seemed so crucial.

"Here," Augie insisted, and Dylan pulled the book to the light for a better view.

High in the corner, Dylan finally spotted it. A scant line crossed the corner of the page and formed an arc. Circles that might have been bolts were welded into the arc.

"Do you think the arc in this picture is a piece of the bridge we're sitting on?" Dylan imagined what it must look like from below. Kati might have crossed beneath.

Augie nodded confirmation.

"But you don't feel like she's here now?"

"Nope."

Dylan craned his neck to make out the bridge behind them. Even if she was not there, Augie knew she had passed this way—less than a hundred miles from Salida. Their search was narrowing.

"I can't keep driving this way." The wipers struggled to keep the windshield clear. "The snow is starting to fall harder. I think we can find a motel in Leadville. It's only about thirty miles from here. Would you mind if we stopped for the night and started again in the morning?" While Kati may have passed the bridge, looking for her in the blizzard was a fool's errand.

"Nope." Augie's reply was simple, but Dylan noticed his tapping heals start to slow.

They took a full hour to reach Leadville. Dylan's shoulders sagged as he pulled into the first motel, desperate to finish the drive.

The car clunked when Dylan switched into parking gear, and Augie pointed out the window. "Is that Lucas's truck?"

"Please, don't make it so." Dylan squinted outside the window.

"It's at the end of the row."

Tell me Augie's mistaken. I need rest.

"I can't be sure. Do you think we should stay somewhere else?" Dylan hoped Augie would disagree.

Augie shrugged, leaving the decision to Dylan.

Dylan wanted to ignore the risk of running into Lucas. But Kati had passed nearby, and they could not let Lucas find her first. Dylan pounded a fist on the wheel before he yanked the car into reverse to gain a closer look.

"Oregon plates," Augie said.

Dylan cursed under his breath and turned the sedan toward the highway. "We're looking for a different place to stay. Maybe on the other side of town."

Chapter 48

KATI

By midday, the wind started blowing in earnest. As the skies grew darker, snowflakes drifted into my cavern through the hole. The gale howled through the pines outside, and once I heard a massive crack that reminded me of the tree that fell in Reval and killed Dylan's father Alevide.

My shoulders gave an involuntary shudder as I recalled scrambling over broken limbs to reach him before his life escaped. But this tree did not slam against the ground like the one in Reval. After it cracked, I heard the Porgu one fall against others, snapping their branches, before it came to rest with a thud. When at last I was free of my prison, I would go to see where it landed.

Once, I transmitted to the chipmunks to see if one might bring me a seed cone. They were buried deep in their burrows, avoiding the storm or the same fate as Felix. My stomach growled in protest.

Late in the evening, a snow cascade fell from the hole high above my head and landed on the floor not far from where I sat cross-legged, stroking Felix's nearly lifeless body. I brought him to my cheek and felt his faint heartbeat—constant but far less frequent than mine.

Be strong. Someone will come to help us. Was I trying to convince Felix or myself?

A seed cone dropped from above and bounced twice before landing nearby. I reached for it and inhaled the nutty fragrance. My mouth watered. With my eyes pleasantly closed, I listened for a shrill chirp from one of

Felix's friends. But that was not the sound I heard.

"Greetings." Hugo's transmission boomed from above. "You are fortunate to be down there. With all the wind and the snow, the weather is brutal. I nearly did not find your entrance."

"Too bad you found it." My response included Sasquatches' images with downturned mouths, tight jaws, and rolling eyes—our inference for scorn and contempt. "You could have taken a misstep and joined me down here. Then Kalev could rescue us both when he arrives."

"A harsh message from you after I brought you something to eat."

Hugo could probably hear me crunching on the cone. "I appreciate the nourishment. I assume you have been communicating with Kalev. When will he arrive?"

"He has decided to wait another night and travel when the storm has passed."

A lighthearted tremor shook my body. I would have one more day of reprieve before Kalev and Hugo decided my fate.

"Enjoy your meal," Hugo transmitted before I heard him slogging through the deepening snow and away from my hole.

"I am glad you're still alive." I stroked Felix's fur. "Maybe we will both live long enough to see another spring. You would probably like to see the changes in Porgu with leaves sprouting from your favorite trees and a crop of new seed cones to eat."

Felix's head moved slightly. Not enough for me to assume he was recovering, but enough to give me hope. I brought him to the crack with the water and touched his nose to the wet rock. Whether from an automatic reflex or his urge to survive, his tongue shot out to lick the water. I held him next to the flow, hoping he would take in more. But he did not.

After returning to my spot in the center of the cavern, I sat cross-legged and snuggled Felix against my shin. I dug into my pack to find the bit of fabric, thinking the extra warmth might help him heal.

Scrounging deep in the bottom, my hand brushed the recorder's smooth wood. I smiled. On the many nights of my journey, I stayed quiet to not attract hunters or other curious halveks. But no one would find me in this place.

I drew out the instrument and put it to my lips. Tansy had taught me so many different tunes. It was challenging to decide which to play. After the first note, I glanced at Felix to be sure it did not startle him. Part of me wanted him to respond, but he lay against my leg—flaccid and unmoving.

Low and with melancholy, I played Tchaikovsky's Dance of the Sugar Plum Fairy. The sound echoed through my chamber and bounced from the rock walls. I enjoyed the tune in the yurt and the van, but here it felt magical and gave me strength.

I had one more night before Kalev came. Perhaps the extra day would bring sunshine and hope.

Chapter 49

LEADVILLE, COLORADO—DECEMBER 20
DYLAN COX

Neither Dylan nor Augie had a good night's rest. The motel's paper-thin walls did little to muffle the next-door neighbors' televisions. The twenty-four-hour news cycle on one side and nonstop laugh tracks from the other did not drown out the wind whistling from the gap under the door.

After midnight, Dylan rose to stuff towels in the crack and found a half-inch of snow crusted near the threshold. After seeing the mini-snowdrift, Dylan bundled up to battle gale-force winds for a sojourn to the office. The motel clerk happily handed over extra blankets and wished him a happy stay. While happiness was out of the question, Dylan hoped he and Augie could stay warm through the night. In the end, the below-the-window heater kept the room mildly warm—enough for any quick trips to the bathroom.

Before five a.m., a snowplow rumbled through the parking lot, scraping and beeping. Dylan cradled his pillow around his head, trying to stifle the sounds. He was nearly asleep when someone broke out a snowblower to clear between the cars.

When the snow removal stopped, Dylan fell into a hard sleep until Augie turned on the television to watch the morning news at eight.

"You can take the first shower," Dylan mumbled with his pillow still clutched over his ears.

"Nope."

"Please?"

"Not my day. I did yesterday and will tomorrow."

"You don't want to shower to warm up?" *Silly question—Augie never deviates from time-honored schedules.*

"Nope."

"Ugh." Dylan rose to grab a steamy hot shower that lasted far longer than usual.

After stopping in the office to return the extra blankets, pay the bill, and retrieve a much-needed coffee to go, they grabbed Augie's snow brushes from the back seat and scraped off a foot of snow from the car. Despite his sunglasses, Dylan squinted to keep out the jarring sunlight reflecting off the fresh snow.

Few cars still sat in the lot. Rectangles of cleared black pavement dotted the spaces where a dozen dispersed cars and trucks protected the surface during the blizzard

The hotel must attract temporary workers from the molybdenum mine up the road in Climax. No wonder they were clearing the lot before dawn.

"I feel good about today." With a flick of his snowbrush, Dylan flipped powdery snow at Augie. "Want to find Kati?"

Augie's pink face broke into a wide grin, and laugh lines creased the sides of his eyes—all but hidden behind his fogged-up glasses. "Yeah."

"Did you see any dreams from Kati last night?"

"Nope." Augie's lips pressed into a grimace. "It's been a long time."

"That's okay. I know she's close. The sun's out, the snow's melting, and I'm optimistic. Today's the day."

"Today's the day," Augie repeated with a firm nod.

As they pulled out of the lot and eased toward the main highway, a white dually blew by. Loose snow billowed behind the tires, leaving a boiling cloud in his wake.

Dylan and Augie stared at the truck, mesmerized.

"Was that Lucas?" asked Augie.

"He's not finding her first!" Dylan gunned the accelerator and jerked the car onto the highway.

"No!" Augie called out and grabbed the dash.

Dylan slammed the brakes.

Beep. Beep. Beeeeep! A red van blasted its horn and lurched into the oncoming lane to avoid ramming the sedan.

Heart pounding, Dylan pulled hard to the right. Concrete-hard snow scraped the side panel and grabbed the tires, forcing the steering wheel to shudder. Dylan held on tight and let off the gas. The car rolled to a slow stop on the shoulder.

"I'm sorry for that." Dylan bowed his head and clasped a hand on his lap. "I didn't want him to be ahead of us again."

"I know." Augie reached to tap Dylan's thigh with a finger—a single touch before retracting the hand and sliding both under his thighs. "I don't know if it was Lucas's truck."

"We've seen a bunch of white extended cab trucks in the area—including one from Oregon at the other motel." Dylan raised his head to look at Augie. "I won't put us in danger again. I promise."

"I know you won't. I trust you." Augie nodded toward the road. "It's okay for him to be in front. He doesn't know where she is."

"Neither do we."

"But we will." Augie smiled. "Today's the day."

"Yes." Dylan straightened. "We'll find her."

When the row of cars behind the sedan grew to four deep, Dylan pulled to the side to let them pass. They had been driving twenty under the limit—slow enough for Augie to concentrate and pick up any transmissions Kati might send.

The plows must have been out all night. The black asphalt steamed as icy remnants quickly evaporated to leave the highway dry and clear. Dylan kept glancing to the side, watching the fields for tracks in the newly fallen snow.

Augie relaxed with his head against the fogged-up window.

Every time Augie moved, Dylan jolted with anticipation, hoping he might have had another dream. This time with Kati close by.

In Granite, Dylan pulled off into the plowed lot in front of a coffee shop. "I need another." He nudged Augie. "You want anything?"

"Hot chocolate," Augie mumbled with his eyes half-closed.

When Dylan returned, juggling two to-go cups and a fist full of sugar packets, he stepped to the passenger door and knuckled the window for Augie to take his cup. Surprisingly, Augie was sitting alert with his hands flat on his bouncing thighs.

Augie lowered the window and reached for the drink marked HC. "We have to go. I had a dream from Kati."

"Where?"

"Not far away. She's inside a hole."

"Is she okay?" Dylan tightened his grip on the cup. *Kati's close but could be hurt.*

"I don't know." Augie's chest rose and fell in rhythm with his short, deliberate breaths.

Once behind the wheel and belted up, Dylan pulled onto the highway behind a massive orange truck with its snowplow raised.

Plink. A stray piece of gravel spewed from the truck's bed. Dylan slowed to stay back and avoid chips in Augie's paint job or the windshield.

"I'm surprised someone out here is going slower than we are." Dylan scoffed. "Tell me if I should turn off the main drag. I'd be surprised if Kati stayed near the highway."

"We need to go right at the next road." Augie's heels tapped double-time. He faced the side window, and Dylan wondered if his eyes were open or closed. But he did not want to interrupt whatever Augie could sense.

Dylan turned onto Chaffee County Road 390 and drove until it ended in a plowed berm—a gray combination of churned snow and gravel.

"This is as far as we can go." Dylan's voice trembled from excitement and fear for what they might find. "Do you sense Kati nearby?"

"I think so. But I am not sure." Augie tilted his head. "Maybe there is more than one Sasquatch."

"As long as Kati is one of them, I'm fine with that." Dylan glanced back along the road from where they'd come—half expecting to see Lucas and Cynthia pull up in his dually.

A couple of bushy blue spruces lined the parking area on one side and offered protection from being seen from the highway. Dylan shifted the sedan close to the trees.

"Do you want to stay here and draw what you saw or come with?"

Augie glanced toward his backpack holding the sketchbooks, seemingly torn between capturing the latest vision and following Dylan outside. "I want to come with you."

"Then let's go find her."

Dylan strapped on his snowshoes and helped Augie with his. Neither had used them before, but the guy at the rental shop in Salida told Dylan snowshoeing did not necessitate lessons.

The guy had said, "You just attach the shoes and walk like normal—snowshoes just extend the hiking season."

Early in the summer, Jen took Dylan hiking all over the trails around Salida. What was there to learn?

While managing to keep his shoes separated and using ski poles for balance, Dylan tested his mobility by stomping forward a few paces with exaggerated marching steps. The snow on the ground sparkled like a mantel of multi-colored glitter. With barely a breeze, the tree branches remained weighted down with undisturbed snow tufts.

Dylan moved in a circle, at a loss on which direction to go. Up a hill to the north, down to the river going south, or continue along the road past the berm? Staying on the nearly flat road seemed most manageable. Making exaggerated steps, Dylan started toward the snow pile to continue on the road.

Dylan suddenly stopped and turned. Augie was not following. Still standing by the car, Augie strained his neck and leaned to the south—toward the river.

"What?" Dylan scanned the valley. The river was not completely frozen, and the previous night's snow was practically blown away.

Augie did not respond, but faint engine noise wafted from the highway, and a fluffy gray jay trilled at them from a protected spruce branch.

Augie said there could be two Sasquatches nearby. In Reval, Dylan had used telecommunication to talk and listen to Sasquatches. Why not try it now?

He opened his mind and tried to capture a whiff of a transmitted image. But he could not perceive any visions or sense the migraines he used to experience when Kalev pushed out his earliest transmissions.

"I've got nothing." Dylan stomped back down the berm and stopped in front of Augie. "Do you hear something?"

Eyes pointed to the woods, Augie ignored Dylan and kept listening.

"Is it her?" Dylan balled and unballed his fists. "Do you hear a message?"

"I hear a song."

"Someone is singing?"

"No." Augie shook his head. "I hear music."

Dylan tried again, straining. A wad of snow fell from a branch to plop on the ground. For an instant, a nearby squirrel chirped. Silence buzzed in his ears. But Dylan heard no music. "Can you tell where it's coming from?"

"From everywhere," Augie responded in a whisper.

"Come and follow me." Dylan tugged at Augie's jacket. "Let's see if it gets louder when we move down the road."

Dylan clomped over the berm with Augie a few steps behind. After marching across the snow and sinking a few inches with each step, Dylan stopped and urged Augie to listen again.

"It sounds the same."

"At least it isn't getting fainter." Dylan gave a weak chuckle. "Come on, let's move forward."

They continued the pattern of moving for a short while and stopping to listen. On their fifth attempt, Dylan gasped. He heard it, too—a flute-like tone with a haunting waltz melody. Dylan stamped one way and then another, trying to locate the source.

"It's louder than by the car." Dylan shuffled to Augie and pulled his sleeve. "Can you figure out where it's coming from?"

Slowly, methodically, Augie leaned in each direction. "There." He pointed farther down the road.

Dylan pushed forward. Soon his thighs screamed from lifting the snow-laden shoes. His heart pounded as he struggled for each breath.

Snowshoeing is like hiking—my ass.

But he forged ahead until he could hear the music above the sound of his shoes crunching through the snow. Dylan cupped his hands around his mouth. "Kati! Do you hear me?"

The music stopped.

Dylan strained to catch a response. He heard nothing.

"There." Augie caught up to Dylan. "Do you hear her?"

"No," Dylan mustered, still panting. "What did she say?"

"She's calling your name from down there." Augie pointed toward the downhill side of the road.

"Lead us to her." Dylan motioned for Augie to go first. "I can't make out her voice yet."

Augie took a few tentative steps on the unbroken snow. Dylan figured following someone's footsteps must have seemed easier—both from a physical and psychological perspective.

"Go slow and follow her voice," Dylan urged. "We're coming to find you, Kati. Keep letting us know where you are. If it hurts to yell, then play the music."

Augie clomped down the hillside with Dylan close behind. Augie stopped next to a mound of snow halfway between the road and the river, and Dylan nearly ran into him.

"What?"

"She said to be careful. Do not fall into the hole."

"What? Where is the hole? I don't hear the music anymore."

"She is under the ground." Augie looked nervously toward the trees. "But she said someone is watching us."

"Who?" Hair on the back of Dylan's neck stood on end. He squinted at the trees, trying to make out who Augie could see. Was Lucas lurking behind a tree, waiting to overpower them and take Kati? Dylan shook his head. How could Lucas beat them here? There was no sign of his truck where they'd parked.

"I do not know him." Augie turned and locked eyes with Dylan. "He's not Kalev."

"Thank goodness for that. Kalev's still in Reval."

The music started again—this time, from below the snow. "Kati's our priority. We'll deal with who's watching if he shows himself."

Dylan knelt and scanned the surface, looking for any evidence of a dip. "There." He pointed with one of his ski poles. "I can see a trail coming from the woods. It ends beyond this pile." With the side of his arm, Dylan scraped snow off the mound and uncovered a small boulder.

He stabbed a ski pole into the ground in front of the rock. Moving it forward a few inches at a time, Dylan poked in a line until it broke through. When he retracted the pole, the snow dropped, leaving a gaping hole.

"Dylan?" Her voice was half whisper and half yell, but it brought a lump to his throat.

Dylan fell to his belly and moved forward walrus-style until his head was above the opening. "Kati?"

Despite the meager light inside, he could see Kati reaching up and jumping toward him. "Be watchful. Hugo is outside. He pushed me into this cavern."

"Hugo?"

"He is strong—and he is a Sasquatch."

Chapter 50

KATI

Images depicting deceit exploded inside my head. Hugo was nearby and angry at seeing the halveks find me.

"Do not hurt them." I sent a vision with Sasquatch mothers comforting their young—touching and caressing. Surely Hugo understood Dylan would fight for my rescue. Hugo could overpower Dylan alone, but I heard another with him. Perhaps Dylan had brought someone as imposing as Lucas with his broad shoulders and violent temperament.

"Do not compare these halveks to our kind. They did not arrive here on their own power. A car brought them to us, and they are too weak to walk in the snow without manufactured platforms strapped to their feet." Hugo's images included a maroon sedan and a close-up of the men's feet.

I willed Hugo to transmit Dylan's face but dared not ask. Would he look the same as in Reval? He had grown quite furry before we transferred to Porgu. After a month of separation, would his eyes still bring a flutter to my chest?

"They travel great distances and have created tools to help them. Why do you judge them for adapting to the horrific conditions in Porgu?"

Hugo did not respond.

I cursed myself for irritating him. Defending Dylan or all halveks would not encourage Hugo to walk away.

I must keep him from interfering with my rescue.

"Halveks have a strong instinct to protect the ones they love."

"Love?" Hugo scoffed. "You are misinformed about their primitive nature. They scrounge and fight over possessions. They continually rut and mate with violence. They do not have the capacity for profound emotions."

Sasquatches' conceptions about halveks were formed from observations made over millennia. I would not change Hugo's mind in the next minutes. I altered my approach.

"Of course—you are right. Dylan sees me as his possession. He acts according to his natural instinct. Once he dominated me, and he will not relent until he controls me again."

Hugo's empathy showed in his images depicting vindication and pride. My plan was working.

"We cannot interfere with his intentions. His actions are appropriate for Porgu, and our kind has committed to observe and not obstruct what they do."

"But you have already interfered." I sensed Hugo's hesitation through his transmission's slowed pace. "These circumstances are unique. You must take responsibility for your actions. I should stop him from helping you escape."

"I understand your view. I am truly guilty and will accept my punishment from the High Council when I return to Reval. But you are innocent, and if you harm the halveks, the Council will accuse you of crimes in Porgu as well."

His silence gave me hope. I continued and sent images of the High Council members when they agreed to my request for euthanasia. "My sentence is confirmed, and I will return to Reval at the next full moon to accept punishment for enacting justice on halveks. I regret my actions and do not want you to suffer my fate. Halveks do not follow our conduct codes."

Hugo sent a vison with Sasquatches shaking their heads and turning to walk away. I breathed a sigh of relief and sent one more transmission to solidify our agreement. "Do not apply your emotions to their circumstances—it will only promote your downfall in our society."

My messages to Hugo reflected long understood ideas within our civilization. I knew how to convince Hugo, but my assertions were disingenuous. I had learned much about the halveks while in Porgu. Each individual was different—some kind like Tansy and others violent like Lucas.

Once Dylan rescued me, I could never go back and live among those who believed all halveks were primitive animals.

Chapter 51

DYLAN COX

Dylan scooted from the edge of the hole and looked around the clearing—no footprints and no one hiding behind the trees at the perimeter. "I don't see him."

"Be wary." Kati urged from below. "Hugo is near."

"We will." Dylan looked at Augie, standing far from the opening with his hands stuffed into his jacket pockets. "Any ideas about how to get her out of here?"

"Z pulley?"

Augie's answer came too fast to be sarcasm or a joke. "What's a Z pulley, and how do you know about it?"

"Jen took me rock climbing in the winter. She showed me."

Leave it to Jen to teach Augie how to rock climb and save the day.

"Okay. Where will we find one?"

Augie shrugged. "In my trunk."

"Of course." Dylan shook his head. "Why didn't you tell me you could rock climb?"

"You did not ask."

Good point. "Do you want to go back to the car to get the pulley, or shall I?"

Augie tilted his head as if considering my question.

"Forget what I asked." Dylan smiled. "You know what it looks like. I'll stay here."

In a half-hour, Augie set up the ropes, anchors, and pulleys. Wearing

Augie's ill-fitting but adequate climbing harness, Kati emerged from the hole while Dylan and Augie steadily hauled her up with the pull strand.

Once free, Kati collapsed on the snow.

"Finally." Dylan's voice shuddered. He dropped to cradle her in his arms.

"Forgive me for not finding you sooner." Leaning within an inch of her face, Dylan traced her cheek with the back of his finger. "We almost got to you in Echo, but we were too late."

Before he could say anything more, Kati pulled him close and kissed him. While the images were faint and faded, he detected her transmission with intimate visions from their time in Reval. She pulled away and mouthed the words, "I love you, too."

"I told you so." Augie giggled as he disconnected the ropes and anchors.

Dylan helped Kati remove the climbing belt and slid her pack from her shoulders to slip it over his own.

"Wait," she whispered and reached for the pack. Kati unzipped a front flap and removed a piece of fabric. She peeled back the covering to reveal a sleeping chipmunk.

"Sasquatches don't have pets. Where did you pick up this little fellow?" Dylan asked as he held out a finger to touch the animal.

Kati's eyes grew wide with sorrow. "Felix died trying to help me escape."

Dylan stroked the rigid chipmunk, then placed a hand on Kati's bony shoulder. Tears welled in his eyes.

She protected me in Reval, and I should have done the same for her in Porgu.

Her cheeks were hollow, probably from a lack of nourishment. She had endured a lot of suffering in the past month. Kati only ended up in Porgu because she tried to help *him* escape Reval. Those who helped her became injured like Tansy or dead like Felix. How could he make it up to her?

"We can bury him here or near the cabin." Dylan held her close, pressing Felix between them. "You decide."

"Not here." Kati rewrapped Felix's body and tucked him into her pack. Kati sniffled and wiped her nose with the back of her hand. "A female halvek helped me."

"Tansy?"

"She told me you saw Joe, but you met her, too?" Kati cocked her head.

"Augie intercepted your transmissions." Dylan pointed to Augie repacking the pullies and ropes. "We traced you to Oregon and found Joe. We made it to Echo, where the van crashed, but you'd already left."

Kati's head dropped, and she stared at the ground. "Is Tansy dead?"

"No. We stayed with her at the hospital until Joe could be with her. She had some injuries but will be fine."

"Halveks can repair without pools?"

"Not as fast, but we recover eventually." Dylan glanced up toward the road. "Are you able to walk? Augie's car isn't far."

Kati nodded and handed the backpack to Dylan. With Augie and Dylan on each side, they helped Kati to her feet. She took a couple of tentative steps.

"Tansy told me about your ankle." Dylan shifted his weight. "At some point, we should figure out how to get that cast off your foot."

"I thought it might break off when I fell." She indicated toward the hole. "It's on tight."

Without another pair of snowshoes for Kati, their way up to the road was slow going. Despite being supported between Dylan and Augie, she sunk to her knees with each step. With Dylan's snowshoes floating on top, he was nearly her height. But Augie stood almost a foot shorter.

Step by step, the men steadied her until they reached the road, where the footing became more level.

After a short distance, Kati stopped suddenly. She looked down the hill toward the hole. "Hugo is watching us."

Dylan turned his head to see. "Should we hurry?"

"No. Hugo will not follow us." Kati sighed and straightened, ostensibly to muster the strength to reach the car. "Hugo will not engage with you and Augie. Sasquatches do not interact with halveks. He believes all Sasquatches should follow our customs."

With shaky laughter, Dylan said, "I'm glad we don't have to worry about him trying to stop us."

"He will leave us alone." Kati tightened her grip on Dylan's shoulder. "But he is not our only problem."

"How so?" Now that Kati was safe, they only needed to steer clear of

Lucas and Cynthia.

"Hugo sent a transmission to another Sasquatch. He is coming here."

"Who?" Another angry Sasquatch? They would have their hands full evading the relentless hunter and journalist.

"Hugo just sent a message to him. Kalev will meet us in Salida."

Dylan groaned. *Not again.*

Chapter 52

SALIDA, COLORADO
DYLAN COX

Dylan pulled into the snow-covered driveway in front of the cabin. He followed tire tracks—gratefully not left by a dually—and pulled to a stop a foot away from Tom's tailgate. Dylan opened the sedan's back door and nudged Kati's shoulder to wake her. She'd slept most of the way.

"We should get you inside. I have sugar and can make you some hummingbird food. Kalev used to eat it when we met at the cabin. I can figure out what else you can eat later. But for now, we need to build your strength."

Kati released a faint moan but did not open her eyes. "Scrambled eggs."

Dylan hardly believed his ears. "Scrambled eggs?"

"Uh-huh. Tansy made them for me." She licked her lips. "They are delicious."

"You realize they aren't vegetarian? Fertilized eggs become baby chickens."

She opened one eye. "Eggs are unborn baby chickens?"

Nothing like being precise. "No. They are not."

"Good." Kati snuggled into the seat. "Then make me some scrambled eggs."

"I will as soon as we're inside. If Tom doesn't have any in the fridge, I'll go into town and buy some."

Slowly, Kati pulled herself upright and stuck a foot out the door.

"Hold on a minute." Dylan realized the futility of his suggestion—Kati was not going anywhere on her own power.

As a team, Dylan and Augie extracted Kati from the back seat and lifted her upright. As they had done on their snowshoes, each man bookended her.

They moved cautiously, one step at a time to the shoveled and swept front porch. *Tom must have cleared it, hoping we'd bring Kati home.*

Despite Kati's emaciated body, Dylan and Augie struggled to walk her seven-and-a-half-foot frame up the three front steps.

When the trio neared the threshold, Tom jerked open the cabin door and raced forward to relieve Augie under Kati's draped arm. "This probably isn't the best time for introductions, but I'm Dylan's friend Tom. We'll help you recover. Don't be afraid of us. We'll keep you safe and protected."

"Thank you," Kati whispered.

Tom's head jerked at her response. He must not have expected Kati to understand polite conversation.

Dylan intervened. "Kati understands how we speak and comprehends what you're saying, but I'm not sure if she'll remember this conversation tomorrow. She's exhausted and malnourished. Imagine eating a few pinecones each day for a month."

"It doesn't matter. I want Kati to know we're on her side."

As Dylan was a full six inches taller than Tom, Kati's dead weight started to slip from Dylan's shoulder. He sluffed her body higher on his neck. They'd be inside in a few more steps.

"Hey, you!" A voice from Dylan's past echoed across the yard, and Dylan froze.

"Not Steadman," Dylan muttered. "Why is he here?"

"Sheriff Austin called this morning," Tom answered with urgency. "Cynthia wasn't the only one who heard Steadman's threats. Austin told me to keep a lookout for him. I promised to let him know if Steadman showed up. Let's get Kati inside and deal with him later."

"I'm talkin' to you, boy," Steadman insisted.

Dylan glanced over his shoulder.

Steadman advanced from the woods while leveling a rifle at the trio. Despite the cold November day, Steadman wore jeans and a faded short-sleeved T-shirt.

He's on something. Meth?

"Stop where you are." Steadman's eyes darted from the porch to Augie's car to the ground. "I came here to take my revenge. You got me in trouble with the law."

Tom grabbed Augie's jacket and pushed him inside.

Dylan felt Tom leaning toward the entrance, trying to pull them away from the scene outside. But Dylan's rage overshadowed Tom's momentum. "You have no right to be here, Steadman," Dylan called. "This is private property. If you don't leave, I'll call the Sheriff, and he'll throw you in jail—where you belong."

Dylan maneuvered to move between Steadman and Kati.

With an earsplitting crack, a bullet shattered a board on the steps below the porch.

Had Steadman shot *at* them, or was he trying to frighten them?

"Turn around. I wanna see what you're holdin'."

Not wanting Steadman to fire again, Dylan nodded at Tom to face the gunman.

"What have we here?" As Steadman spoke, the rifle tip lifted and dropped as if on its own power. "Looks like I'll be getting' more payback from you than I expected." He cocked his head as he appraised Kati. "What's wrong with it? Can't it move on its own?"

Dylan held Kati closer. "She's got nothing to do with you. Leave us alone."

"Not likely." Steadman chuckled with a low rasp. "A female, huh? I can see from here she's got a nice set of tits. You boys taking her inside to have a little fun?"

Dylan bristled.

Tom whispered through his teeth. "On the count of three, let's make a break for the door. We can barricade inside until the Sheriff gets here."

"It's too risky. I'd take a hit for either of you. But if Steadman fires again, you or Kati could be hurt."

"What are you two mumbling about?" called Steadman as he took two steps forward, only yards from the porch steps. "We can do this the easy way or the hard way. But in either case, you're gonna help me. You owe me."

"We're not doing anything for you," Tom said.

"What I hear you sayin' is that you'd like to hear your choices."

Steadman sniffed. "You boys can either move that critter to my car and let me drive off with her, or I can shoot all three of you and drag her dead body to my car. She might be easier to deal with if she's dead." He brought the rifle butt to his shoulder to peer down the sight. "Your choice. I'll give you five seconds to consider your options."

Tom turned to talk into Kati's neck—loud enough for Dylan to hear. "I don't like those options. On three, we'll make a break for it."

"Agreed." Dylan nodded. With each movement, Dylan breathed the count. "One, two, three."

They spun Kati around and leaned toward the door to gain momentum. As Dylan stepped over the threshold, he heard a bang—not once, but two shots, and then a third.

The trio fell through the doorway in a heap, and Augie slammed the door shut.

"Were you hit?" Dylan called out. He disentangled himself from Kati and Tom to run his hands down Kati's limbs, looking for any sign of blood.

Her limp body was either dead or unconscious. Trembling, Dylan put an ear to her chest.

"Well?" Tom hovered over the pair.

Dylan glanced over his shoulder to see Tom nervously wiping his hands down the front of his jeans. "Her heart's beating strong. I think she passed out."

As Dylan turned back to stroke her cheek, Kati opened one eye and then the other. He struggled to find words.

She smiled up at him. "What about you? Were you hurt?"

"No." Dylan relaxed to sit on the floor. "I'm fine. Steadman must be a terrible shot." Gently, he moved her head onto his lap and brushed her cheek with a kiss. "Don't worry. We'll hide you before the Sheriff gets here. Stay strong for me."

Augie bolted the lock and handed Tom a cell phone from its place on the center island.

"I'll make the call." Tom tapped the phone.

A knock rapped against the front door. Not a bang like a rifle butt or a boot slamming into the wood, but a gentle strike Dylan might expect if a friend were paying a social visit.

"Are you going to let me in?" Cynthia's voice pierced through the door.

Dylan swung his head toward Tom. "Don't call Austin just yet. Cynthia's outside. We should find out if Steadman is holding her captive."

"Shouldn't we call him no matter why she's outside? What if we open the door, and she's working with Steadman?"

Cynthia knocked again. "I'm not kidding. It's cold out here. Let me in. We need to call the Sheriff about the dead burglar in your yard."

Tom inched his way to the window and peeked around the closed blind. "She's right. Steadman is lying in the yard with a big red spot on his back." He turned toward Dylan. "I think she killed him."

"Cynthia killed Steadman?" Dylan's jaw dropped. "Is Lucas with her?"

"I don't see him outside."

The door handle rattled. Cynthia was not taking *no* for an answer.

"I appreciate Cynthia stopping Steadman, but we can't let her see Kati. Once Cynthia finds out about her, everyone will know." Dylan clutched Kati's head closer. She moaned in response.

"Come on, fellows. I saw you on the porch with our furry friend. Let me inside to help take care of him," Cynthia pleaded. "Or now that I've gotten a peek at it, maybe it's a *she*. I always believed Kalev was a male— at least that's what Erle told me."

"Where's Lucas?" Dylan called out.

"I'm here, too," Lucas confirmed. "Open the door now, or I'll find another way inside."

"Neither one of you is coming in here." Dylan looked at Tom and whispered, "I don't trust Lucas not to kill Kati, and Cynthia would create a circus at Kati's expense."

"What should I do?" Cell phone still in hand, Tom looked from Augie to Dylan. "What if I call the Sheriff and open the door after he gets here? At least that way, Cynthia would be busy talking about what happened with Steadman."

Knowing Cynthia, she wouldn't want anyone else to hear about Kati until she had total control of the situation. Having the Sheriff nearby would keep both Cynthia and Lucas at bay.

"I agree." Dylan nodded.

Tom stepped to the window to make the call.

"Augie, there are pillows and a blanket in the bedroom. Please get them for Kati while Tom calls the Sheriff. I'll get her settled, so I can make up some sugar water for her before we decide what to do."

"Scrambled eggs," Kati murmured.

"Later." Dylan touched her cheek. "Right now, you need something to boost your strength—in case we need to make a run for it."

Dylan glanced to the front to see Tom lifting one of the blinds as he spoke into the phone. "Sheriff, there's been a shooting. We're holed up in Augie's cabin. Cynthia Waters and a guy named Lucas are outside with a gun. Either she or Lucas shot Kirk Steadman." A pause. "They aren't threatening us." Another pause. "Okay. I'll try to keep them on-site until you get here." Tom poked his phone before turning to Dylan. "Austin's leaving right away and should be here in about fifteen minutes. He wants us to keep them engaged so they won't leave."

"We're not letting them inside." Dylan scoffed.

"Agreed. I'll go out back and walk around the front to meet Cynthia and Lucas on the porch."

"What if they threaten you?"

"I assume they killed Steadman because he planned to harm Kati. I don't believe they'll hurt us."

Augie returned with the bedding. After slipping a pillow under Kati's head and tucking the blanket around her, Dylan moved to the kitchen to melt sugar. While he worked, Dylan struggled, thinking of ways to keep Lucas, Cynthia, and the Sheriff away from Kati.

A rap on the window startled Dylan and nearly made him drop the wooden spoon into the syrup. He needed to get his act together—his nerves were fried, and Kati was depending on him.

Cynthia's voice echoed through the glass. "I don't know why you're hiding. Please, let me in. I have resources that can help her. They'll be discreet."

Tom walked to the back hallway, toward the rear entrance.

As Dylan watched Tom leave, he slipped an ice cube in the pot with the hot syrup and stirred. After filling a cup, Dylan dropped to the floor in front of Kati. He slid a hand under her head and called to Tom, "Approach them cautiously. I don't trust either one."

Dylan scooted around to lift Kati's head into his lap and heard the back door click closed. Augie followed behind Tom and slid the deadbolt shut.

"Take as much as you can," Dylan directed as he leveraged a spoonful into Kati's lips. His shoulders sagged with relief as she swallowed and opened her mouth for more.

"This tastes good." She smiled up at him. "Not as good as eggs."

"How did you get so fussy after only one month on your own in Porgu?"

"You are not going to believe the journey I've taken to find you," she rasped. "I want to ride on one of these." Kati sent a vision with a snowmobile.

While her volume was low, her intonation sounded nothing like the coarse whisper she'd had when they talked together in Reval. "I can tell you've been practicing your speech. You and Tansy must have had a lot to talk about."

"We mostly talked about you." Kati's chin dipped. "She thinks I am in love with you."

"You said it, so it must be true."

"And you?" Her eyes filled with questions. "You said it to me before we left Reval. Have you changed your mind?"

"My feelings for you haven't changed. I don't know how we'll manage, but we'll figure out a way."

"We will. But now, I need more food."

Dylan rose to fill the cup. He heard voices outside but could not understand what Cynthia and Tom were saying. Her tone seemed crisp and demanding. He heard nothing from Lucas and pictured him standing to the side with a rifle pointed at the ground. Maybe they were figuring out what to tell the Sheriff. It would be good to have a consistent story about why Cynthia or Lucas shot Steadman in the back.

While it wasn't self-defense, they were clearly defending us. Maybe that should count for something.

As he knelt in front of Kati with a full cup, a Sasquatch transmission boomed into his head from somewhere close by. "I know you are hiding in the cabin."

Dylan's stomach clutched, and Kati grabbed his arm. They had both intercepted Kalev's message.

After spending a month in Reval, Dylan clearly understood Kalev's first transmission and the one that followed. His messages included images and words all mixed together. "I am willing to forgive you both for making a fool of me in front of the High Council. I've transferred from Reval to bring you back with me."

Dylan set aside the cup. Kalev knew the woods around the cabin like the back of his hand. He understood how to hide in plain sight and avoid detection. Despite wanting to hold Kati forever and never let her out of his sight, he knew Kalev could offer her protection from Lucas—at least until she regained her strength.

But could he trust Kalev?

"This is our chance for you to escape." Dylan said the words he dreaded to admit, "You can go into hiding with Kalev. He can help you recover."

Eyes wide, Kati's grip grew firm. "He is deceiving us," she whispered. "I want to stay with you."

"People are after me and know they can find you through me. I can't keep you safe."

"I've fought within an inch of my life to come back to you, and now you want me to leave you again?" Kati wrapped her arms around Dylan's neck.

Her body trembled. How could Dylan find the strength to let her go?

Chapter 53

TOM MORROW

With balled fists on his hips, Tom stared at Cynthia. She tried to convince him that she and Lucas searched for Kati alongside Dylan and Augie, but Tom knew she was lying. Cynthia only had her own interests in mind. She did not want to help Kati—Cynthia wanted to exploit the Sasquatch.

"Why should I believe you?" Tom asked.

"That beautiful creature," Cynthia pointed to the cabin door, "needs our help. If she likes raw food, I know people who can sell us wild game meat. If she'd rather kill her food, they can deliver live animals here. You'd be amazed at my resources. Please, let me help."

Lucas's cocky smile belayed his confidence in Cynthia's approach. But he kept glancing at the cabin. Door. Windows. Lucas was sizing up the place for weak spots.

Tom moved to place himself between Lucas and the door. "Tell me what you know about her, and maybe I'll open the door."

How much time had passed? Would the Sheriff come to the house with lights flashing or sneak through the woods like Cynthia and Lucas had done?

"I only know what Dylan told me." Cynthia straightened.

Does she think Dylan and I haven't spoken?

She continued. "Dylan wants to protect her, and so do Lucas and I." Cynthia waved a dismissive hand. "The creature is smart and strong and somehow learned to communicate with Dylan and a nutcase in Oregon named Tansy."

As Cynthia slid a hand into the back of her waistband, oblivious to his delaying tactics, Tom leaned against the door frame.

"You know," Cynthia rambled on. "If we handle this right, she'll make the cover of all the major magazines and probably the prestigious science ones, too." Her head bobbed, and Tom could almost hear wheels turning as she plotted out a strategy. "People have already seen her."

"People?"

"Well, at least Lucas and me. But people have heard about Dylan's rescue in Oregon. He's already famous, and I'm certainly not the only reporter who thinks there is a bigger story than what Dylan told the officials. How hard will it be for other journalists to find him in Salida? Once they start camping out by the cabin—they'll uncover the Sasquatch story. She won't be safe here with you and Dylan."

"What do you propose?"

"Give her to me," Lucas injected.

"That's not an option." Cynthia shot Lucas a look. "*We* need to move her somewhere safe." She tapped a finger against her chin. "Nobody's after Lucas or me. Let *us* take her away. We'll find a spot to drop her off, and no one will find her."

"I thought you wanted to bring her food and help her recover."

Does Cynthia believe we'd fall for her rescue ploy?

"Oh, come on!" Cynthia pushed Tom aside to grab the door handle. "Just let me see her."

"Will you promise not to take any photos?"

Tires crunched the gravel on the main road—no sirens or flashing lights. Before Cynthia and Lucas had a chance to react, a Chaffee County Sheriff's car pulled into the drive and stopped short of Steadman's body. Cynthia's eyes went wide, and Lucas moved a step away from her as if distancing himself.

Gotcha. Tom smiled.

Sheriff Austin and Assistant Deputy Erle Hodges jumped from the car with their firearms drawn.

Austin called, "All three of you—put your hands where I can see them!"

"Damn it," Cynthia muttered under her breath as she placed both hands on top of her head.

Lucas bent to lay his rifle on the porch and turned toward the Sheriff to assume the posture. "My name is Lucas Edwards. My rifle is loaded, but I have a permit to carry it."

Both officers slogged through the snow and passed Steadman's unmoving body before approaching the porch.

"Space yourselves out on the porch, find a spot, and sit." Austin pointed his weapon from Tom to Cynthia and finally settled on Lucas. "Don't take your hands off your heads."

"Hi, Erle." Cynthia gave him a flirtatious nod as she sat down and placed her hands in her lap.

Erle tipped the end of his Glock 22 toward Cynthia. "This isn't a social call. Keep your hands up."

Tom stifled a chuckle. *It seems like Erle's figured out how to handle Cynthia.*

While the three captives sat silently, Austin noded at Erle, who picked up Lucas's firearm with a gloved hand and secured it in the car.

Austin moved to stand in front of the trio and pointed to the body in the yard. "Erle's going to have you stand up one at a time and search you for weapons. While that's happening, I want you to tell me what happened to Steadman."

"I'll start." Cynthia nodded. "Lucas and I had a meeting with Dylan at the cabin. As we neared the driveway, Lucas spotted Kirk Steadman leaving his car parked on the road and heading into the woods. He was carrying a rifle. So Lucas pulled past until Kirk entered the woods. Then we doubled back to park and followed him to the cabin."

"Did it enter your mind to call emergency services?" Sarcasm laced Austin's words.

"How long does it take to get from your office to out here? If we'd waited until you or your team arrived, Kirk would have killed both Tom and Dylan." She huffed. "We probably saved their lives."

"Did you shoot Steadman?" Austin asked Cynthia.

"No," Lucas injected. "I did, Sir. I took reasonable actions to protect Tom and Dylan. Steadman had already fired a shot." Lucas pointed to where Steadman's first bullet struck the porch.

"Thank you for cooperating, Mr. Edwards. We'll need to question you further." Austin turned to Erle. "Secure him in the car, please."

Austin scanned the yard. "Where's Dylan?"

"Dylan locked himself in the cabin." Cynthia's lips formed a pout. "He's a bit fragile and refuses to let us in. Augie's with him. But why don't we all go inside and see if he's okay?"

"No." Tom glared at Cynthia. "I don't think that's a good idea. Cynthia's vigilante act shook him up. Dylan went inside to use the toilet. He'll be right out." Tom rose to stride across the porch. He banged on the door. "Dylan, the Sheriff's here, and he wants to talk with you."

No response.

Tom started to pound again. But the deadbolt slid, and the door opened.

Dylan stood in the entrance, as white as a sheet. "Sorry, I'm pretty rattled." Dylan gave a slow catatonic nod. "First Steadman tries to kill us, and then Lucas stops him in his tracks. Do you need us to come into the station to give you a statement?"

"Nobody's going anywhere for a while." Austin secured his firearm. "Come outside until more officers get here."

Augie followed Dylan onto the porch. At the steps, Dylan rested a hand on Augie's arm, seemingly to steady himself.

What could have happened inside?

"I'm freezing out here, Sheriff." Cynthia rubbed her hands down her arms. "I'm sure your other deputies and the coroner will be here soon. You'll probably need to give them instructions. Can't we wait inside for you to take our statements?"

She never quits. Can't she see that Dylan's hurting?

When two patrol cars pulled into the drive, Cynthia stood and edged toward the door.

"Stay here and wait for the Sheriff to decide what to do," insisted Tom.

Austin waved instructions to his team about photos and preparing the site for the forensics team. To Cynthia, he said, "All of you can wait inside. Erle will go with you." He turned to Erle. "You know the drill. No chatter until we get statements."

Tom looked at Dylan, expecting him to argue. But Dylan shrugged and opened the door. Cynthia rushed inside.

Erle followed the group into the cabin. "Go ahead and sit where I can watch you."

Once Tom closed the door, everyone found a place to sit except Cynthia, who dashed from room to room. "Where did you hide her?" She opened closet doors and slammed them shut.

"I said to sit." Erle took Cynthia by the arm and pulled. She resisted but finally complied, staring at Dylan as Erle led her to a chair.

"She's not here," Dylan said from the sofa.

Tom placed a tender hand on Dylan's shoulder. Tom whispered, "She can't last long outside in her condition. Where did she go?"

"Maybe she'll come back to me someday. But for now, she's with others who know how to hide her and can keep her safe."

"I can't believe you let her go."

"It's not what I wanted." Dylan's chin trembled.

Chapter 54

Kalev pulled my arm and dragged me into the woods behind the cabin. Once we were a reasonable distance away, Kalev yanked my pack from my shoulders.

"No!" I made a feeble attempt to grab it but missed.

He tossed it into the brush on the creek's far side. "You do not need halvek belongings."

I crumbled into the snow, forcing my muscles to go slack. "I'm not leaving until you recover my pack."

In a swift and decisive movement, Kalev scooped me off the ground and heaved my body over his shoulder. I tried to wriggle free but lacked the strength to fight.

Tears welled in my eyes.

Before long, the voices near the cabin faded into the distance. Bird songs and rodent chirps replaced them—all sounds that had become familiar over the past month.

Kalev stayed close to the trees as he ducked under limbs hanging low from the snow's weight. My added bulk did not slow his pace. As he walked, Kalev shook the branches, and falling snow covered our tracks.

I could hear Kalev's transmissions to larger animals, directing them to follow us and destroy remnant evidence of our passing. Soon we were deep into the forest and far from Dylan and his cabin.

Silently, Kalev walked until dusk. I strode beside him a couple of times. But Dylan's sweet syrup soon lost its potency—my feet started to drag, and, finally, I fell to my knees.

"We must keep moving," Kalev insisted.

"I have outrun Lucas before. He even had dogs tracking me." I turned to look back. "I did not hear his dogs today."

"How did you allow dogs to follow you? You were trained to control lower animals before your last transfer."

If my mind were still as open as when I met Hugo, Kalev would have known about the dogs. My telepathic skills were continuing to improve, but I was unsure how much I'd recovered. "When I arrived in Porgu, I tried to transfer back immediately. But I could not and hit my head. I was unconscious for a day."

"You attempted to return?" Kalev's eyes narrowed. "I assumed you left Reval with Dylan and intended to stay with him in Porgu."

Just as Felix's responses told me when my animal controls skills had returned, Kalev's unawareness of my circumstances in Porgu told me I could again hide my thoughts from another Sasquatch.

A further test was in order. I recalled but blocked an image about lying on the cot in Tansy's yurt. I pictured the comfy blanket and the heater's hum.

Kalev looked at me with a blank stare. "Well? Tell me whether you attempted to return."

I closed my eyes and offered a silent thanks for my recovery. As long as I kept Kalev apart from Hugo, maybe my recent transgressions in Porgu would not filter to the High Council. But at some point, Hugo would return from his mission and inform the Council.

I sighed. If I kept my promise to undergo the euthanasia ceremony, I might be long dead before Hugo returned to Reval.

"Well?" Kalev asked again.

"I *did* try to return." I transmitted images from when I stood in the clearing in Oregon and raised my hands to the sky to capture the moon's power. I sent him a vision of the lightning and the final image from when I fell to the ground.

"To be clear—you only intended to transfer Dylan to Porgu?"

"Yes. He does not belong in Reval. He should be with his kind in Porgu." I did not admit my feelings for Dylan.

Now that I can block my thoughts—let that be my secret.

Kalev looked back at the direction we had come. He likely reflected on Dylan, but he kept his thoughts to himself.

"I have been on my own since I arrived in Porgu and have barely eaten." I held up my arms so he could see my thin, wasted body. Let him assume I traveled alone from Oregon. He did not need to hear about Tansy's assistance and my love of eggs. "Can we rest for a while before you take me into hiding until the next full moon?"

"I understand." Kalev looked from me to the landscape. "I know this terrain well. There is a cave nearby where we can stay for a few days until I decide how we will wait out the time."

"I am grateful for the rest."

"I will bring you berries, seed cones, and tree bark to give you strength."

If the cave was nearby, we would not meet up with Hugo. I pressed a hand to my heart in silent gratitude. "May I assume we will not go back for Dylan?"

"He and I agreed." Kalev's eyes narrowed. "I would take you away and keep you safe until we return to Reval. Dylan would not attempt to contact you again. I plan to stick to our arrangement."

Neither had asked for my input, but it was the best decision. While I longed to stay with Dylan, I understood a future with him would be riddled with dangerous confrontations from halveks like Lucas. Self-serving Kalev had not saved me to help Dylan—more likely, he wanted to keep our society secret from the halveks.

"Why did you come after me?"

"That is a story for another time. Be satisfied that for now, I will be your protector."

I recalled my discarded pack lying unprotected next to the creek. Felix's body, Tansy's flute, and other halvek trappings—had they made my life better or worse? My journey taught me much about halveks and my kind as well.

Could I accept my fate to stay with Kalev until we returned to Reval and faced my destiny?

That is best—for my family and the Sasquatches.

ACKNOWLEDGMENTS

I must start by thanking my writing partner Susan Bavaria. From reading early drafts to giving me suggestions on character development and scene-setting, she was vital in my journey to complete this book.

Two special beta readers, my sister Tina Pickell and brother-in-law Bruce Iannuzzi, provided in-depth comments that resulted in this book's complexity and consistency. Sherry Richardson, Laurel McHargue, and other beta readers spent countless hours reviewing drafts and providing helpful comments.

Feedback from the Rocky Mountain Fiction Writers' Spec Fiction and the Chaffee County Writers Exchange critique groups also helped me fill plot holes and deepen my characters.

I appreciate procedural advice from C.J. Meseke. His descriptions of officer responsibilities and weaponry helped to make scenes more realistic. But don't blame him if I diverted a bit to stay true to the plot.

My final thanks are to my loving husband, David. For all the times we've been hiking, and I've asked you to remove my phone from my pack so I could record an idea and take hours away from our vacations to write and edit—I give you my sincere thanks.

L.V. DITCHKUS is the author of the award-winning *The Sasquatch Series*, which includes *Crimes of the Sasquatch, Mission of the Sasquatch, Legacy of the Sasquatch,* and *Passage of the Sasquatch.* While writing these books and her new Sci-fi series, *The Chrom Y Chronicles,* about time travelers working to save humanity by repopulating the world with men, L.V. leads adventure travel trips, hikes and snowshoes hundreds of miles, and volunteers for wilderness advocacy and writing organizations. She and her husband live in a rural mountain community in central Colorado, where she gains inspiration from the five 14,000+ foot tall peaks viewable from her window.

Check out her blog at LVDitchkus.com